Ethos

A Mason Briggs Mission

Annette Goeres

This book is a work of fiction.
Any resemblance to actual events or
people is beyond the author's
intention.

To M.M. (Because it's still your fault)
and B.G., always

Prologue

Mason Briggs walked into the corner deli. He had received the phone call earlier in the week, and he was there to collect the envelope he knew would be there for him. This time, there was no awkward passcode exchange. He merely went up to the counter like a normal customer.

"Good morning," He greeted the young man behind the counter pleasantly. "I had an order in, but I seem to have lost my ticket."

"Oh, I am sorry. Do you happen to remember the number?" The young man asked.

Mason smiled. "It was 423 B."

The young man looked through the various containers and bags waiting for pick up. He pulled a nondescript white box from one of the stacks. "Here it is, sir. That will be $5.56, please."

Mason paid for his package and left. He tossed it into his briefcase in the car. It had been almost six months since the last job, and he thought that the team was sufficiently recovered. Just to be sure, he would ask them all tomorrow night, when they got together to play poker and shoot the breeze.

Until then, he would do the usual initial listen and get his general ideas in order. Since it was his lunch break, Mason considered going back to his office and going over the information immediately, but he found he wasn't that interested in it yet. He wanted to devote full attention to it. Instead, he turned towards Porter's jewelry store. Maybe he was in.

Once outside, Mason fished out his cell phone and called.

"Hello?" Porter answered.

"Hey, it's Mason. You busy for lunch?"

"Nope. I was thinking of going out with James though."

"Bring him. I like James. Plus, I am feeling generous today."

"Shit, I better jump on that gravy train right now. You tend to get all tight-fisted quick." Mason heard Porter move the phone away from his face and say, "James, you bored and/or hungry? Mason wants to treat us to lunch."

There were some muffled sounds, then Porter said to Mason, "We'll be right out. Sienna and Karen will hold the store for us until we get back."

"Awesome. I'm outside." Mason hung up.

True to his word, Porter came striding out of the front door within five minutes, James, his young blonde assistant or apprentice or whatever the hell he was, a few minutes later.

"Where to?" Mason asked as he eased into traffic.

"Who cares?" Porter shrugged. "I'm just hungry. James, do you care?"

"No."

"Then you decide, Mason."

"Okay. No fucking complaining though."

Porter assumed a look of exaggerated innocence. "Us, complain?"

"All the fucking time." Mason parked by a good steak house.

The interior was dimly-lighted and personal. Mason liked it here.

Porter hit his forehead on a low-hanging chandelier that he didn't see in time. "Goddamn it! Who hangs a fucking piece of iron only six feet off the fucking floor?"

Mason snickered. "Oh, shut the fuck up. I am six feet tall and I never hit it."

Porter rubbed his forehead. "Fucking stupid." James was grinning. Porter scowled at them both. "Just fucking say it, James. You're not going to feel better until you do."

James, still grinning, shook his head. "I have no comment at this time."

"Fucking idiots, you two."

The hostess came up to her podium. "Good afternoon, gentlemen. Are there three of you for lunch?"

Mason smiled back. "Why, yes, thank you."

The young woman looked curiously at Porter. "Are you all right, sir?"

Porter sighed. "Yes, I seem to have hit my head on one of the chandeliers. I am perfectly fine, otherwise."

The hostess shook her head. "I have asked that those be raised, repeatedly. You are not the first to have that problem. Anyway, would a booth work for you all?"

Mason looked at James, who shrugged, and Porter, who also shrugged. He turned back to the hostess and said, "As long as there are no other low-hanging obstacles in getting there, that should work fine."

The hostess laughed. "No, sir! This way."

She showed them to a booth in the back, away from all traffic. "I will be back with some menus. In the meantime, may I bring you something to drink? Especially you, sir?" She asked Porter directly.

Porter glanced at Mason quickly, then said, "Just water, I think."

Mason and James also asked for water.

The hostess left.

Mason smiled at Porter. "She totally thinks you're hot."

Porter rolled his eyes. "Mason, fuck off with it."

James shrugged. "He's right, sir. She does."

Porter covered his face with his hands, digging his fingers into his curly dark hair and muffling his voice. "It doesn't fucking matter."

"It does, but not in the way you are thinking of it." Mason said quietly.

"Fine, I'll ask. Why does it matter?"

"Because, you still haven't fully accepted who and what you are. I know you don't much care if girls think you are attractive, seeing as how you have Sienna, but it is important that you realize that others recognize you as an attractive and worthwhile person outside of your group of friends."

Porter finally put his hands down. "Okay, fine, I get it, Mason." He sighed. "I have a lot to work on, and I didn't think through that part of it yet."

Mason looked at him closely. "How are you doing, really?"

Porter shrugged. "It's hard for me to say. You should ask Sienna. She might have a better read on it. It is hard to gauge any improvement from the inside."

Mason nodded. "All right. I will ask her, but later."

The hostess brought back the menus and the water. She hesitated for a moment and then said, "You know, you look quite familiar to me, for some reason." She was looking at Mason.

Mason shrugged. "I look familiar to lots of people. I think I have an evil twin running around somewhere."

The hostess laughed and moved off.

Porter shook his head. "How does she know you?"

"I have no idea."

"That worries me, Mason."

"Me, too, a little, but if we leave now, it will be that much more memorable."

Porter sighed. "You're right, of course. Anyway. James, did you get the design mapped that you wanted to get done?"

They talked shop for the rest of the meal.

As Mason was driving them back to the store, he said, "By the way, I might have a job. We'll see tomorrow night if it's something for us all."

Porter looked interested. "Really?"

"Well, I haven't looked into it yet, but I have a contact. James, you were coming out, right?"

James nodded. "Yes, but if you would rather I didn't…"

"That wasn't what I meant to imply. I want you to be there if you think you should. Have you considered Callie?"

"Yes, she wanted to come, too."

"Well, she can, but I meant if she can handle this sort of thing."

"Oh. Well, I think she can. I honestly trust her."

"Okay. That is good enough for me, for now. I will check into her background and all. Here's the store. You two have a good day and I will see you both tomorrow night. Porter, if you get there early, you can cook."

"Ooh, that is tempting."

"I know. Actually, if everyone gets there early, we can all bitch and moan about your cooking the whole time."

"That's pretty damn tempting, too."

Mason laughed and Porter and James got out.

Later that evening, Mason texted Porter to ask what he wanted to cook. Hopefully, he would have a list to go by soon. In the meantime, there was this box to take care of. He went to his study and pulled his privacy shade, humming to himself. The cat he had recently been given followed along curiously. Mason hadn't had an animal in a long time, but he liked this cat. It kept to itself most of the time and liked to play. Plus, it was completely black. All spies needed a black cat. He had named it Ninja.

Mason opened the cardboard box. It had a tape and a sheaf of papers and pictures.

"Damn. This is a lot." Mason said softly.

He pulled out his tape player. The technology was rubbish, but it didn't leave a digital copy anywhere. That was important to Mason. No computers meant nothing would be stolen digitally and no traceable trail, either to him or back to whomever employed him.

"Good evening, Mr. Briggs. This assignment is a departure from the normal work you and your teams are accustomed to.

"These are the pictures belonging to an online presence. This group is a loosely connected group of crackers and hacktivists known as Phalanx. There are similarities to Anonymous in that hackers can join or leave as they wish. The big difference is that Phalanx is headed by a group. There is a head, and we need him removed.

"Phalanx is elite. You have before you the profiles of those we know for certain are included. They have all fled to either the Netherlands or Sweden. We are unsure of which, and, while we have various treaties with those countries, it is simply not viable that we search in them for the leaders.

"These people have planned several detrimental and devastating attacks on governments, most recently on the Israeli infrastructure and the Iranian core development program with devastating internally launched DDoS attacks. It is obvious that these leaders do not subscribe to a single ideology, but they have been posting more and more violent calls for members. They see themselves as a great army standing up to the corrupt and backwards first-world. Our indications are that they have been directly courted by both extreme

9

Islamists and the North Korean government. Anarchy is the name they are operating under, but they are advancing a program that is much more in line with total dictatorship.

"Mr. Briggs, we know that you have someone uniquely positioned to enter the ranks of Phalanx. If you decide to accept this mission, you and your agent must be fully willing to engage, possibly for some time, the agents of Phalanx on their playing ground. You must both be able and willing, with any other members you see fit to include, to fly to where the leaders are and to bring about their capture. We have in our custody a cracker of the name of 'CommanderRED', along with all his equipment.

"If you are willing to accept this mission, the stakes are high, and the rewards are likewise high. You and your team will receive five million dollars, plus any electronic support that can be given.

"Please destroy this message when you have finished with it. As always, good luck, Mr. Briggs."

Mason stopped the tape, thinking hard. This was going to be a difficult one. And the first part was all going to be on Juan. Mason hated to drop it all on one person, but that was how this was shaping up.

After listening and taking extensive notes, Mason burned the tape in his fireplace. Fuck the environment; no one would be able to reconstruct the thing after that.

Ninja was lying on top of the papers on Mason's desk and cleaning his paws quite industriously.

Mason picked him up and pulled out the papers then set him back down. The cat glared at him. Mason ignored it.

There were photos of seven people, six men and one woman. They had bios, of course, but Mason was most interested in getting his own information. Juan was going to have to gather it, by himself. The bios were a good start, but they were short and not complete. They needed more.

Mason put the shade back up and stared out at the night. This was going to be one hell of a job.

Part I

Chapter 1

Juan's cell phone buzzed. He had just gotten out of a long and boring meeting. Thank God this call came afterwards. He'd have had to ignore it if it had gone off during.

Juan went out on the patio outside the office. It was Mason calling. Fuck yes. "Hello, this is Juan."

"Juan, are you able to get off early today?"

"Shouldn't be a problem. I was going to anyway. Maybe another hour left."

"All right. Would you come out as soon as you can, then?"

Juan perked up. This was interesting, indeed. "Yeah, what's up?"

"Later, man, later."

"Ooh, something exciting. All right. I should be out in an hour and a half, tops. I wanna change after work. I look kinda stupid in these clothes."

Mason laughed. "I doubt that, but whatever you want. See you then."

"Hasta." Juan wasn't really very Hispanic, not after several generations of his family had legally been in the United States and he didn't speak Spanish even semi-fluently. Sometimes people assumed that he did, or that he was an illegal immigrant. Juan got tired of that. He had, in fact, gone to MIT and graduated there within the top five percent. And he had done graduate work at Stanford. He especially hated it when vendors talked really slowly to him. As if brains were determined by what a person looked like. Fuck them all.

Juan finished writing his parts request and filling out his purchase orders for the week. This he didn't much like, but he had to do them. Just because he understood why didn't make him like them any more than he did. Boring as hell. Once they were all submitted, he grabbed his jacket.

"See you Monday, Mitchell!" He said in the general direction of a coworker's cubicle as he walked purposefully out.

"Hey, Juan, wait!" He heard someone who was not his manager say. He smiled to himself.

"Gotta go! Got a hot date!" He yelled back over his shoulder, then he was out the door. In the hallway, he started to run. He made the stairs and was sliding down the banister before whoever had asked after him would be able to catch up. Yes, he was free for a few days. Now about that hot date...

It didn't take very long for Juan to get cleaned up and out to Mason's house. He noticed that there was car he didn't recognize parked in front. He shrugged to himself. Mason could have someone else out. Whatever. Juan would let him do that in his own damn house.

He rang the doorbell. Mason opened the door. "Hello, Juan. Thanks for coming early. The others should be out in about an hour, but I wanted to float something past you first."

Juan nodded, coming in. "Okay, Mason."

"Watch out for Ninja. He's feeling all excited."

"Who the fuck is Ninja?" Juan asked as a small black blur ran out from behind a corner and wrapped itself around his ankle. "Uh, scratch that question." He said, shaking his leg gently to dislodge the cat.

Mason smiled. "That is Ninja. He's my new cat. My neighbors gave him to me when they moved. I like cats."

"So do I, just not as ankle decorations. Hello, Ninja." Ninja growled menacingly at him and high-tailed it back down the hall.

Mason nodded. "Also, I have someone to introduce you to."

"I already met him, or did you mean besides Ninja?"

"Yes, besides Ninja." Mason led the way to his study. There was a lovely young woman sitting there already. She had short, black curly hair and cocoa skin. She smiled at Juan and he was startled to see that her eyes were very light hazel. The effect was striking. "This is Gabriella Wright, Juan. Gabriella, this is Juan Cardoza. Gabriella had worked in my office for several years now, and she has been involved, lightly, with several of our missions before."

Juan grinned at her. "Well, shit, I like this one already then." He bowed to Gabriella. "Lady."

She laughed. "You are quite outrageous."

"I know. I try. So what is this about, Mason? I mean, I don't mind being introduced to beautiful ladies, but…"

Mason smiled. "You might want to sit down; this might take a little while."

"May I get a drink first, Mason?"

"Of course."

"Gabriella?"

She smiled. "I would like that, thank you."

"Scotch or something else?"

"Is there any bourbon?"

Juan nodded and poured two drinks. He handed one to Gabriella and sat.

Mason glanced up. "Here's the assignment. You know I have been instructed to have you setting yourself up as a hacker for a while, and now it pays off. Juan, they want you to penetrate Phalanx."

"Phalanx? Fuck." Juan was surprised. Phalanx was the best. He wasn't that good. "I don't think I am up to that, Mason."

"I know. We can work around that a little though. They want the leaders of Phalanx. That means you have to become trusted enough to meet up, physically, with them. That in turn means we have to boost your credentials, preferably to insane-high levels. I was thinking that if you had access to CommaderRED's machines, you could show what a badass hacker you really are, to get a hold of them from under the government's nose."

Juan nodded. "Yeah, that might do it. But why do I need Gabriella then? No offense, lady, you are really pretty and all, but I don't want to put you in danger for no reason."

"She is going to pass messages from the rest of us to you. Subtly, of course. She is going to be your girl, Juan."

"Damn, I am lucky this time around, for sure."

Gabriella smiled again.

Mason nodded. "Yes. Porter has worked out a good system for passing messages that doesn't rely on code words or anything spoken. He is going to have to train you both, as well as the rest of the team.

We have to assume you will be watched to make sure you are clean. Gabriella has a job in a café, and you are going to suddenly become a frequent customer."

"Gotcha. By the way, are Porter and Michael going to be a part of this?"

"The second half. The first part is on just you two, I am afraid, and mostly on you, Juan."

Juan sighed. "Damn. Well, Gabriella, you'll have to get to know us all here. We are fucked up beyond belief, but at least we are fun." He looked at Mason knowingly. "You must have known I told someone I had a hot date tonight."

She laughed gaily. "I think that will be quite acceptable."

Porter and Michael showed up about fifteen minutes later. Porter had a bag of groceries. Michael had several bottles of wine. Michael, as usual, had the amazing ability to make almost any room feel too small. He had a truly phenomenal physique. Juan figured he would make the goddamn Superdome feel too small.

"You know, I bought food for this." Mason said, pointedly.

Michael shook his head. "You never buy near enough. I don't want to be fucking hungry all night."

"What, are you training again?"

"Maybe."

Porter laughed. "He means, 'yes'."

Mason nodded solemnly. "Ah, that explains so much then!"

Porter set down the bag and bowed to Gabriella, his eyes curious.

"Oh, allow me to introduce a new member; Porter and Michael, this is Gabriella. These are Porter, the tall one there, and Michael, the wide one there."

Porter laughed merrily. "Charming! Well, Gabriella, I don't quite know why you cast in with this group of losers, but we are lots of fun."

She smiled mischievously. "That's why, silly."

Michael smiled. "I like her. Anyone who cuts you down is someone I can get to like."

18

Porter nodded. "Yes, God knows I need cutting down."

Mason shook his head firmly. "Enough with that. Both of you. I thought we had agreed there would be no self-inflicted put-downs tonight."

Porter looked away quickly. "All right, Mason." He said softly. Gabriella looked at them both curiously. She didn't say anything though.

Juan started to dig through the bags. He knew that both Porter and Michael were embarrassed to have to be reminded. While he sometimes played up his enthusiasm, he wasn't stupid, and he could usually tell what his friends were feeling. "Hey, you brought some good shit, Porter. Whatcha making?"

"A mess of things, evidently. Also, some kebobs."

Juan gave Porter a warning look. Porter sighed softly. Juan looked at the bottles Michael had supplied. "Dang, you got some even better shit than Mason usually has, Michael. This will make for a more funner party!" Juan knew if he could get the emphasis off Porter, they would get past that hurt.

"That's not a word, Johnny."

"Who the fuck cares? You know what I mean."

Porter smiled. "True. And why not make up random words to express the inexpressible?"

Mason sat at the bar. "When are Sienna, Karen, James, and Callie getting here?"

"In about an hour. Sienna wanted to change. Her feet sometimes hurt after standing behind the counter. What do you want with the meat, Mason?"

"Whatever you feel like, chef."

"Mason, I thought I asked you not to call me that." Porter said with a pained look.

Mason shrugged. "I get to do whatever the fuck I want. That's the fun part about being your leader."

Michael smiled slightly. "I knew there had to be some perks to it that you weren't sharing."

Mason nodded. "Of course."

Porter sighed again. "All right, then may I ask you, as a friend, to please not call me that?"

Mason looked at him very hard. "All right, Porter."

"Thank you."

Gabriella was very confused, Juan could see it. She looked at him. "What the hell just happened?"

"That's a trifle hard to explain." Juan said softly as Porter and Michael started making various dishes. The noise of them talking, laughing and preparing covered up Juan, so he continued. "Porter and Michael are having trouble accepting who they are. I think it might be something common to all men really, but they are worse. Both of them have tried to erect walls around their feelings and then ignore them. Of course, feelings have a way of not being ignored and busting out at inopportune times. So Mason has had the two of them examining feelings and getting in touch with that side. It is hard for them both though."

Mason had been listening. "Fuck yes. I am still a bit worried about them, but they are doing much better. They aren't channeling everything into self-hate or anger anymore."

"Good." Juan said. "I hate having to guess when they are going to blow up."

Gabriella still looked confused but she let it lie. "Juan, would you pour me some of the cabernet?" She asked, smiling slightly.

"But of course!"

Porter didn't even look up. "Would you pour me some, as well? I would like a glass."

Juan nodded and poured two glasses. "Mikey? I have the cork out and everything."

Michael hesitated, then shook his head. "Nah, man, I can only have two glasses and I want to save them for later."

Juan looked at him quite steadily, one eyebrow raised.

Michael flushed a little. "It's a therapy thing, Johnny."

"Ah." Juan looked at Mason and held up the bottle suggestively. "Mason?"

Mason shook his head. "Not right now, Juan. Thanks."

Juan poured himself a small glass and put the cork back. He handed one glass to Gabriella and put the other within easy reach of Porter.

"Thanks, Johnny." Porter said, although he didn't take it right away.

"How many do you get tonight, Porter?"

"As many as I fucking want. But I will take two."

Mason snorted. "You only get fucking two, bitch."

Porter returned the snort. "I thought you didn't talk to Dr. Mitchel."

Mason smiled beatifically. "I didn't. I fucking talked to Sienna. Two. No more." He got up and left the room.

Porter shook his head in disgust. "Fuck you. And fuck you too, God. I hate being fucking dry."

Juan found that very odd; why would Porter be pissed at God? "What the fuck you talking about, Porter? What does God have to do with any of it?"

"God has everything to do with it, Johnny. I made a very solemn promise to Him about all this. I can't keep my promises very well to anyone else, it seems. He's the only one I can be accountable to. Fucking sucks."

"You are one hell of a complex guy, you know that?" Juan noticed that Mason had come back in with Sienna, Porter's beautiful fiancé, and Karen, Michael's lovely girlfriend. They both worked in Porter's jewelry store, they were both very nice on the eyes, and they were both experts at keeping male egos in check. Porter didn't see them.

He shrugged. "Whatever fucking works. I have to get better, if only so I don't hurt Sienna again. I can't do that, never. She has suffered too much of my shit, and I don't want to put her through the dirt ever again." He looked over, saw Sienna, then closed his eyes in resignation. "God damn it! This is not my fucking night!" Sienna smiled slightly, but it was a gentle smile, not a mocking one. Karen was looking on, wide-eyed. Porter exhaled sharply. "Well, since I am doing such a fantastic job of fucking myself over, any other questions people have?"

Juan shook his head. He hadn't meant to put Porter on the spot like that. None of them had realized that Sienna and Karen were there except Mason, obviously. Gabriella was staring around the room at them all. Juan smiled suddenly as a humorous thought hit him.

"No, Porter, I think we have revealed enough to Gabriella to give her nightmares for at least a month."

Porter smiled slightly at that. "Yes, well, sorry, my dear lady, but that is the way we are in this group. I wish we could change but obviously we can't."

Gabriella also smiled. "Well, I do hang out in Mason's office all time anyway, Porter. He has some seriously messed up people coming through there. I just didn't quite expect so much philosophy tonight. I will make the mental readjustments necessary." She closed her eyes and put her fingers to her temples. Then she opened her eyes and grinned at him. "Okay, I am ready now."

Michael laughed. "Awesome. Now that's squared away, let's get the rest of the food ready. Then we can contemplate our existential crises and how we can establish a metaphysical response."

Karen laughed. "You are being silly now."

"Of course I am. Care for a drink, lovely?"

Sienna was still smiling at Porter. He was looking at her without saying anything. Finally, she took a seat. Mason cleared his throat. "May I offer you a drink, Sienna?" He asked gently to break the moment.

She nodded. "Water would be fantastic right now, thank you."

"So." Michael said, pouring a glass of wine for Karen. "Why all the secrecy, Mason?"

"You know why. I have a proposition, but it is going to wait until James and Callie get here."

"Huh. You trusting them, too? This is a large group then."

Mason shrugged. "It'll probably be a couple of months in the making."

Chapter 2

James and Callie showed up within the half hour. Porter and Michael had relaxed enough to be ridiculous and Juan noted that, while Mason had said they couldn't put themselves down, he didn't enforce it on each other.

"Michael, why are you always in the fucking way?" Porter said impatiently, trying to get into the refrigerator while Michael was trying to get out some wine.

"Must be fucking talent." Michael retorted. "Just like your talent of being fucking annoying."

"Whatever man, I think it is just physical mass. And right now your physical mass is in the fucking way."

"Bitch, bitch, bitch." Michael said in a whiny voice, but he did move.

James shook his head. "I guess we came at the wrong time."

Juan shrugged. "There is no right time with these two in the kitchen."

"You are probably right about that." James noted.

"I seem to hear the generally insulting and yet highly dulcet tones of my associate James." Porter said without looking around.

James smiled. Callie laughed. "You two work together too much! Sometimes I would swear you are the same person!"

Sienna laughed as well. "You can hope not."

"It's more than a hope!"

Porter sighed in mock despair. "You see what I have to deal with, Mason? And you wonder why I am so fucking messed up?"

"Oh, no, Porter," Mason shook his head. "You are not putting me in the middle of your own fucking domestic problems."

Gabriella smiled. "I think Porter is more than enough to handle his own problems, self-inflicted or not."

"Hey, now." Porter said warningly, pointing his knife at her. "Nothing out of you. I am not quite up to your sallies yet. I haven't adapted myself to you, so you have an unfair advantage."

"Oh, what a tragedy." She said with mocking regret.

Porter shook his head.

Sienna laughed gaily. "She is going to be great to work with!"

Porter looked at Sienna steadily. She grinned at him cheekily. "Yes, my love?"

Porter shook his head again. "Nothing. Why the fuck am I surrounded by manipulative women who like to get what they want out of me?"

Juan snorted. "Because you're fucking lucky. Who the fuck cares what they get? There are worse things than getting used by beautiful women, you know."

Porter smiled slightly. "Hmm, good point, Juan."

"Of course. I am always right."

"Except when you aren't."

"Those times don't matter. When the fuck is the food going to be ready? I'm starving!"

"When it is fucking done and no sooner, now calm the fuck down."

The food was ready within fifteen minutes. Porter and Mason had done a great job, with Michael's help, of course. Juan privately felt that they should open a restaurant, what with how good at this they were. Admittedly that would cut into Porter's time at the jewelry store, but it would mean that Juan could have really good food more often. Maybe he should bring that up. Again. If he did it often enough, maybe they would cave in.

Michael looked amazingly happy as he sat next to Karen and was joking with Mason. Karen looked very content. Juan was glad; his massive friend totally deserved to catch a lucky break in the love department. From what he knew of her past, Karen did, too.

Gabriella sat next to Juan. While he didn't know her very well yet, Juan admitted that he was secretly pleased that she chose to be nearer to him. He may not be an expert when it came to the female mind, but he was reasonably sure that women don't tend to choose to be in close physical proximity to people they don't like or find attractive in some way.

Towards the end of the meal, Mason stood formally. "Friends, there has come my way a new assignment. I want all of your help. I've already spoken to each of you privately, so let's get the general plan laid out so we can start moving on it."

Michael raised his water glass. "Hear, hear!"

Porter clinked his to Michael's. "On to Valhalla!"

"Yeah, they have good drinks there." Juan snickered.

"Indeed they do. And they tell stories all night after fighting all day. What's not to like?"

Mason sighed. "Are you finished?"

"No!" Several people said at once, and then there were muffled laughs. Mason rolled his eyes.

"Okay, well, here is how this one goes down. Juan is going to infiltrate an elite hacker group. Gabriella is our contact point with Juan, and perhaps you other ladies as well. That might depend. These guys are going to have ears everywhere, so Porter is going to teach everyone his and Sienna's code. It isn't spoken, so there won't be anything to intercept that way." Mason looked at Juan and Gabriella very seriously. "These guys are dangerous. They've been contacted by radicals. They have access to international agents. You two must be expecting to be followed and watched. This is going to take a while to set in motion, and as of right now, you need to be careful."

Gabriella nodded. Juan, who was capable of being serious, said, "Okay, Mason. If you need us to be safe, we can be safe."

Mason inclined his head. He passed out pictures. "These are the Phalanx members. These are who they want. The problem is that they are not in this country. Juan is going to have to get a personal contact with them, somehow. Then, we'll have to extract Juan and take these leaders at the same time. It is going to be tight, but I don't want Juan arrested. It will get more in focus the closer we get to the time. Porter, Michael, James and I are going to be back players this time. It is mostly on Juan and Gabriella with support from the other ladies. Juan, you are going to turn into quite the player."

"I always knew I had it in me, anyway."

Porter laughed.

Mason smiled and continued. "Okay, heart-breaker. What is

your handle?"

"'Poniard' is what I have been using, although I occasionally go under 'Harold Hutchins'."

Porter laughed again. "You do not! Harold? Awesome."

James looked confused. "Who is 'Harold Hutchins'? Some cartoon character?"

Juan smiled. "Sort of. He's one of the wise-ass kids in <u>Captain Underpants</u>. I don't use that one as often, mostly because almost no one gets it. Inside jokes are only funny if people get them."

"Okay," Mason decided, "Then use only 'Poniard' from now on. Also, do you need anything to keep your hacker life separate? I don't want you using any of your personal stuff for this; it all has to be disposable. All of it."

"I get it, Mason. I will make a list and get it to you tomorrow afternoon."

"Good." Mason glanced at Gabriella. "You too, Gabriella. If you need something, you need to let me know. You can't be using your own cell phone or anything. I'll get you another. And you two are going to temporarily move. New apartments."

"I will, sir."

"Not 'sir'. You call me 'Mason'. I'm not your boss anymore."

She shrugged. "Whatever. I get to call you whatever I want."

Michael snickered. "Good. But don't fucking call him 'lenient'."

"Nor 'perceptive'." Porter joined in.

"Nah, and definitely not 'subtle'."

"Are you two fucking idiots finished?" Mason asked, exasperatedly.

"Nope. But you may continue."

Juan laughed. Mason shook his head. "Anyway, this one will take a lot of planning and a long time. Juan, get in on some low-level attacks, specifically aimed at Homeland Security areas. I can blanket you. Also, I will arrange a meeting with an official to get you the hard drive and perhaps hard case of CommanderRED. Once you have some actual hits under you, and his stuff, you should be able to start floating yourself with real credit."

Juan nodded. "Once I can analyze some of what he has, I can definitely boost myself."

"Good."

Porter looked very sharply at Mason. "You can blanket him for illegal shit?"

Mason shrugged. "To a certain extent. It's kind of like how nobody has any fingerprints on file anywhere."

Callie looked a bit alarmed. "None of us?"

Mason smiled slightly. "None of us. I got yours and James pulled last week."

"You must have some clout." James suggested.

Mason shook his head, still smiling. "No, James, you won't draw me that easily."

"Too bad. Oh well, I tried."

Porter was still looking hard at Mason. Mason sighed. "Porter, come on, you knew I had some sort of high-level security clearance."

"Yes. But I wish you didn't have to keep secrets from us."

"I can't help that; I can't just share everything with you."

"I'm not asking you to, Mason, but it kind of hurts that you keep a lot from us. Or, if you want me to be all healthy and shit, it hurts my feelings a lot that you don't share this shit with me. Better?"

Mason looked at Porter for a long moment. No one else said anything. Finally, Mason sighed again. "Okay, I admit that I kept it from you because I wanted to. Why? Who the fuck knows? You are a smart guy, probably even brilliant. I have always been a bit intimidated by you, and I guess part of me wanted to have something that you didn't know. To prove that I was good enough too. Good enough for you?"

Porter shrugged. "I don't know, Mason. How much more are you holding back, really?"

"I don't know, Porter. I never thought about it consciously."

Juan looked between them both. He whistled. "You two are acting like to fucking starving wolves sizing each other up. What the fuck? I was pretty sure we were all friends and on the same fucking side, once. Has something changed?"

"Stay out of it, Juan." Porter warned.

"Fuck that, Porter." Juan said softly. "Mason has every right to keep some things to himself. Besides, why the fuck do you even care? It doesn't really concern you."

"I know that, Johnny. I never said it did. I said it hurt."

Juan smiled a half-smile. "It hurts because you don't like not being in control, or it hurts because you feel like Mason isn't acting like a friend?"

Porter slapped his hand on the table loudly and shouted, "I don't fucking know, Juan! It just hurts!"

Mason held up his hand for silence. "Well, it should. I have no fucking good reason for hiding it from you all. And especially not from you, Porter. What I said is still true. I feel intimidated and inferior to you often. However, that is no excuse for me to be a fucking idiot. Therefore, I apologize to you all, and I ask you to forgive me, Porter, especially. Please, I am very sorry. I should not have done it."

Porter seemed taken aback but he nodded. "Okay, Mason. And Juan, I hate to say it, but you are right. We are on the same side. I'm too fucking touchy. I'll get over it."

Juan shrugged. "I know you will. But seriously, it should hurt a little; friends sometimes hurt each other. Real friends are the ones who say, 'sorry' and mean it."

"I'll try to do better." Mason said gravely.

Porter nodded. "I will, too."

"Good." Juan said. "Anything else, Mason, O Great Leader?"

"Juan, I really wish you wouldn't do that." Mason said.

"I bet you do; too bad."

Mason shook his head. "Ah, fuck... I can't remember now if there was anything else."

"Well, I can. Phalanx is the best of the best. They aren't going to just be tailing me. They're likely to check out everyone I have contact with. It might be a good idea to get all the ladies different identities. And gentlemen, they will look into you too. "

"I thought you were the best." Michael protested.

"I'm not a hacker or a cracker, Michael. These guys and girls are. I am probably one of the best at what I do, but this ain't it. Plus,

28

these people live to find data. I don't mind coding and shit, but they live it. Like, some don't even go outside, if you catch my drift."

"Uh, sort of. These are more like the movie versions, right?"

"Sort of, but not really."

Mason nodded. "Porter, we will need to make sure all of you are clean, again. Will you help me with that?"

"Sure, but why me?"

"Because you are the best and I can't think of a fucking good reason to have someone else do it. Michael, while we're on the subject, you can't enter anything for a while. Those competitions might be too dangerous."

Michael shrugged. "Okay, Mason. I wasn't really planning on it anyway. I have other things to think about right now."

Juan raised his eyebrows at Michael. Then he glanced suggestively at Karen and grinned. "Oh, I just bet you fucking do."

Karen blushed deeply. Michael laughed. "Lay off, Juan."

"No way, man."

"Anyway." Mason continued. "Juan, we need you to have a new name and identity. Gabriella as well. She already has a new name, but I need help with the paperwork."

Juan shrugged. "I can help with that, too, Mason, if you and Porter want help."

"Of course. What do you think, Porter?"

Porter smiled. "Always needs that Juan touch."

Juan laughed. "You know, I would say 'thanks' but I have the distinct feeling that I was just insulted."

"Take your pick."

Juan laughed again.

Mason sighed theatrically.

"I'm just keeping him in line." Porter protested. Mason gave him a long steady look. Porter smiled back. "Well, I am. Who wants dessert?"

This was enthusiastically accepted, so Porter got up to get it. Mason followed, and, on a hunch, Juan did, too.

Porter pulled some bowls out of a cupboard. Mason got some

spoons and glasses out. They all started getting the crisp dished up.

"Porter, really, I am very sorry." Mason said softly.

Porter paused in his spooning. "I know, Mason. I didn't really mean to be such an asshole about it. It caught me by surprise, but, like Juan said, it doesn't really matter and I already kind of knew it anyway."

Juan shrugged. "Porter, I know you and Michael are still a bit touchy from that last mission and the one before it. Look, I don't mean to say that you should feel great about it or anything, but you are acting a bit erratic. I don't want to put you on the spot, but is there something wrong?"

"I don't know, Juan. This whole being dry thing is really hard for me. And I am worried about the ladies passing messages, and I am really worried about you. I know who Phalanx is, and frankly it scares me. I don't like sitting on the side when you are all in potential danger. Puts me on fucking edge, not being able to act. Don't go out of your way to be a hero."

Juan shook his head. "No, man, I won't. I appreciate your concern though. I appreciate it a lot. I know I am flippant and make jokes; that doesn't mean I don't understand what it means to be a real friend."

"Good, because I will do permanent and bad things to those guys if you get hurt."

"Aw, thanks, man." Juan grinned at him.

"I mean it, Johnny."

"I know you do. I completely appreciate the fact, and I appreciate that I will be responsible for myself and Gabriella, as well as Sienna, Callie, and Karen. I am capable of being serious, Porter, and I do love you, man. Now, let's get this food out before Michael chews through the tablecloth."

Mason laughed. "You are both irrepressible."

"Well, duh, Mason. What did you expect?"

"Nothing more, or less."

Porter smiled a half smile. "All right. Well, Mason, you were man enough to apologize for something. I would like to reciprocate. I am sorry that I was such a jerk. Please forgive me and help me to not do it again."

Mason also smiled slightly. "Of course, Porter. I completely understand and forgive you."

"Thank you. I also forgive you. How are we going to get this all out there? We have a bunch more people than usual."

"I have some trays under that counter. Pull out some."

Juan opened the cupboard indicated and pulled out some plastic trays. "These?"

"Yeah, those. Who cares what they look like? They just have to work."

"True that." Juan loaded three trays. "Let's go, boys. I want to eat this shit soon."

Porter shook his head. "You have such a fucking way of putting things, Juan."

Juan shrugged. "Whatever. You two should open a restaurant. I like it when you make the food."

"No, Johnny. I am far too touchy to handle doing something that public. Witness how bruised my fucking ego got when I thought Mason was holding out on me? No way can I handle that."

Juan sighed. "I thought you would think that. Too bad. It might be good for you, too. Have you considered that?"

By this time, they were back in the dining area with the crisps.

"No, Johnny. Let it lie. I was never meant to be a world-class chef."

"Damn."

Michael looked up, seeming to follow the conversation back. "It is our loss. I wish Porter would at least cook my food more often."

"For as much as you fucking eat, I bet you wish anyone would be willing to cook for you."

"Yes," Mason joined in. "I cannot even imagine how you go through the day without consuming more. You know, pets, paving blocks, pedestrians..."

"What?!" Michael looked outraged, and everyone else laughed.

Juan sat down by Gabriella again. She leaned closer to him. "Did you get it all worked out between Mason and Porter then?" She

31

said in a low voice.

Juan smiled at her. "I didn't have to, lovely lady. They actually worked it out on their own. It only makes sense, really; they are like best friends. They love each other an awful lot, which is why such a piddly little thing was such a big deal between them."

Gabriella looked like she wanted to say something else, but Mason set a dish in front of her and she desisted. Juan glanced at Porter and noticed him looking at the two of them. Very little got past Porter. Juan looked at him for a second or two, and then winked rather deliberately to let him know it was all right. Porter nodded ever so slightly. Sienna said something to him then, and he turned to answer her.

Juan ate his dessert, again mourning the fact that he couldn't cajole Porter into being a chef. It made no sense when he thought about it, except that he wanted good food more often.

"So, Gabriella, where is this café you'll be at? I want to start frequenting it as soon as possible."

She smiled. "It is on Center Avenue, small place called 'The Little Bread Shop'. They have good enough food, I think, but nothing compared to this."

"No, but little is! Porter is a genius in the kitchen."

Porter said from further up the table, "I heard that, Juan. I still won't do it."

"I'm not saying anything like that!" Juan protested.

Porter looked at him very skeptically.

"I'm not! I'm innocent!"

Michael laughed. "Those are two completely different statements, Juan, and you know it."

"Yes, that is why I said it." Juan smirked at Porter. "I win this round."

Porter grinned back. "Want to bet on the next round, boy? I think I can manage to turn your luck sour."

"Oh, fucking bring it, big man. You don't scare me."

Mason smiled. "Well, since this is the last time we will be together for quite a while, let's make this a tournament to remember."

32

Gabriella looked confused. Juan smiled at her. "Know how to play poker?"

"Well, yes, but I am not very good."

"You're about to learn to be a lot better. Ready?"

Chapter 3

Several hours later Juan had not won, and he didn't much care. Porter probably hadn't cheated much, despite the obvious temptation. James the unassuming had taken them all, which was only worth bragging rights; they only played for the lowest possible stakes most of the time.

Juan wandered out onto the deck. The moon was very bright and mostly full, and Mason had a great view. Juan admired the fact that there was a large expanse of no development for perhaps half a mile. It made Mason's house feel secure and safe. Also, it made it much quieter at all times of the day and especially at night. Mason said his neighbors moved out. Maybe Juan should look into that.

He heard a light step behind him. Turning, he saw Gabriella come out. "Gabriella." He nodded.

"Juan." She smiled. "The view here is amazing."

"Yes. Mason mentioned his neighbors moved. That's how he got Ninja. I was just thinking I might need to look at that. I like it out here, away from all the city."

"Do you have money to buy a house?" Gabriella sounded surprised.

"Probably. I have lots in various accounts." Juan shrugged. "I will look into it. Anyway, that is for later. For now, I very much enjoy your presence. I am quite lucky that you are part of this mission."

She laughed. "I am glad, too. You are pretty damn hot yourself, you know."

"I have heard that before, but it is not always easy for men to believe."

"Well, you are. I was thinking, though, that if we are supposed to be involved, it might not be a bad idea to practice."

"Uh." This was a bit beyond Juan. "Practice? Practice what, exactly?"

Gabriella stepped up very close to him. Juan realized she smelled very good, and that made him a bit nervous. "Well, we are going to have to be intimate, you know. I don't want there to be an awkward first kiss in public, so maybe, I thought, we should practice a bit and get over the awkwardness in the dark. Alone. Now."

Juan smiled. "I like this idea."

"Oh, good. I like it too. Besides, I like kissing attractive men."

"Just so we're clear, that's all I do."

Gabriella moved right up to him and put her arms around his neck. "Good. Then let's get to know each other."

Juan hadn't kissed lots of girls. He certainly hadn't recently, but the fact that no one could see them and the fact that it was night made him feel less apprehension. Gabriella was a very attractive woman and she did smell really good.

They had definitely gotten a lot less awkward when there was a loud cough from the doorway.

Juan jerked his head up. Porter was there, a slight smile on his face. Juan suddenly blushed very red.

"Wanted to see if you two were up for more cards. I had also considered commandeering this balcony, but you two beat me to it."

Juan laughed slightly. "We were trying to be natural around each other."

Porter's smile widened. "Oh, you were both hugely fucking natural!"

Gabriella laughed gaily. "Good! Would you be willing to give a full critique?"

Porter shook his head. "No, because that is really all personal preference and I think the less opinion that goes into making out, the better."

"You probably are right. Cards sound fun." Gabriella kissed Juan on the mouth one more time and moved back inside.

Porter came out to join Juan, his eyes twinkling. "Well, you certainly looked natural. I completely understand, and it is probably a good idea. Plus, this is really a beautiful spot for that kind of thing."

Juan looked back out at the view. "Did you know Mason's neighbors moved?"

Porter came to the railing and looked out too. "Yes. I was wondering if it would appeal to anyone else."

"Are you looking at it?"

"Not right now. These houses are kind of big for one guy."

"Porter," Juan said gently, "You aren't one guy anymore. Besides, these houses are big enough so you and Sienna could both have your own space in one house. You wouldn't have to share a room, even. I mean, I know that would be fun and all, but I also know you are both virgins and not interested in that yet. The reason I asked is because if you are looking then I won't. There are other houses around."

Porter considered that. "Hm. You might be right. I will talk with Sienna and think about it. You are right about other houses, too. Mason may not want me living close."

"You could ask him, but I think Mason would not mind. Friends do that."

Porter shrugged. "I think I will think about it. But I won't think too long, in case you want it, or something."

Juan turned back towards the house. "Porter, think as long as you want. I'd rather not be moving on something for a couple of months, you know."

"Good point. Let's go win money from James or else he will be insufferable for fucking days."

Juan laughed. "Yes, let's!"

Porter smiled at Juan as they went in the door. "By the way, Juan, Gabriella is very pretty. Maybe you should not toss it all off on one mission."

Juan shrugged. "It's possible, Porter, but I am not banking it all on that. We'll see how it goes and maybe it will turn into something after all. If not, it is better for both of us if I am not pressuring her to something she doesn't want."

"True that. And that way, you can always work together. I would imagine that this type of job is impossible if there are jealous feelings behind it all."

"Ask, Sienna. She would know better than anyone."

"Ask me what?" Sienna had come out from the hallway, a curious look on her face.

36

Juan shrugged. "About people being jealous and working with that happening."

"It fucking sucks. Why do you ask though?"

"Uh, no reason." Juan felt self-conscious all of a sudden.

"Oh really?"

"Let it lay, Sienna." Porter said calmly. "I will tell you later, if you are that interested." Sienna stuck her tongue out at him. "Yes, I love you, too." Porter agreed.

Everyone else was wandering back to play poker. Juan slid into his seat beside Gabriella. She smiled at him and he caught a whiff of what she smelled like. All of a sudden, it seemed kind of hot in the room. Porter winked at him from across the table.

James and Callie came in holding hands. "Did you see that moon tonight?" James asked. "It is phenomenal!"

Porter nodded. "Indeed it is." He began to deal expertly.

Callie gave James a long, sly sidelong glance. "Yes, damn-near seductive, that moon." She said.

James blushed. Juan laughed. Michael also nodded.

"By the way, Mason," Porter said, looking at his hand. "You mentioned your neighbors moved?"

"Yes," Mason said, rearranging his cards. "That's how I got Ninja."

"Anyone bought the house yet?"

"No. I think it is a bit remote for most people, and it is kind of expensive. Are you looking into the market?"

Porter shrugged easily. "I might, but it is not just me making the decision this time. Also, I don't know if you would want us, me, as a neighbor." It was just a slight slip, but it was a very telling one. Juan smiled slightly to his cards.

"Of course I would, you ass. What did you think?"

Porter shrugged again and the talk drifted off in other directions. Juan noticed that Sienna looked extremely pleased about something. Porter might be more in the market than he anticipated. Damn. That meant Juan would have to look at another place, but his original thought still held; he wanted to be done with this mission before he started another phase in his life. Besides, Porter and Sienna would throw one hell of a housewarming party, and they deserved to be happy.

Juan looked at his hand. Evidently, he would not be teaching James a lesson this hand, since his cards fucking sucked. He folded.

The next hand was better. Juan managed to win it. That continued for the rest of the night. By the end of it, Juan had won the most. Michael and Karen had disappeared after they were both eliminated.

"Ah, man." James said, throwing his last hand. "You win, Juan." He stood up and was joined by Callie.

"Thanks so much!" Juan grinned, raking the pot towards him. "I just got the luck this round."

"Oh, that is what you call her now?" Porter said softly, his eyebrow rose suggestively.

Juan blushed. Gabriella did too, but she laughed.

"I see." Porter said.

"I can't help it if you walk in on stuff you would rather not see, Porter. Learn to fucking look first."

"What's this?" Mason asked.

"Oh, Gabriella and I were practicing being more natural around each other and Porter had to witness some of it."

Mason laughed. "I see, indeed. As long as it worked, I suppose."

"Oh it worked." Porter said gravely. "They were all sorts of natural. I could almost see the pheromones shooting off, that's how natural it was."

"Lay off, Porter. Like you never kissed somebody on a beautiful balcony."

"Okay, true, I will stop. Besides, maybe the balcony is open again. I wouldn't want to let that go to waste."

Sienna laughed. "Let's go find out!" she stood up and offered a hand to Porter. He also stood. She looked rather directly at Juan and Mason. "Don't come looking for at least an hour, unless you're looking to join in. Consider yourselves fucking warned."

Porter smiled. "You heard the lady."

"So have you; put up or shut up."

They left the room.

Gabriella smiled at Juan. "We could probably improvise. Mason does have a nice couch and he might not mind giving us advice..."

"Whoa! No! Never mind!" Juan said, just a touch too loudly.

She laughed. Mason smiled. "Should I leave? Go fucking lock myself in my room or something?"

"No, Mason. Just gimme a second." Juan said. He was way out of his depth here and he needed to change the subject. "How would you suggest I get into Homeland Security, since everyone else appears very interested in making out in various places around the house? I need to start thinking about how to do this. I really don't think I am a good enough hacker to do any real damage."

"That doesn't matter. I think you just need to be a presence. They need to know you have skills in the area, and if you can make it look like you somehow have breached real security, and physically, that is going to up your value immensely."

Juan thought about it, staring into his mostly empty wine glass. "Well, most attacks tend to be denial of service attacks anymore; I would rather not do that. They are traceable, for one thing. Also, I am not really interested in being a hactivist. I think I am going to leave a subtle message for others in the signatures. I think that will be subtle enough for them to see and yet show that I have skills enough. Also, I will need to show some damage in the physical systems monitoring the likely location of CommanderRED's stuff. Where should I target?"

Mason thought that through, also staring into his glass. "How about you focus on the warehouse on Fifty-first for that? It has some stuff in it, and they won't know what is and isn't there. The only recorded list is a physical one, but they won't know that. There is actually rampant speculation as to what is in that warehouse online."

"What is in there?" Juan asked, interested.

"Mostly old tanks and parts seized in the Pacific, but they don't need to know that. The reason it is so well guarded is so that no one goes in there and accidently sets something off. There are potentially

39

live munitions."

"Ah, gotcha. Okay, so I will get the machines from there. Gabriella, make sure you know all this, too. You can collaborate on it if they ask you."

Gabriella looked a bit skeptical. "I have almost no idea what you are talking about, you know."

"Good. They will assume you aren't lying then. Just keep your knowledge at that level and you should be fine. And keep your hotness there, and you will distract anyone from looking deeper. For some reason, people assume that beautiful women cannot also be smart. Lame-ass punks. But let's use it to our advantage. When do you start at the bakery?"

"I actually started there last week. You better start coming to visit soon. I want to show off for you."

Juan flushed a little. "Um, okay. I won't notice what I am eating though."

"You'd better not, or else I will have to try harder."

Mason laughed. "I am going to miss you around the office, but I think I have lost you to a much better person. Juan will take good care of you. I would trust no one more with your safety than these men. I mean that."

Juan inclined his head in gratitude. Gabriella smiled. "Well, at least you have put me in the protection of a fucking awesome kisser."

"Dammit, Gabriella!" Juan said loudly, dropping his glass on the table and spilling the rest of his wine. "Don't say things like that!"

"I can say what I want, and it is true. You are one of the best I have ever had."

Juan shook his head violently, beet-red.

Mason laughed again. "Should I leave you two alone for this?"

"Fuck no! Just give me a second to get over it!" Juan dabbed furiously at the stain caused by his red wine, still deeply embarrassed. Mason passed him some salt and Juan poured it over the spot. He took a deep breath. "I think I all of a sudden understand what Porter was saying earlier about you pretty girls getting what you want. Damn. That was way too easy."

Gabriella shrugged. "I don't know; if it were second-nature to you then I wouldn't want to do it. Half the fun is in the surprise, you know."

"Maybe so; it still is a bit unsettling how quick you did it."

"I am sorry, but I still hope it never gets easy for you to ignore."

"We'll just have to see, won't we? Anyway. Damn, before that mess, I was going to ask Mason something. I hope to hell it wasn't important, because I can't fucking remember anything now."

Mason smiled. "Might it have had something to do with meeting up with Porter?"

"It might have. I honestly am fucked on this right now. When do you want to meet up?"

"Well, let's see. Porter is occupied right now, and I think he might be a little late getting to bed. Maybe eight?"

"Okay, you want to do it here?"

"No, Porter has the stuff we'll need. Gabriella, did you want to come?"

"Yes, I think I had better. I need to be comfortable with the names and all, plus Porter needs to teach us the code."

"Oh, yeah," Juan said. "I know about it. He told me about it once. But I can still use some pointers on how to use it and practice."

"Is it hard?"

Juan smiled. "No, but it will require practice. It also requires physically touching the person you are communicating with."

"Hot damn, I like the sound of that."

Juan blushed again. Then he smiled. "Oh, I do, too."

Ninja wandered in, meowing curiously. Mason looked over. "Oh, I guess I need to get him some food. He's probably annoyed with me for that."

Juan was getting tired. He'd been working for most of the day, and it was starting to get close to bed time. Gabriella leaned her head against his shoulder. "I'm tired. Maybe I should go to sleep." She confessed.

"I'm pretty tired, too. I think I need to leave soon or else I will have to sleep here. I can't drive too tired or I am unsafe."

41

"Think Mason will care if we sleep here?"

"We've done it before."

Mason came back in. "Done what?"

"Slept here."

"Oh, yeah, you can always sleep here. I will make sure the guest bedroom is all ready for somebody."

Juan was close to dozing when Mason came back. "Too late, Johnny. Michael and Karen are asleep on the bed in there. It's probably just as well; Karen still needs a nightlight. I have the other bedroom, and then you are stuck with the couch and recliner."

"Mason, you know I will just take the recliner. That thing is damn comfortable, even if it is fucking ugly."

"Mm. Me, too." Gabriella yawned. "Right after I wash up." She got up.

"I'll get some pillows and blankets, but I warn you that you might end up with Ninja, too."

Juan smiled. "I like Ninja. Maybe I need to get a cat. Once I buy my new house, and all."

"What new house is this?"

"I don't know yet. I was thinking about the one next door, but then Porter sounds pretty interested in that. So then I guess I will have to look. I like it out here, and I would like to live near a group of friends. That seems really cool to me, somehow."

"I would like that, too." Mason admitted. "I hope Porter and Sienna buy that house."

"I have a hunch that they will." Juan stood up. "I have gotta get some sleep. Sorry, Mason, I am just tired."

"Making out will do that to you."

"Damn straight. I haven't had that much excitement in a long time. Best night ever, Mason. Thanks for the hot date."

Mason bowed. "It was my pleasure, sir!" He went to get the blankets and Juan washed his face and brushed his teeth quickly. He always had a toothbrush in his briefcase, which was weird, but he had needed it on occasion. When he came out of the bathroom, he saw the pillows and blankets Mason had left there.

"I should probably tell Porter and Sienna that I am going to be here. Fucking inconsiderate." Juan muttered to himself.

"Beg pardon?" Mason said from right behind him. Juan jumped.

"Fuck, Mason!"

"Oh, oops. You were saying?"

"I said that I should probably warn Porter and Sienna so they don't come barging in here and wake me up."

"Good idea. I will let you do it though. Sienna has a bad habit of springing embarrassing invitations on me."

"You're just scared of her." Juan accused.

"No shit, Johnny."

Grumbling, Juan walked out to the balcony. Porter and Sienna were just sitting and talking softly, which made Juan very relieved. "Hey, lovebirds. I am going to be sleeping in the living room. Don't turn lights on in there when you come though."

"Is it that late?" Porter sounded surprised.

"It is for me. Night, Porter. Night, Sienna."

"Goodnight, Juan."

He went back to the living room and got his bedding ready. He did like sleeping in that recliner. Gabriella came back in quietly. She looked at him quite speculatively. "Hm, that looks comfortable."

"You may have it, if you want."

She laughed. "Oh, no! Only if you are in it! That is what looks comfortable!"

Juan flushed a little. "Oh, um, okay."

"You are wondering if I always act this way, aren't you?"

"A little, yeah. You seem pretty forward. I hope that doesn't offend you."

She shrugged. "No, I don't normally act like this, but I figure, why wait? You interest me and I think I like that. You are very attractive and you seem really nice. Therefore, why wait? Like me first, get to know me and love me later."

Juan grinned. "Okay, I can buy that argument." He turned the lights off. "If you want, you may sleep with me. I would like that a lot."

"I think I will!"

Chapter 4

Juan woke up to his watch buzzing the next morning. He'd forgotten to turn his alarm off. Dammit. He'd wanted to sleep in, too. Fuck. He awkwardly reached around Gabriella and managed to shut it off. Of course, it wasn't as if he could get up anyway. He smiled up at the ceiling. Maybe it was his lucky day after all.

Gabriella snuggled into his shoulder without waking up. She still smelled good. Juan wondered idly if girls always smelled good naturally, or maybe there was some vast conspiracy where they all got together in about sixth grade and traded this kind of information. That would actually explain a great deal, in Juan's mind. Well, whatever they did, he was almost helpless in the face of it. He had always had a good sense of smell, and when he liked the scent of something, he had strong reactions to it. Gabriella was, for better or worse, one of those things.

He closed his eyes again. Maybe Porter was onto something with this whole relationship thing. He drifted back to sleep still thinking about it.

An hour later, he woke back up. This time, he was really awake. He looked over at the rest of the room. Porter was in the kitchen. Of course Porter was in the kitchen. Juan wondered if the man ever slept. He was going to ask.

Very carefully, he slid out from the chair, carefully covering Gabriella back up with the blanket.

"Do you ever sleep? I think you got up early just to be here." Juan asked softly as he poured himself a cup of coffee.

Porter smiled at him. "Well, of course I do. I slept more last night than I usually do. We used Mason's other room. I didn't even get up four or five times."

"As Mason says, making out will do that to a person."

"That's God's own truth. Although I could have used a little more of that and a little less talk, to be honest."

"Really? What did you talk about?"

Porte shrugged. "Buying a house, living in it, minor changes like that."

45

"Oh. Well, changes that big probably need to be discussed."

"Probably, yes. Of course, it also brought up the somewhat tricky subject of actually getting married, too."

"Fuck, you covered lots of ground." Juan said, somewhat awed.

Porter smiled. "Yes, well, if I am going to be uncomfortable, I guess I had better make it the worst I can."

"Just don't let Mason hear you say that. He'll tell you off."

Porter nodded.

"Well, what did you decide?" Juan asked impatiently.

"Nothing; at least, not yet. We are going to look into the house next door. But marriage... well, that is a bit stickier. You know I am nominally Catholic. Well, that is hard to get around, and I don't know if Sienna is up to that, yet."

Juan thought about that. "Well, it has to be her choice, regardless of what you want. I do know that about the Church. She won't accept people half-heartedly."

Porter looked at Juan, his eyes twinkling slightly. "And why would Johnny know that?"

"After I saw you after the one mission, I looked into it. If it is something good enough for you, then it is worth looking at, in my opinion. So I did."

"Really?" Porter sounded very surprised.

Juan sighed. "Porter, seriously, how many fucking times do I have to tell you I respect you and look to you for guidance? Yes, when you find something that is that fucking important, I will look into it. What the fuck, man?"

"I didn't... I guess... Ah, fuck. I am sorry, Johnny. I guess I didn't really connect what you said with what you might do."

"It is okay, Porter, but like you once told me, I get tired of saying things over and over."

"I know. I am sorry. I should be listening better."

"It takes time, and it takes acceptance of the self, I think. Once a person can accept who they are, then they can start to give the other person the gift of listening. Or something. You know, that made sense in my head. Came out like shit though"

"I think you are onto something, Juan."

Juan sipped his coffee while Porter put things together. "After breakfast, I guess we better get the technical crap all figured out. And you need to teach Gabriella and me the code."

"Oh, the code is easy. It is just Morse code, and you tap it out on a hand or leg or arm. Whatever. It takes a bloody long time to get anything said, but it works well for this sort of thing. You really need to practice together though, so you understand each other's little idiosyncrasies."

"Yeah, that makes sense. I love using old technology to fool new technology."

"You would."

Juan suddenly remembered what he had not communicated last night because Gabriella had distracted him too much. "Oh, I wanted to talk with you and Mason about something. Once he gets up from his fucking beauty sleep, that is."

"Go easy on him. The best-looking person he got to sleep with has four paws."

Juan laughed softly. "Point for you, there. Do you want some help making something to eat?"

"Sure. I was doing my usual eggs. Want to put in something vaguely healthy, like fruit?"

"Sounds good to me. Let's see what Mason has in this house."

Mason himself appeared within a half hour. He poured some coffee, surveying the breakfast and subsequent mess that Juan and Porter were making.

"Morning, you two idiots." He said softly.

"Same, fearless leader." Juan grinned. "I wanted to talk with you and Porter before we get into this whole alternate personality thing."

"Go ahead. The caffeine will kick in soon enough."

"Well, they're going to know where I work; I can't hide that. I also don't want some underling coming after me after this goes down. So I thought that I should assume someone else's identity from there."

"I assume you already have someone lined up for this?"

"Why, yes, yes I do! There is an engineer named Michael Douglas who is basically AWOL. I don't work in engineering, I work in IT, and they will expect me to be an engineer, so it will tally with what they want. Then maybe they won't look far. Plus, his name is a liability for him, but will confuse the scent, as it were. There are tons of guys with that name."

Porter nodded. "I like it, Mason. They will get frustrated if they try to dig too deeply."

Mason also nodded. "Yeah, go it, Juan. But I want you to change your hair for a while."

"I was going to anyway. Get something all angled and jaggy and shit like that."

Porter smiled. "You'll have to go to Emma, Sienna's go-to. She is the best, plus she showers compliments on you and that makes it better."

Juan shrugged. "Okay. Maybe I should get some color. I think at least one big swatch of bright red. Not subtle, but it will look way different. Plus, I can cover it with temp color for work."

Mason smiled. "Whatever you want. Where is this real Michael Douglas?"

"No one really knows. We don't have a picture of him in the directory or anything. Very convenient. He works remotely, usually. I have seen him about once, but there are tons of engineers at GH. I doubt that anyone not trained in observation by the great Mason and Porter would be able to pick him out of a lineup."

"He is perfect, then."

"Yeah, I thought so. I would have brought it up last night, but then Gabriella threw me hard-core."

"Oh?" Porter asked, way too interestedly.

"Let's just say I totally understand what you said about being manipulated by beautiful women. She made me completely lose track of what I was saying."

Mason nodded gravely. "You looked like a fucking twelve-year-old. It was awesome."

"It was not!"

Porter laughed softly. "And once they know it, they never let off. Oh well. It is one way to make them happy, you know."

"Fucking sucks! It was way too easy for her. And then she smells good, too. I am so bombed, aren't I?"

"Fucking buried." Porter agreed.

Juan sighed mournfully. "I guess I better surrender while there is still dignity in it, then."

Porter poured the eggs into the hot skillet. "Just don't turn tail and run. Women don't pursue. That's the men's prerogative."

"Oh, I'll pursue, dammit. It is gonna be like I have no fucking choice. I can probably sniff her out from half a fucking mile away now."

Mason smiled as he poured himself more coffee. "Good. She will like that. I guarantee that Gabriella is very interested in being pursued by you. She can shoot a male ego full of holes almost as quickly as Sienna."

"You're probably right." Juan laughed suddenly as something occurred to him. "Isn't it funny how we have these mental guidelines that we compare to? Like Sienna is the standard we measure other women by. Stuff like that."

"I think it is perfectly normal, Juan. Even though none of us like to be labeled per se, we all have to categorize and therefore compare others. Not to do it would be chaos, because to compare means that there is something that is held as a standard."

"Yeah, and there goes the conversation. Poof, off to philosophy. Why do we have to do that all the fucking time?"

"Because philosophy is fun, and you fucking asked."

"That was before I realized I needed more coffee."

Mason passed him the pot. "Feel free."

"Fucking cheap shot, Mason." Juan poured himself another cup anyway. It wouldn't hurt.

Porter put the eggs onto three plates. "Breakfast, boys." He said, turning the burner off. "I'll do more when everyone else shambles through." He sat down to eat.

Juan found he was quite hungry. "You know, you'd think I didn't fucking eat at all last night; I am starving today."

Mason shrugged. "As I said, making out will do that to you."

"Good. It's the best workout I have found, then." Juan observed calmly. Porter choked slightly. Juan laughed. "You know it was a good statement when I can catch you off-guard, Porter."

Porter smiled. "You're probably right. I do think I am too fucking clever for my own good."

"You're at least too fucking clever for my good. That is damn sure."

"What will we need to do the documents, Porter?" Mason asked, pushing his plate aside.

"I have the engraver and embosser at the store. I was helping James figure out if he wanted his own brand name for recognition or not."

"Did he?" Juan asked, curious.

Porter shook his head. "He's still unsure of his marketability. He wants to be under my umbrella a little longer. But we did come up with some fun stuff."

"I bet."

Gabriella woke up soon after, and then Sienna and Michael wandered in. Porter put more eggs on.

"How's Karen this morning?" Juan asked Michael.

"She's okay. Nights are often hard for her, still. Thanks for your room and the nightlight, Mason."

"It's no problem, Michael. I hope you did more than just sleep in there, though. I hate changing sheets for just sleep." Michael slowly flushed. Mason nodded. "Oh good. Then it won't be a waste." Michael flushed redder.

"Mason, that's not nice." Gabriella admonished.

"I'm not trying to be nice; I am trying to make a fucking point."

"Oh. Sometimes I miss your points, since they're so fucking subtle."

Mason laughed. "I believe you, too!"

Michael, still red, said, "And what was the fucking point of making me embarrassed?"

Mason smiled at him. "You really think you are all the fuck

better? You have to accept that we are your friends and we love you and we fucking want you to be fucking happy. That includes kissing a beautiful woman, idiot."

"You have such a way with words, Mason." Gabriella said in mocking admiration. "I bet you talk like that to all your patients."

"Of course not, but then most of my patients aren't this fucking dense."

Porter shrugged. "Just go with it, Michael. There are much harder ways to make them happy than kissing beautiful women, you know. If all therapy was that easy, I would be so damn healthy they'd throw me out."

Michael laughed. "Maybe I should get better some more later!"

Porter grinned at him. "I believe you once offered a rather interesting idea involving doubles..."

"And you fucking shot it down."

"I might be willing to reconsider."

Juan laughed. "Not til after we get the work done today."

"Oh, damn."

Gabriella leaned in close to Juan. "I bet we could make a triple." She whispered.

Juan almost dropped his cup again. Damn! His hands were shaking slightly. He was going to have to do something about that, sometime.

She laughed softly and sat up again. Sienna was sitting on the other side of Gabriella and heard it all. She smiled as well. "Just don't talk about stripping, Gabriella." She suggested, also quietly. "They all lose it, completely and totally."

"Really? This is good information to have."

"Sienna, please stop! You are going to make this impossible!" Juan pleaded.

Porter looked over. "What's this?"

Sienna looked far too innocent. "Oh, nothing, why?"

Porter just looked at her for a second or two. "You know when you look that innocent I know you are doing something. What is it?"

Sienna laughed at him. "I was just advising Gabriella on

something."

"Uh-huh."

"I was!" Sienna protested.

"You know I don't believe you."

Gabriella raised her eyebrows. "Oh, but she was. She said to never talk about, mention, or even allude to stripping, because it upsets you all terribly."

Porter closed his eyes and sighed. "Yes, it does. And yes, I bet she said exactly that."

"Well, perhaps not exactly that..."

"It shouldn't bother you that much." Mason said to Porter.

Porter opened his eyes and looked at Mason. "Really? Then you can fucking watch the two of them do it."

"Uh..." Mason got a little red. "Never mind, then."

"Exactly my point. And, Sienna, I really wish you wouldn't do that."

"I know, which is why I do it, Porter. I don't want to be predictable, not even to you. I value the shock it gives you because it means that I am still interesting to you, even after all that we have been through. I have told you before that I do not want you to go looking elsewhere, and as long as I still can surprise you, I know you won't. I cannot stand thinking you might not want me. It would absolutely destroy me."

Juan shook his head and drank some more coffee. He definitely needed more of that. Too much damn philosophy.

Mason raised his eyebrow at Porter, then looked at Sienna, but he said nothing.

Karen came out shortly after. She sat next to Michael and smiled at them all in greeting. Porter slid her some food.

"Are James and Callie here, too?" Juan asked Mason.

"No, he had work he wanted to get done. They left, uh, sometime last night. Not sure when, though. It seems like they might have been observing the moon, as well."

Gabriella smiled. "Yes, your view is enchanting, Mason. I may need to visit more often, just to enjoy it."

Mason shrugged. "Come when you like, but make sure you bring a distraction. I don't do chaperoning."

Juan smiled. "I can't come until this one is over. I am not putting you in more danger, Mason. Or any of the rest of you."

"You seem awfully concerned, Juan." Michael said.

"Michael, imagine some very upset people who can get into computer systems and trace where you have been. If I get rid of the head of Phalanx, there are going to be underlings who are pissed. Really pissed."

"Oh. Okay, you are the expert. I trust you."

"You have to. I will be trying to keep Karen safe."

"We need to get going." Porter interrupted. "I can't spend all day doing the papers this time. I have to work. Lame, I know, but I do. James wants to try another line, perhaps a lower target, and I need to get some things ready. Mason, Juan, Gabriella, are you coming?"

Chapter 5

Monday rolled around. Juan was still pretty excited about the prospect of seeing Gabriella at lunch time, even though he needed to get his hair done, too. It would be a long lunch break. Oh damn. The new names were in place. Gabriella had been going by "Sarah White" since she started work, which, given her coloring and hair, Juan found inexplicably funny. He would get his hair done first, then go to the bakery and eat. And flirt. And whatever else presented itself.

One of his coworkers seemed to notice his mood. "Hey, Juan, why are you so high today?"

"I said I had a hot date, didn't I?"

"That was like three days ago, man!"

Juan shrugged, smiling. "She is smokin'. Three days means nothing with her."

"Wow. What are the chances of..."

"No. I don't share." Juan cut him off. "Especially not her."

"Aw, damn." His coworker muttered. "You get all the hotties."

Juan smiled to himself. "Well, not all of them. But this one is special."

He hummed to himself in his cube as he blasted through his meager work for the day. Mondays were traditionally slow for him. It usually took a day or so for people to fuck up their systems and need him to fix them. He took a quick break to make sure no one was paying him any attention, noted that all the people in his immediate vicinity had headphones on: talking on the phone or listening to music, or gaming. Hey, Mondays were slow for everyone in IT. Then he went back to his own cubicle and looked up a number for a tech position inside the area he was targeting. It was right before lunch time, a good time to catch people with their guards down. They would be hungry, and they would also be looking to resolve issues quickly.

The phone rang. "Clarissa speaking." A woman answered. Juan grinned. He usually could fool girls more easily. Women were more likely to want to be helpful and nice. Not always, of course, but often enough for him to bet on it.

"Hello, this is John from the IT department calling. I received a message that there was a security problem that I needed to investigate?" If he sounded helpful, she might reciprocate.

"Oh, I don't know anything about that, sir. May I transfer you to my supervisor?"

Juan reworked his mental script a tad. He did not want to be transferred to someone with authority. "Well, if you think that would be better, you might, but if it is a problem that we can fix at this level, that might work out better for you. Some supervisors don't like to be bothered with little problems." He laughed in a conspiratorial manner. Wink wink, he thought.

"Oh, you're right about that. Well, what can I do to help you?"

"Hm. It looks to me that your internet might be a bit slow. Have you been receiving any attempts to access your files recently?" That was safe; all internet connections seemed to be running slow. All the time. It was one of his least favorite IT problems to receive. That, and the vaguely helpful 'but it was working fine yesterday and today it doesn't'.

"You are sure right about the slow! What can it be, do you think?"

Oh, bingo. He had this. She didn't have enough knowledge to know better. He was fucking in.

"Well, it can be from a coordinated attack from a DDoS server." Juan made it up on the spot, sounding highly competent. "I will need to know the sign in name and password so that I can check all your settings and make sure the security is updated with all the latest patches. It seems likely that one or two might be outdated. Would you like to help me, or would you prefer take it to your supervisor?"

"Oh, um, no, let me get that for you. The sign in name is cpowers and the password is Cat$2Meow."

"Awesome, thanks so much Clarissa." Juan said, mentally dancing around in a crazy fashion. "Once I have accessed what I need, I will reset your password so that you can login again under it. I will put it to Pa$$W0rd, all right? I suggest you don't change it back for three days or so, so that we can be sure that everything is working appropriately."

"I won't. Thank you for helping me."

"You are most welcome. You have a good day now."

"You too, sir."

Juan pulled his headset off. "Whooo! Yessssss!" He glanced at his watch. Time for lunch! "Bye, Mitchell! Got another hot date for lunch!"

"Yeah, yeah, you suck man!"

"I know!" Juan grinned and quickly left the building. He had some time before his appointment. Hopefully this Emma chick could see him early.

Emma, who seemed very excited about doing hair, had an early chair. "Sure, sugar! Just walk your fine self this way!"

Juan smiled, even as he felt his cheeks heat up a little. This whole thing was still a bit raw. Emma led the way to her styling corner. There was a young lady reading a magazine under a dryer. She didn't look up.

"We'll just put you at station one. What can I do for you, gorgeous?"

"Uh, I wanted a new cut. I kind of wanted to try out some manga or anime looking stuff, you know?"

"Oh, yeah, that'll be fun! You have enough body and it's long enough, too. You want it a lot shorter?"

"Yeah, I think so. And, this is gonna sound weird, but can you throw a big ol' streak of blond or red right across the front here?"

"Ooh, yeah, I like that! That's going to be smoking hot. Love the idea! I think red will be more shocking, but I will have to bleach it first. Then the red will totally pop!"

Juan smiled. "You are the expert."

"Sienna says that all the time!"

"She is pretty damn perceptive."

Emma laughed. "I think I will cut it first, then we can decide on where to put your personal mark, there, sugar."

Juan shrugged. "Whatever. I don't shove my nose in where it won't do any good."

56

"All right!" She started cutting, although Juan, who knew how long and thick his hair was, would have called it "mowing" or something. It didn't take very long. Juan stared at the job she'd done.

"Damn! You are amazing!" He marveled. It had taken her almost no time, but he looked all edgy and Japanese-inspired. "Do I need to do anything with it?"

Emma smiled. "Of course not! I try to be as hands-off as I can with my cuts."

"No wonder Sienna calls you the best. Damn. This is awesome!"

Emma positively glowed. "Now, about that red..." She said.

Twenty minutes later, Juan looked totally different, even to him. Juan couldn't get over how fast Emma was at this. He smiled as he stepped out of the shop. It meant he had more time to hang out with Gabriella. Hot damn, yes!

He walked into the bakery, noting that there were people lined up, but it wasn't totally crowded. Good. He waited in line for his turn, glancing over the menu. Ooh, a crusty sandwich; he liked those. And a café latte, of course.

Gabriella was taking orders today at the counter. She looked up at him expectantly. He winked at her. She smiled extra nicely. "Hello, Sarah. I'd like a roast beef sandwich, a café latte, and to talk to you when you have a break."

"Of course, Michael!" She laughed. "I have a break for lunch in about ten minutes."

"Good! Come sit with me."

"I will." In a soft whisper, she added, "I love the hair."

He grinned, handing her some money. Then he took his number and sat at a small table by the large window. He liked sitting in the sun, and there was a nice amount streaming in there.

True to her word, Gabriella brought his plate and drink over and sat opposite him. Juan could smell her even when she was not right by him.

"And how are you today, Sarah? You look as fucking amazing as always."

She smiled at him. "I am fine, and you?"

"Fabulous!" He took her hand gently. They had practiced with the code all weekend and they were getting pretty adept at it. Porter was right; it was easy. It was also very difficult to detect, if they did it right.

"Any news?" Her fingers asked.

"Yes. I got a password and login. I will do some minor damage. We can wait. I will start boasting soon."

"Fast."

"Have to. The government will shut that window. I will move on it. Put the signatures around. Be out. Then they will see I was there. I am too good to show them where."

She smiled at him. "Got it. Anything else?"

"Not yet. Let me know when Mason has the machines."

Out loud, she said, "I am glad you finally stopped by. I told my manager all about you. She is dying to meet you."

"Not all about me, I hope."

Gabriella considered. "Well, I might have not told her what a stupendous kisser you are." Juan sighed as he blushed more. Gabriella, looking far too innocent to be believable, said, "I said I didn't tell her that part."

"You just like doing that to me." Juan accused.

"Of course. I don't want to be predictable to you, any more than she does for him, you know."

Juan shook his head. "Women." He muttered under his breath. Her smile widened. "You're all evil."

"Of course we are. That's part of the fun. Now, are you going to kiss me?"

"Here? Now?"

"Yes."

"Then yes!"

Juan noted that they were a lot more natural than he might have expected. Practicing paid off. Maybe he should practice more, though. A hell of a lot more.

"Did you want to come over tonight? I work until 5:30." He

asked softly.

Gabriella pretended to think about it. "Hm. Well, let's see. I have work tomorrow. And it's Monday. I think I am going to have to say, 'Hell, yes!'"

"Awesome. I will make you dinner. And I have a bottle of wine."

"God, you are going to spoil me."

"Good. Beautiful women deserve to be spoiled."

She laughed and kissed him again. Another woman, older, came out from in back. "Wow, Sarah, this is your young man?" She asked, perhaps a little loudly, but Juan didn't much care. The more attention other people called on him, the better.

Gabriella smiled and stood up. "Yes. He stopped in for lunch today. I was just saying goodbye, in fact, Mary."

Juan took his cue. He stood up, picking up his empty plate and cup. "See you tonight, Sarah."

"Bye, Michael." She went back behind the counter.

Juan whistled all the way back to the office. He had some of that colored gel stuff to cover the red over. He couldn't hide the cut, but the color he could. He put it in his messenger bag and went up the stairs after a quick bathroom trip to use the gel. It wasn't terrible, and for as observant as his coworkers were, it would do the job. They hardly noticed when someone wasn't in. For days at a time.

There wasn't much to do this afternoon, either. Evidently, all the people who usually fucked their computers up were out sick. Or maybe they were all at a convention. Juan didn't much care. He had his new laptop from Mason. He set it up quickly and logged in with his stolen username and password. He quickly went through the limited access he had. The girl didn't have high security clearance, but he could get some places. He really only had to modify and insert some lines of code. That would be enough. If he did it two or three places, no one would likely notice from the inside, but Phalanx would be looking. They would notice.

Besides, he had to set up some sort of mirror site somewhere that looked like a security list that he could use to show he hacked it.

He would insert some code that Phalanx would find and follow. Too bad he didn't like coding that much. However, once he knew what he wanted to do, he could set it all up fairly quickly. He would do as much offline as he could, then throw the stuff all up together. Juan carefully took some screen shots of lines of code. He could write something pretty easily.

And then there was dinner. Fuck yes. It had been a while since he had looked forward to a date this much. Who cared if it wasn't all pleasure and was a fair amount of business? She at least seemed pretty interested in him. He would ask her about it, though. He didn't really want to get infatuated and piss her off.

Juan quickly shut his laptop down. He couldn't be scrolling around in there too much and he had what he needed. He didn't want to be detected. Mason said he could shield him, but that was no reason to tempt fate that much. Besides, Juan didn't like being caught. It hurt his pride.

His phone rang. It was a customer. Juan was busy with work-related projects for the rest of the day. By the time it was 5:30, he had finished what he needed to and was ready to be gone. He shoved his stuff into his messenger bag again. Then he frowned. He should probably get another bag to carry his shit around in. That shouldn't be a problem. Maybe something flashy. Then he could ditch it along with the identity after this shit went down.

Juan went down the stairs fairly quickly. He stopped by the bathroom and quickly washed the gel off. It had worked, and the red was kind of cool. Gabriella was waiting inside the lobby, pretending to not notice the admiring looks of the other engineers.

She smiled as Juan came up. "Hello. I thought I would meet you here."

Juan also smiled and kissed her. "Works for me! Ready to go?"

Gabriella laughed and put her arm through his. Mitchell stared at Juan. Juan winked at him outrageously. "I told you. Smokin'."

"Goddamn. I never should have doubted you."

Juan led Gabriella to his car. She rode the bus to her job, so she didn't have her car around.

"What did that one guy mean?" She asked curiously.

"I told my coworkers that I had a hot date. I think they didn't really believe me. You solved that."

"Glad to help."

"Not nearly as glad as I am. They won't be onto us yet, so we can probably talk in the car. Actually, this is a spectacularly dumb car, so we can always talk in it. I turn my phone off in here, and you should too. No one can listen in, if it is turned off."

"Gotcha." She pushed the power switch and the phone shut down.

Juan exhaled. He hated feeling like he was being watched. "We might need to go driving at night sometime, just so I can relax."

She looked at him with a suggestive smile. "If we go driving at night, you won't be relaxing."

He laughed. "That wasn't what I meant! But while we are on the subject, I do have a very direct and serious question for you."

"Okay." At least she didn't sound worried. That was good.

"You can probably guess that I find you very attractive. In fact, you are almost completely distracting. But I don't want to be pressing you into something you don't want, so I want to know if you want me to pursue this beyond the job." He'd done smoother jobs of explaining things before, but hopefully that was direct enough.

Gabriella examined her fingernails, thinking about what she was going to say. "Well," she said finally, "I won't deny that I think you are very attractive, too. As to beyond this job? Well, would it be all right if we wait and see? I don't want to say, 'no', but I can't commit to, 'yes'. At least, not yet."

"Good enough for me! I'm all for a nice long courtship. I'd love to get to know you."

"So long as this courtship includes making out."

"I think I can allow for that. Also, one other question: do you wear perfume?"

"Uh, no. Why?"

"Ah, damn, I was almost hoping you did." Juan sighed.

"Are you going to explain that?"

"Well, see, I have a really good sense of smell." That should cover enough, Juan thought.

It didn't. "What the hell does that have to do with anything?"

Juan sighed again. He hated giving hints to girls; they always used them. Evil women! "Well, see, I, uh, you smell really good." He said, lamely.

Gabriella smiled. "Oh. I think I get it. You think I smell good and it turns you on?"

"Yeah, pretty much. I was going to ask you to not wear perfume, but since you don't, I am totally screwed."

Gabriella kept smiling although she didn't say anything else. Juan was experienced enough to know she was probably categorizing that and storing it away somewhere. Might as well dig his own damn grave and shoot himself all at once.

"Since I have just fucked myself worse than usual, what would you like for dinner?"

"I don't care. Make what you want. I eat anything."

"Awesome. I figured Mason wouldn't pull someone who was picky or a Vegan or something, since when we go other places we have to blend in and all. If there is something in particular you wanted though..."

She shook her head. "No, I don't mind at all. I don't eat tons."

"That's fine. I don't have tons to offer you. How about a steak and a salad? I don't usually churn out the fancy shit like Porter and Mason and Sienna do."

"Sounds fabulous. The plainer, the better. I eat too much of that fancy stuff when it is around. That was one reason I couldn't drive home, besides the alcohol. My stomach hurt!"

"You should have said something. We would have helped."

"You did help. You helped all sorts of ways."

Juan pulled up to his new, temporary apartment. "By the way, I will drive you home, if you want. Or, if you are up to it, you can always sleep at my apartment. I don't have lots of furniture, but I do have a really comfortable couch. You can have my bed and I will sleep out there."

"Aw. I was kind of hoping to share with you."

"It's not that big, and this way, we can keep the whole courtship thing up. Besides, if you end up not liking me, then there is less for you to regret."

She sighed dramatically. "Oh, all right. We'll see how it goes. You are probably right about all that, but I am still going to ask you to sleep with me a few times, even if not right now."

Juan smiled. "I'll probably accept, too. I just think it would be good to have that as the exception not the rule."

"Whatever you think best. I'm hungry."

"Let's go then!"

Chapter 6

Juan got all his code written over the next two days. He inserted it quickly, with some references to the mirror site he was going to set up. There was no way to know when the woman would reset her password, and he had to get it in there before she did. The mirror site would have to get sorted later. He simply didn't have time to put it up now.

Then there was the part where he didn't want to code the site on the laptop. If Phalanx cracked his computer, they would find it there, and that would destroy some of his credibility. He would need another machine to do it from. His work computer was not a good one, either; GH monitored internet use, although not very strictly since there were games being played in the IT department all the fucking time. He made jokes about it but Juan didn't game much there, and when he did he used his own laptop. He also tried to keep it to lunch time. No point in using work time for games, especially since that meant he could actually get his work all done during the day and go home at night. He knew some of the others had to take it home sometimes, especially on weekends. Suckers.

Gabriella would pass his information, but he needed to get another machine to code that site on, and soon. He didn't want to use Mason's work computer; that would put Mason in too much risk. Then he remembered that Porter sometimes had a laptop with him. It was a long shot, but maybe he could use it.

Juan called from his work line. He only hoped Porter wasn't off somewhere today.

"Hello?"

"Hey, Porter? This is Juan."

"Hey, what's up, man? I didn't recognize the number."

"Nah, it's my work's landline. Hey, I have a huge favor to ask."

"Go on."

"Do you have a laptop I can borrow for an hour or two?"

"Yeah. When do you need it?"

"As soon as I can get there."

Porter paused. "Uh, okay... It'll take you about fifteen minutes now. I will have it waiting."

"Thanks, man."

"No problem."

Juan knew Porter was very curious about this whole thing, but he was too professional to ask over a landline. He had to make sure that he explained it all once he was there. It might be that Porter wouldn't want him to use the thing once he knew.

He grabbed his new messenger bag, covered with Star Craft characters, and quickly left. He was caught up with work and it was almost lunch time. He could hopefully get stuff done and over with today. That would be fucking nice.

At The Diamond Nest, he walked into a crowd of frantic people. He had to literally push his way in. That was new. Porter, who was usually a head taller than everyone else, motioned him back.

"What the fucking hell did I just walk into?" Juan demanded as Porter shut the door to his tiny office in the back corner of the workshop.

"A launch, idiot. Next time, ask what you are coming into. James is launching a line today; he is becoming a real contender in the sector. It is limited-run, and that makes it more desirable, you know."

"Good for him. Does he give discounts?"

"You could ask him, I suppose." Porter pushed his laptop across the desk towards Juan.

Juan put his hands behind his back. "Before I do anything, I want you to understand what I am proposing. If you don't want me to do it, I will try to find something else."

Porter looked at him very oddly. "Juan, I don't fucking care."

"I'm serious, Porter; you might. I want to set up a decoy site of a homeland security office that shows an artificial list of made-up shit in a warehouse and then I want to hack it from my laptop."

"You're going to hack your own site?"

"I have to show that I got into the warehouse and got the machines out."

Porter nodded. "Okay, I think I get why you are telling me. It is possible that Phalanx will access my computer and find that you wrote that site on it, correct?"

"Yeah. So, it is up to you."

Porter tapped his long fingers gently on the desktop, looking off into the distance. "Well, fuck, I think you can use it. I know they could crack it, but why would they? You aren't going to be coming in here every day or anything, and once this starts to heat up, you won't come in at all unless it is an emergency, so I don't quite see that they will connect this up with you. Sure, go ahead. If I really get worried, I will get another one." He picked up the laptop and handed it to Juan. "Just do a fucking good job."

Juan grinned. "I will. Can I do it here? I don't want to use the company bandwidth for it."

Porter smiled. "As long as you don't mind the noise from the idiots in front. They should die off shortly. They can only remain hysterical for a little while. Amateurs. Some of us can stay at fever pitch for fucking days."

Juan shrugged. "It takes too much practice and stamina. They couldn't dedicate that kind of effort."

Porter laughed. "Oh, so fucking true!" He moved to leave, then hesitated for a moment. "Juan, thanks for coming by. I know I won't see you for a while. I won't feel better about this until you are back with us, you know."

"You're welcome. Is that a message from Mason?"

"No. It is a message from me, and only me."

Juan suddenly felt himself tearing up. What the fuck? "Well, thanks, man. You better go or I am gonna fucking bawl all over your damn office."

Porter did something completely out of character for him: he reached out and hugged Juan. "Just be careful, you fucking idiot." He said, not sounding totally steady himself. Then he left the office, shutting the door softly behind him. Juan sniffed, grabbing a tissue.

"What the fucking hell is wrong with me?" He mumbled, taking off his bag and putting it on the chair. He went around the desk and sat down, taking several deep breaths. "All right, Internets. Prepare to be fucking hacked, bitches."

The site was actually easy to write. Juan didn't have to do anything fancy. In fact, he made it a boring html document link. It would be overlooked by everyone, except people who were hoping for a conspiracy. And if some nut job found it on accident that would actually help. The paranoid leading the paranoid. May they both jump off a fucking cliff. Juan thought that probably wasn't Biblical, but it should be.

He had the thing written and up within an hour. It was masterful, he thought to himself. It would pull up an access denied message first, then, once they cracked that, which wouldn't take too long, there was password-protected, tantalizingly vague list, which he would use his laptop to go into and modify some code with to show that he had bypassed it all. Fuck yes. He could see how this stuff could be addicting, but he still didn't like it as much as building circuits and troubleshooting them. Now those were exciting.

Juan shut Porter's laptop down, humming softly to himself. Now he needed to eat something and get back to work.

There was a soft knock on the door. "Yes?" Juan said warily, standing up and ready for doing something if he needed to.

Porter opened the door again and came in, shutting it behind him. "They are still out there. When you leave, we'll get you out the back door so you can bypass them all."

"Thanks. I was conspicuous enough coming in."

"Yeah, well, since you don't have that red showing right now, no one is going to have noticed you today. They are all frothing over James. He looks fucking terrified." Porter laughed. "It is good for him, though. If he goes out on his own, he will have to deal with this."

Juan smiled. "Good. Let him get too scared to leave now!"

Porter laughed again. "Damn straight! Now, since it is lunch time, I thought you might like something to eat."

Juan perked up. "Fuck yes. What do you have?"

"Nothing, yet, but I expect developments in a few minutes." Porter smiled, his eyes twinkling. He picked up Juan's messenger bag, glancing at it curiously, and setting it aside. Then he occupied the chair.

Juan sat behind the desk. "You should really be here, since it is your fucking store."

Porter shrugged. "In case you hadn't noticed, I don't much fucking care who is pretending to be in charge. If you want the truth, Sienna does more running of this place than I do. I started it so I could use my creative energy, but I am not a great manager. Don't bother asking her; she fucking denies it. It's true though."

"You are a great team in many ways." Juan smiled.

"She deserves much better than me, in all ways."

Juan shook his head gently. "Porter, you and I both know we can't tell women what they deserve. They decide what they want. Here's the thing, though: I think they instinctively or somehow know exactly what they need and want, and that is what they get. She may deserve more, but she needs you."

Porter sighed and closed his eyes. "You're probably right, Johnny. It sucks that I am not that great, though."

"Porter, if you think about it, none of us deserve any of the women we have. I sometimes think no man deserves any woman. They are so much better than we are, so much more intuitive, grounded, and fucking awesome. And then there is us men, all carnal and beasts. How the hell did that happen?"

Porter shrugged. "Dunno, but when you put it that way, it sounds right, somehow."

"You guys keep forcing all this philosophy on me. It's your own fucking fault."

"You're right, but like Mason said, philosophy is fun."

There was another soft knock at the door. "Come in," Porter said, without bothering to get up.

Sienna opened the door. "Here, Juan." She smiled at him and handed him a bag. It smelled delicious.

"Wow, thanks, Sienna. Service with a smile. How fucking lucky can I be?"

"I'd love to stay with you two, but they are mobbing poor James and Karen. I have to go beat them back, possibly with a bull whip."

Porter smiled. "Interesting mental picture, my love."

"It's true. At least they will have bought it all soon, then we can throw everyone else out."

Porter nodded. "I will be out shortly."

"No rush, Porter. I can manage them. You take the time with Juan. I am not stupid; you have been wound tight for days, and I know it is because of him." She left, closing the door.

Porter sighed. "Proof positive that she is far too good for me."

"Whatever, man. You bring out the best in her. Didn't you know that?"

"Whatever."

"I'm serious, Porter. She never acted this way before she met you that first time. You know, you have made us such a better team. You are so fucking brilliant we have to up our game to keep up. Didn't you know that?"

"No. I think you are exaggerating."

"You can think whatever the fuck you want. I know I am telling the truth." Juan opened the bag. "What the fuck do you want? Besides a fucking crab sandwich?"

Porter smiled a half-smile. "What did she get us?"

"You mean you don't know?"

"Johnny, she offered to go and get it. I don't tell Sienna what to do. What the fuck, man? First you say I am brilliant then you say I order her around? Way to be fucking inconsistent."

"Okay, you win. Looks like French dips. And salad."

"Then hand one over, idiot."

"Fine, asshole." Juan handed the bag across.

"Did you get the page up?" Porter asked as they ate.

"Yeah, it was easy. But, seriously, Porter, if you are worried…"

"I'm not, Johnny. Not over that. I am worried about you. If you think this will compromise you, then I will ditch that thing right now. I care less about my precious files."

"Oh." Juan hadn't really expected that. He thought about it for a few minutes. "Uh, sorry man, I didn't really think about it like that."

Porter smiled. "No, you were worried about me, not yourself. We are similar in lots of ways, Johnny."

"Yeah, we are. That's why we are so fucking awesome!"

"Exactly! I am going to miss you."

"Same, especially since you cook such amazing food. Which reminds me, are you buying that one house?"

"Well, Sienna totally loves it, and I like it enough. I have a little trouble committing to anything, but she really wants us to be there. Besides, I like the idea of living close to Mason. He is the guy who understands me better than anyone else, really. So, yeah, we are probably going to buy it within the next few weeks."

"Awesome. I can't wait to see it. And I can't wait for you to be happy."

Porter smiled again. "You might put too much pressure on a poor little house."

Juan grinned. "It isn't the fucking house, idiot. You better invite me out when you get it."

"Once you have caught these guys."

"That goes without saying, Porter. How big is it?"

"Big enough. It has a guest room, for when you are done with this shit."

"Pencil me in for a day, then."

"Of course. I probably shouldn't say anything, but the house two down from Mason on the other side of the street might go on the market. It's a little up the hill."

"Ooh, well, I hope it hangs around until I can get to it!"

Porter hesitated, and then said, "You know, Juan, if you are serious, Michael and I can look it over, if it does go on the market, and if you authorize us, we could buy it for you."

Juan was very surprised. "If you two would do that for me, that would be amazing. I completely trust you, especially if you have Sienna and Karen reining you in."

"Well, we will see."

Juan looked at his watch. "Shit, I have to go. Porter, man, thanks. For everything. And I am going to start crying here in a second, so just let me go before I embarrass us both."

Porter shook his hand and opened the door without saying

anything more.

Juan hurried out of the back room into the alley. He swiped at his eyes quickly. "Seriously, you need to fucking pull it together, boy." He said to himself. "Fucking get over it."

Self-talk usually worked for him and by the time he was back at his car, he had regained his outward stability. He had been deeply touched by Porter's offer to be an intermediary, as well as his extreme concern for him. He hadn't realized how much Porter worried about the team members before. It made sense though. Porter acted like an older brother to them all, and he was damn smart. Juan hadn't been joking about having to up his game. He understood what Mason said about feeling inferior. Juan didn't like being caught doing something stupid when it was his own area of expertise. So far, Porter hadn't pointed anything out to him and Juan wanted to keep it that way.

Chapter 7

The next time Juan saw Gabriella was Friday. She came by his work again at quitting time. Juan really liked coming down the stairs and seeing her there. It made him very happy. Besides, she always looked amazing, and he didn't even notice anyone else for several seconds when he saw her. Talk about uplifting.

Once they were in the car and driving, she said, "Mason said he will get the machines to you tonight. It will be an unmarked box that says something about wineglasses on it. It'll just be on your front porch, so you better get it as soon as the doorbell rings."

"Got it. Are you hungry, beautiful?"

"Starved. Working around food all day makes me not hungry while I am there and then I am so hungry afterwards."

"You should eat more. You are going to waste away."

She shrugged. "Whatever. It'll even out sometime."

"We'll just have to wait until they contact me now. I can't do more without being too obvious, and leet hackers like me don't show off."

She laughed at him. "You're not a hacker."

"They don't know that."

"Where are you from, anyway? You don't seem as puffed up as a lot of smart people do."

"California, the northern part. My family has been legal in the US for four or five generations now, and I don't even know if we have relatives in Mexico anymore. I went to MIT and Stanford. You?"

"I'm from Ohio, a place called Troy. It is smallish, love that feel. I don't really like big places, but that is where the jobs are. I went to Ohio State. Got a degree in psychology, but not clinical. I ended up in a few jobs, and I remember Mason coming for a conference to the hospital I was working at. He was really nice, just the same as always, and he seemed really good at getting information. I somehow told him my degree and he promised to look into his own clinic and see if there was an opening for me there. A few weeks later, he called and asked if I would work there as an administrative assistant for him. At first, I was kind of worried that he might have some sort of designs on me. I've had that problem before, but he has always been most professional in that matter."

"He would be. Mason doesn't mix work with pleasure like that. Boring that way. I sometimes wonder if he has even kissed a girl at all."

"Probably. But that is how I ended up here. How did he find you?"

"Through GH, of course. He called up looking for help, and eventually he asked Michael to work with him and Michael recommended me. Michael has been my friend for about ten years now, so that wasn't as weird as it could have been."

"Oh, yeah, that makes more sense."

"You have any family?"

"My parents live back in Ohio still. I call them once a month or so. And I go back for Thanksgiving and Christmas, if I have the money. You?"

Juan shook his head. "My parents died. There was a car accident. It was fifteen years ago, or so."

"I am very sorry."

"Yes, it was hard for awhile. I doubt I would have gone to graduate school at all if I weren't trying to shake that. I never finished out my degree, anyway. I don't really have any family that I am close with."

"Maybe that helps you be close with your friends, then?"

Juan shrugged. "It might, it might not. I can't say. Maybe I can tag along to Thanksgiving with you sometime."

"Maybe so. We'll just have to see."

"Yes, indeed. Do you dance?"

She smiled. "That was quite a subject change. Dance? Who doesn't?"

Juan also smiled. "I meant ballroom."

"Oh, well, now I can't say that I have much experience with that."

"Too bad. I like ballroom dancing."

"Hey, don't write me off that fast. I might be willing to learn. If, you know, the teacher is hot enough."

"I would love to teach you some, if you want."

"I will try it for you."

Juan grinned. "Then maybe we can give Porter and Sienna a run for their money during a tango or salsa sometime. I swear she is like watching a strip show, and she never even takes anything off."

"Ooh, I like the sound of that. I always wanted to try a sexy dance."

"We'll have to start with something tamer, first." He warned.

"I think there are probably ways to sex up the tame ones, too."

He laughed. "Oh yes. The other reason I asked is because usually, on a formal dance floor, people are always moving around, unlike a club party. So it would be very hard for someone to overhear anything. Just another option."

"Makes sense."

After dinner, Juan put on some waltz music. "We start like this." He said, holding Gabriella's hand and demonstrating the basic box step.

It had been about ten minutes or so when there was a single, soft knock at the door. Juan immediately and carefully pushed Gabriella off to the side of him and out the line of sight with the door. He put his finger to his lips and moved to the door. A quick glance through the peephole showed no one outside. Juan unlocked the door and opened it quickly. A plain box sat on his doormat, marked "Wineglasses, Fragile" on the top. He pulled it inside and shut the door again. After locking the deadbolt, he shoved the box out of the way with his foot.

"Well, where were we?" He asked, coming back over to Gabriella.

"Don't you want to open it?"

"No, I know what it is. And if it isn't that and is a bomb or explosive, I don't want you here when I open it. One of us is enough. Would you like to dance? And then I can take you home, if you are tired."

Gabriella smiled. "That would be very nice. I have some cake at my apartment, if you would like to stay for dessert. Maybe a little television?"

"I don't watch anything."

Her smile turned a touch wicked. "I didn't mean watch television."

"Oh. Yes, I think I would like that. Dessert, and uh more dessert."

"Exactly."

"Hot damn. Then, if you want to get together tomorrow, we can dance and maybe learn something else."

Several hours later, Juan finally got back to his own apartment. He knew that he could have stayed at Gabriella's but he wanted to keep that as a rare, special option, rather than the norm. Besides, that way he would be more able to keep himself under control. She was just too damn hot! Now his sweater smelled like her. As he pulled it off in his place, he noticed it. Damn women. They had too much power.

Oh well. Tomorrow, maybe they could start something new, like a salsa. He liked those, too.

Now there was this package to open. Juan hadn't been joking about the bomb. If it was something other than what he thought it was, he did not want Gabriella anywhere close. As he examined the box, he noted a tiny initial "MB" under the words. Good. It was from Mason after all. No one would put that unless they knew about the connection, and no one should know that. He put the box on his table and cut the tape. It looked like a professional job, straight for the factory. He carefully made sure to rip the initials as he opened the box. Oops. Now no one could see them. Damn.

Inside, there was a disassembled hard drive and some cards from a computer, as well as a motherboard. Juan was going to have to be careful putting it back together, but he had the skill for this. It was so much better than coding. Hacking it after that might be hard.

A single sheet of paper fell out as he picked up the hard drive. It had some numbers in two columns, and at the bottom it said, "CommanderRED" and "G0lD*leAder76".

"Fuck yes, Mason. You are so awesome." Juan whispered to himself. He was going to have stop doing that pretty soon, since he was sure he was going to be spied on. His evening, while not better than earlier, was at least still interesting.

Juan glanced at his watch. It was 10:00. If he got this stuff all connected into a box, then he could at least turn the damn thing on and see what happened. He could always run it on a standard power supply and leave it open. Besides, if it burned up, he wanted to see that right away. This stuff had been out of commission for two or three years. Who knew how long it had sat in some box? There could be all sorts of strange stuff with that. Oh well.

"Okay, computer. Let's get you going. Then, if you actually power up, I will call that a night."

It didn't take too long to connect everything. This was stuff that Juan liked. Well, okay, he liked all of it, but this was the stuff he liked the best. Holding his breath, he powered it on. It spun up right away.

"Fuck yes! Okay, tomorrow, my pretty. Tomorrow I search for something concrete, some pictures, maybe. Or, maybe I will just take a picture or two. Then I will sit back and await developments. Phalanx, your ass is so mine."

Glancing at the numbers, Juan thought most of them looked like IP and IPv6 addresses. His hunch was that these were some of the sites that CommanderRED had either frequented or written, or both. Juan would check into that tomorrow. Tonight, he was done. He had danced with a beautiful woman, and he had got this shit to work. Enough was enough. Maybe he would dream up some answers to the problems he still had, but he was pretty sure he wouldn't care if he didn't. It had been a terribly successful evening already.

Juan got ready for bed, humming to himself and mentally planning out his strategy. He absently noted that his shirt also smelled faintly like Gabriella and briefly considered sleeping in it. He smiled to himself. He probably wouldn't dream up solutions to his computer problems that way, but it might make for a very interesting night.

Chapter 8

The next morning Juan, who wasn't good at sleeping late, was up early. There was a problem to fix, dammit! He had to get it addressed. After a quick breakfast, he fired the computer up again. He also opened his laptop. Whatever he did had to be online and traceable. Hopefully, the Commander had used some sort of signature, or some identification mark somewhere. They usually did. It was one of the trademarks of hackers: they both simultaneously wanted to be anonymous and demanded instant recognition.

Juan hummed to himself for moment. Screw it, he opened Pandora and put it on a new hits station. He wanted mood music.

It looked like the entries on that sheet were the username and password to something. CommanderRED didn't lock his computer. Stupid move, that. Juan cruised right on in. On his laptop, he began to check out the numbers. They mostly went to different websites, several no longer in operation. There were some forums, as well. He skimmed through those pretty quickly. They seemed like the usual crazed hacker shit. About that paranoia, Juan thought. Still that might be one way to get his message out, if Phalanx was really so dense. Juan thought they would be smoother than that, though. He would give it one week, then he would start posting insulting, broad hints that he had the machine.

He shifted attention to the other machine. Sure enough, right across the desktop, there was sprawled a copy of CommanderRed's signature code. Juan stared at it incredulously. This had to be a fucking joke. The guy was unbelievable. He must have had one hell of an ego before they caught him. Juan would never do anything that blatantly obvious.

Oh well. That just made his chore so much fucking easier.

The next two URL's went to defunct government websites and redirected immediately. The third went to a sign-in page. Juan stared at it for a minute. What the fuck was this, then? Whose page was it? Ah, what the hell. He typed in the username and password from the sheet.

"All Hail the great Commander!" His computer said, in what

was probably supposed to be a suggestively sexy female voice. To Juan, it sounded way too mechanical, like Siri, but whatever. He had his own sexy voice to talk to him. She never said anything scripted, either. So much the better.

The main page was a manifesto. A long, staggeringly, egotistically, boring manifesto. Several parts seemed to be lifted right from <u>The Conscience of a Hacker</u> without citation, of course. Hackers and crackers didn't need to cite other people's genius. They assumed that everything was free to whoever lifted it, it seemed to Juan.

The section below the boring ego fluffing was a forum. The last date was June 12. There was no year tag. It was a call for a hit on a nuclear plant. There were responses from several handles, but they all ended up eventually asking what had happened to the Commander. Then they stopped. Juan knew CommanderRed had been hit in a high-level sting operation, and that whoever he was he had his ass hauled off to jail pretty damn quick. Hacktivists had that happen with depressing regularity.

Juan smiled slightly. Time for the Commander to reawaken.

He started a new forum. "The Commander seems to have lost his way. Fortunately, Poniard found a weakness and hit it."

That was it. It was egotistical enough and vague enough. Juan thought it would work. He would just have to sit back and wait. One week. Then he would start hitting other forums.

His cell phone buzzed from the floor beside him. It was Gabriella. This was going to be a good day.

"Hello, this is Michael."

"Michael, are you up?"

"Why, yes, Sarah. I was finishing up a little project, but it is at a convenient stopping point now."

"Oh, good. I hoped I wasn't interrupting."

"You may always interrupt me!"

"You are being ridiculous. Did you have any plans today?"

"No, but I notice that the weather is gorgeous outside. Would you like to go on a picnic in the park later?"

"Oh my God, that sounds amazing."

Juan grinned. "Sure, what time?"

Things were quiet for the next week. Juan did not monitor the Commander's website. He wasn't going to look that anxious. Work went at the usual pace. There was nothing interesting there. Juan went to the little bakery Gabriella worked at two times, and she came to his work for a dinner date once, on Tuesday. They kept dancing.

Friday, Juan went in for lunch again. They were going to get damn used to seeing him there if he had to live there. Fortunately, there was some really nice scenery. She smiled up at him. "The usual, beautiful?"

"Of course, lovely Sarah!"

"I'll bring it right out!"

True to her word, she had it right there.

"That was quick." Juan said, impressed.

She smiled at him cheekily. "I had it all ready, Michael. I knew you'd be in today."

"You must be psychic as well as beautiful beyond the right anyone should have. I had a proposition for you." She looked interested at that. "There is a ballroom dance at a little dance studio I know. Would you like to go? It is very laid-back, intimate, no pressure."

"Ooh, that sounds like lots of fun! What should I wear?"

"Anything you want. There is no dress code, except that shoes are clean on the bottoms. I recommend bringing a pair just to dance in."

"All right! What time?"

"It starts at 7:00, but we can show up at any time."

"I'll meet you after work then. Maybe we can get some dinner first."

"Okay, but how will you get your clothes then?"

"We can stop by my apartment."

Juan smiled. He was looking forward to this, far more than he let on. Half the fun of dancing was showing off, and showing off with ballroom meant having a good partner. Gabriella was quite good, better than she thought she was. And Juan liked showing off.

It was time for him to get back to work. Gabriella looked at him with her eyebrow raised. "You better not think you are leaving without at least one kiss, Michael."

"Of course not. What kind of idiot do you think I am? Wait, don't answer that. But I am not that kind of an idiot."

Besides, she was a lot of fun to kiss, especially in the sun. It made it all edgy, like doing something forbidden.

When he quit for the day, she was waiting for him. He noted, again, the jealous looks of some of the guys who worked in his office. As he walked towards the bottom of the stairs, Mitchell whispered despairingly, "Does she at least have a sister?"

"No, man, sorry. She is an isolated incident, like a unicorn."

"Damn." Mitchell sighed.

Once they were in the car with the phones turned off, Juan said, "I have been expecting developments from Phalanx anytime. I can't say for sure what they will do, but I kind of think it will be extravagant. So just be aware, sexy lady, that you are in their line-of-sight. I had some nibbles at my laptop a couple of times. I think they will try to contact me soon. At least, I hope so. I don't like waiting."

Gabriella nodded seriously. "I understand, Juan. I have been very careful this last week, and I won't let my guard down."

"Good. I would never forgive myself if something happened to you because of any of this."

"It wouldn't be your fault."

"It makes no fucking difference."

At his apartment, Juan quickly started some food and went to shower and change, letting Gabriella do what she wanted in the kitchen. Black was a good color. Black on black, tie and shirt.

Gabriella raised her eyebrows appreciably when he came back out. "Wow, you look smoking hot."

"Thank you, lovely Sarah. Ready to eat?"

"Why, yes, I am. Then I need to get changed. I guess I will have to aim a little higher than I had originally thought. You look much too handsome and distinguished for what I had planned on."

"You may wear whatever you want. I can always change, you know."

80

"Don't you fucking dare!"

"Okay then." Juan moved to pull the manicotti out of the oven.

While Gabriella showered and changed at her apartment, Juan looked around. She had some books from the library. He glanced through them, secretly glad that she wasn't reading that romance crap that was marketed to women. All it was, really, was porn disguised as a book. Lame.

Gabriella came out in a stunning fuchsia dress. She held out a gold chain to him. "Would you put this on me, please?"

"Of course. You look amazing." Juan carefully put the necklace on her. "I might not be able to concentrate anywhere else."

She smiled. "I kind of hope not. Shall we?"

The studio was not large, and the owner opened the floor on the second Friday of each month for a dance. The cover charge was five dollars a couple, and a lot of the couples were clients there. They were all good. There were some others, singles and couples, who had heard of it and came. Mostly, they were good enough. Juan smiled as they walked in.

"Don't worry about watching anyone else, if you don't want to. Dancing is more fun if you enjoy what you are doing."

Gabriella still looked a bit nervous. "Um, okay. I feel a little out of my league though."

"There's no league here, just fun."

"Okay. Let's have some fun, then."

"That's my girl!" Juan laughed.

"Are you sure you want to say that?"

"Well," Juan considered it. "I think so, but if you would rather I didn't..."

"I don't know, yet."

"Okay, I won't say it."

"Just maybe not right this second."

Juan shrugged. "Easy enough. Sometimes I don't do a good job of censuring my tongue. Would you like this dance?" He bowed as a waltz started up.

They danced for about an hour and a half. It was fun, once they got used to the atmosphere and the feel of the floor. About halfway through, Juan noticed Porter and Sienna come in. He knew they came here occasionally, but he hadn't expected to see them tonight.

"Porter's here." He whispered very softly to Gabriella. "Don't look; he and Sienna are going to dance, like we are, and we are not going to pay any attention."

"I understand. Unless they do something really hot. Then I am taking notes."

"That goes without saying."

Porter caught Juan's eye once, but neither acknowledged the other beyond that one glance.

The next waltz, though, Porter came over and bowed to Gabriella. "May I have this dance, lady?"

"Oh, um, of course." She said, glancing quickly at Juan.

Juan smiled at her. "Go on. I won't monopolize you, Sarah."

"Thank you, sir." Porter said gravely.

Juan asked a giddy college-age girl to waltz. She blushed cherry red and agreed much too quickly.

The dance after was a tango. Gabriella asked if Juan would go with her to get some water. As they stood on the sideline watching, Gabriella snuck her hand into Juan's. He smiled slightly.

The studio closed down at 10:00. As he was driving them back, Juan said, "Did you want to come over?"

"Sure! By the way, Porter, who is way too good at that whole code thing, asked how you were getting on. I told him what I know, which is nothing."

"Nothing to tell, yet."

"He seems worried."

"He is. He is worried about us. He could care less about the mission otherwise."

"That makes sense. He asked me to tell you to be careful still and, now let me get this right 'the house is his and the other might go.' I hope that makes sense to you."

Juan smiled. "Yes, it does. He and Sienna bought the house by Mason. There is another house in that area that might be for sale soon,

82

and if I am not available to purchase it, he and Michael will buy it for me."

"They would do that for you?" Gabriella sounded surprised.

"Well, yeah, he offered, in fact."

"You guys have enough money just sitting around to buy each other expensive houses?"

Juan laughed. "I'll pay him back, you know! But Porter has lots of money. He is one of the best and most exclusive jewelers in this country. He only makes what he wants to, not what anyone orders. And these missions pay extremely well. Didn't you ever ask Mason what we are getting for this one?"

"No, it never came up."

"That's probably just as well. We'll both get something like two million."

"What? That's insane!"

"Well, half of it goes to taxes and all, but yes, it is a lot. None of us are hurting for money. Of course, none of us really care about the money, either. It's all a game, and we're playing it with our best friends. The money is just the bonus."

"Holy shit."

"I'd do it without the money, just to play. And I never even consider it when we start the thing. I only asked this time to make sure you would get a just compensation."

Gabriella smiled slightly at him. "I have a more than just compensation. I get to meet the most interesting people and I have gotten to know you."

Juan blushed. "Well, thanks."

At his apartment, Juan took off his shoes with great relief. "Ah. My feet start to hurt after a while." He also took off his tie and undid the top two buttons. Then he threw himself on the couch. He smiled up at Gabriella. "Care to join me?"

She smiled down at him and deliberately straddled his legs with her own. "You are not getting away from me now, Michael. I can do whatever I want."

It was later, much later. Juan was dozing with Gabriella still in his arms. It must have been close to midnight when there was a scratching noise at the door. Juan was fully awake in a second; someone was trying to force the lock. He shook Gabriella gently. Then there was a crashing blow to the door. Gabriella woke up with a scream and she started to fall. Juan caught her quickly. His heart was hammering. Someone certainly wanted his attention.

He put his finger to Gabriella's lips gently, giving at her with a warning look. She nodded, her face still shocked.

Out loud, Juan shouted, "What the fuck!"

Outside, there were some muffled sounds of people conferring, and then a man's voice said louder, "We want to talk to Michael. He has something we want."

Juan nodded. He put his mouth very close to Gabriella's ear. "Phalanx." He breathed. She nodded.

"Well, give me a fucking minute." Juan shouted back. He waited a few seconds, then got up and undid the deadbolt. The regular lock was already open.

He swung open the door. Two men stood there, one fairly non-descript and wearing glasses, the other had tattoos all over his arms. Juan noted briefly that one was a butterfly with pink wings on his left hand flying into an open-mouthed skull right above it. The tattooed guy reached out and grabbed Juan by the front of his shirt. Too bad for him, Juan had trained extensively with Michael and Porter. He stepped into the grab and slammed his forearm on Tattoo's wrist at the same time as he buried his left fist into his stomach as hard as he could.

Tattoos let go immediately, doubled over and coughing.

"Don't let your friend vomit all over my mat." Juan said coldly to Glasses. Glasses was staring at him with a calculating look. Juan returned it. "Well? You gonna pound my door in and throw up all over my steps and leave, or you wanna come in and pretend to talk like a man?"

Glasses jerked his head in assent.

Juan stepped back. "Just take your damn shoes off when you do. Don't go tracking shit all over my place."

Glasses and Tattoos came in and took their shoes off

resentfully. Juan glared at them the whole time. "Listen, idiots, I don't like it when people try to scare me and I don't like it when they scare my girl. Now, what the fuck you want? Better speak up now. I am not going to be lenient for long."

Glasses glanced at Tattoos, who looked back blankly. Irritably, Glasses said, "We were asked to come recover a machine."

Juan laughed harshly. "Took you guys fucking long enough. I only cracked it a whole week ago."

"Well, I don't know shit about that, man. They just sent us."

"Who did?"

Tattoos nudged Glasses warningly. Glasses nodded at him. "We can't tell you."

Juan smirked. "Well then I guess we're done here. If you can't give me a name, then I can't give you jack shit."

Gabriella moved up beside him and slipped her hand into his. "Be careful." Her fingers warned.

Glasses looked at Tattoos helplessly. Tattoos sighed. "Fine, we'll call him and see what he says." Tattoos pulled out a phone and dialed. "We're here, boss, but he won't give it up."

Tattoos listened for a minute. He handed the phone across to Juan. "Hello?" Juan said, not taking his eyes off the two guys nor letting go of Gabriella.

"Hello, Michael. Or should I call you Poniard?"

"Call me whatever the fuck you want." Juan said rudely. "You can't just send two guys here and break down my goddamn door and expect me to give up the goods without even a name."

"I can do what I want."

"Good. So can I. So I'm hanging up. Goodbye."

"Wait!" The man on the other end said, but Juan ended the call and handed the phone back to Tattoos.

Tattoos stared at him. "You are fucking crazy." He said, a touch of awe in his voice.

"Whatever, man. He won't tell me who the fuck he is, we're done. For all that, I don't even know who you two are."

Glasses cleared his throat. "I'm Black Adder."

Tattoos said, "I'm Ink."

"Ah." Juan remembered his biography searching. "Toby and Clarke." They both jumped a bit and stared. Juan laughed harshly. "Oh, come on, boys. You knew I had skills."

Gabriella touched his fingers slightly again. "Dangerous."

"I know. Keeping off-guard." Juan signaled gently back.

She squeezed in assent.

There was the sound of a phone ringing. Clarke with the tattoos jerked. "Oh, it's for you." He handed the phone, still ringing, across to Juan. Juan took it and put it on speaker.

"How about we don't have any secrets here, gentlemen?"

"What do you mean?" the voice on the other end asked, obviously irritated.

"Oh, I put this call on speaker phone. You say what you want to all of us."

"And who is 'all of us'?"

"Why, Toby, Clarke, Sarah, and me, of course."

There was a pause on the other end. "I see. You have Sarah with you?"

"Well, shit, man, you sent your goons here on a Friday night. What the fuck did you think? You're goddamn lucky you didn't send them into something they would have loved to see."

"Oh?"

Juan snorted. "Use your fucking imagination. I don't do public shit like that. I'd have done something a lot worse to them both if they had."

"Worse than what?"

"Not much. Now, what the fuck you want? Start there, then we can negotiate."

"We want CommmanderRED."

Juan laughed. "Sorry, I don't have him. I have his machine though."

"That is what we want."

"What are you going to give me in return?"

"Prestige."

"Sorry, no deal. I have all I want. I can always get more. If that's all you have, then…"

"Money, then."

"Don't want any more. I have enough. You know what I get paid."

"What do you want?"

"Oh," Juan pretended to think it over. "I want to know who I'm dealing with, to start with. Then I will know what to ask."

There was a long silence on the other end. Finally the voice answered, "Fine. You're dealing with Phalanx. But you knew that."

"Of course I did. Making you speak the name gives me power though. Now, as to what I want… I want in. I can take my skills anywhere, but I like your style and I want in."

There was another long pause. "I can't just agree to that."

"Then I suppose I will have to go shopping somewhere else."

"Wait! Is there any way we can convince you to give us the goods?"

"Hm. Nope, not without me. Besides, I have enacted security on the hard drive now. Did you know the Commander hadn't even password-protected that thing? Ridiculous. I bet the feds pulled all the shit they could off there before they chucked it in a box."

"Yes, we know where it was."

"Of course you do. But you won't know exactly what I did to it, and you won't want to take the time to figure it out. Besides, do you want me as a rival?"

"Hm. No, I don't. But I can't make the decision myself. We need you to meet a group. We'll need to make sure you are clean first. How about we call you when we want you?"

Juan paused again, pretending to think about it. "Oh, all right. But I keep the command post with me. Now, if you'll excuse me, I was doing something a lot more interesting than talking on the phone when your boys frightened my girl."

"Of course. Later, Michael."

Juan ended the call. He handed the phone back to Clarke. "Now get the fuck out. Next time fucking knock."

Toby and Clarke were staring at him, both in fear and awe. Toby finally said, "I never heard anybody talk like that to any of them."

"It's probably refreshing for them, then. Don't forget your shoes, gentlemen, and please knock next time."

Clarke suddenly grinned and nodded. "You are fucking crazy." He said in admiration. They put on their shoes and left. Juan relocked the door.

Gabriella looked at him as he put his finger to his lips again. He came back and tapped on her hand, "We can't talk in normal tones here anymore. Your apartment either. They will be watching. Only the code or in the car is safe. Maybe dancing."

She nodded. Out loud, she said, "Well, since we're both awake again anyway..." She put her arms up around his neck and kissed him quite seriously. Juan wondered, somewhat irrationally, if he would ever get used to that. Then he fervently hoped he wouldn't.

Chapter 9

It took about a week for Phalanx to call again. Toby and Clarke came around the same time but they didn't try breaking in the damn door. They knocked politely. Fortunately, Juan and Gabriella were awake.

"Oh, hello, boys." Juan stepped back. "Please come in."

Clarke grinned and took his shoes off. Toby was a bit upset looking about something.

"Bosses want to meet you." Clarke said, pulling his phone out of his pocket again and dialing. "You must have intrigued them last time."

Juan shrugged. Gabriella again came up beside him and snuck her hand into his.

"Hello, yes, we're here. You wanna talk to him?" Clarke listened for a second and nodded at Juan.

Juan took the phone and put it on speaker again. "Hello. This is Michael."

There was a pause, then a new voice said, "We don't use real names here."

"I do what the fuck I want. You know who I am, why act all secret?"

"It's not something we discuss."

"Oh, my bad. I didn't realize that I was intruding on some special kabala shit. Do I have to wear a red string bracelet, too? What is this, fight club?"

"I do not find your tone humorous." The voice was frosty.

"And I don't find your little stupid rules worth following. Let's cut to the chase, whoever you are. You guys still won't give me names, then I am out. You want to trust me, fine, but you trust me all the way, not some arms-length shit. I have the command post. You want it. I cracked it, and what's more, I cracked the government. Now, you can either throw in with me, or you can try and bluff me out, but I tell you this now: I don't bluff. You know my hand, but you don't know how I will play it. It's up to you guys. You decide."

There was another long pause. The frosty voice said, "I think we cannot afford to let you get away. My name is Fredrico. We are willing to meet up with you, in Amsterdam, if you can get here soon."

"This is shit." Juan said dismissively.

"How so?"

"You want me there? So give me a goddamn timeline. I have a job, and I want to keep it. It is excellent cover. Also, I have Sarah, and believe me when I say that I refuse to leave her where your boys can get at her. You either take us both or you can fuck off."

"All right, the lovely Sarah can come, too. But the offer holds. You have to get here on your own. Within two weeks. You will find the usual instructions on the forum. Good night, Michael."

"Night, asshole." Juan ended the call and tossed the phone to Clarke.

Toby looked less preoccupied. "Whoa, man, I have never heard any of them say a real name before."

Juan shrugged. "Whatever. They think using handles is more cool, like using passwords and secret handshakes. What is this, elementary school? Man up and use names. Anyway, thank you for knocking this time. If I were you two, I would make myself scarce, maybe real scarce. Also, you might rethink this line of work. They let you stick your necks out and then treat you like shit. That ain't right, boys. Ain't right at all. Night."

He could see that he had them thinking. "Night." They put on their shoes and left.

Gabriella still held his hand. "Are you sure you want me to come?"

"My dear, if I didn't bring you, my hunch is that someone would apprehend you and bring you as blackmail. If I bring you with me that is one less chip they have to play."

"If you say so."

He put his finger over her lips gently. He said meaningfully, "Did you want to spend the night here, or would you like me to take you home?"

"You may drive me home, but only if we spend at least ten

minutes kissing goodnight."

In the car, Juan said, "I definitely want you with me for all this. You're far too important to me to chance anything happening to you."

"And after?" She asked lightly.

"Well, I promised to wait and see about after. Besides, I don't want to pressure you on anything."

"You aren't. I want to know what you want."

"Okay, well, I want you with me after all this, too. I think I want you with me always. But that has to be your decision."

"If I say no, would you be upset?"

"Would I be upset? Fuck, yes! It would destroy me for weeks! I think I would cry for a long time if you left. I might never stop! What kind of question is that, anyway?"

"A really good one, apparently. Let me ask one more, then. If I said 'maybe', would you still try?"

Juan sighed. This was not going to make him sound very manly or whatever, but it he already admitted to crying a lot, so it wouldn't be worse. "Yes I would try. I would probably make a fucking nuisance of myself, too. Then you would go away because I was so damn annoying."

"Oh, I doubt that."

Juan shook his head. "I don't."

"Have you ever thought about being this exclusive with anyone else?"

"No, have you?"

"No. But then I haven't had too many other boyfriends."

"Other? Does that mean I get to claim the coveted official boyfriend title?"

"I think that would be appropriate at this point, yes. We've been on enough dates, and you haven't been scared off by me yet."

"I really think it would be me scaring you."

"Well, either way. I think this sort of conversation definitely goes with the whole boyfriend/girlfriend thing."

"Awesome!" Juan grinned widely. "Best night!"

Gabriella laughed. She snuggled her head on his shoulder as he parked in the quiet parking lot of an overlook. "Besides, I can't really imagine a life without you in it now. I haven't known you very long, but you already are such an important part of it. Crazy, huh?"

Juan slid his arm around her waist. "I don't know; I feel the same way. That's one reason I would be so upset if you left now. I will have to get the new info on to Mason. I am going to write it on a note and pass it to Sienna tomorrow. I will go in to the jewelry store for a present. Either Karen or Sienna, or maybe James or Porter will be there and I will get help and pass it then. We'll need to get tickets, too. I know Phalanx won't give us money for them, which is no big deal, but annoying. Anyway, let's do that at your place when we get there. Anything else?"

"Clothes?"

"Oh, yeah. Anything you take, be prepared to leave there. I don't know how Mason will get us out, but I can guarantee he won't be able to spare time for us to go back to the hostel or hotel or wherever we are staying. It will probably be a quick exit, and possibly dramatic. Also, and this is really up to you, I would suggest you pack extremely sexy and provocative clothes, if you have them. They are unfortunately going to see you only as an object. To them, you are toy I happen to have. I am sorry for it, but I know how they think. You aren't a computer whiz and therefore you are nothing. Their type tends to be extremely elitist and closed-minded."

She smiled. "Oh, I can do that. I think you might be terribly distracted though."

"Oh well. The hazards of being me."

"I think I will brush up on my dancing skills, too. I might have to distract the masses, or something. Want to give me some pointers?"

"Uh, no. You don't even want to tempt me with that, right now."

"Oh, but I do."

"Please don't. I am a little stressed and that tends to make my fucking adrenaline go up anyway."

"You are only giving me more incentive, you know."

Juan sighed. "You women are so damn evil!"

"Well, now, seriously Juan. What did you think? Of course we are. We like having the eye of men, and we like to be chased, even if it is only by those eyes."

"I am so completely fucked, aren't I?"

"Probably, but do you really mind?"

"No, not really. You should know that I will chase you anywhere, though. Even if you were stolen by Olympus, I would climb the fucking mountain and storm the gates to come for you."

"So damn romantic." She laughed softly, running her fingers gently through his hair. "I guess we should probably get back to the apartment soon, or they might get bored watching and come looking."

"Yeah, that would be unfortunate." He reached for the ignition. "Oh, and before we go, it is possible that I may need to see one of the other ladies before we go. That means I may have to kiss another girl. Is that all right with you?"

"Sure. I know you aren't going to do more. Even if I wish it were otherwise with me, sometimes."

"Sorry, love, but I am a virgin still."

"You are? Wow."

"Everybody is in the group, except maybe you and Karen. It doesn't really matter, you understand, but I have kept it this long. I don't think I will give up anytime soon, even to the hotness that is you. Sorry if that offends you."

"No, it doesn't offend me. Are you kidding? That takes all sorts of pressure off! I was a bit worried, to be honest. I mean, sex is really fun and all, but it hurts when the other partner leaves. Now, I don't mean to say that you are leaving or anything like that, but you might, and I already want to keep you. If I wasn't good enough in bed you might not want me after that. I've had that happen before."

"Not good enough? What the hell was wrong with that guy? Men are lucky, or blessed, to be even allowed to look at women, let alone have sex with them! I'm damn blessed to be allowed to say I might love you. Sex is just a physical way to do that and certainly not the only physical way. Maybe it is the ultimate way, I don't know, but it certainly isn't something worth rating. Fucking messed up."

"I didn't think you would get this angry about it."

"Yeah, well, any guy who is willing to tell a woman that she didn't do exactly what he wanted is a self-centered idiot. That's basically what he told you."

"Well, I suppose. I hadn't really thought of it that way, just that I wasn't good enough."

"Who the fuck is allowed to say that? You're good enough, and if he didn't think so he's the one with the problem. Sex isn't supposed to be some big performance with judging at the end, damn it. It's supposed to be special. And private. And a fucking gift to each other, not to one's self."

She smiled. "Whether or not it is, I am still glad that I don't have to worry about that."

Juan shrugged. "Besides, if we ever get there, I think we'll both know what we both can do for the other."

"Probably true. Should we practice a bit later?"

Juan smiled. "Of course. Perhaps after I check the forum and see if they left instructions yet."

Gabriella sighed dramatically. "Oh, all right. Business before pleasure, I suppose. But don't take too long."

"Why, you'll cool off?" Juan asked as he eased the car back and headed for Gabriella's apartment.

"No, just the opposite. I'll heat up too much. You definitely don't want that, now do you?"

Juan's attention had been divided between listening and driving. When she said that, though, he jerked. "Fuck!" Then he had to recorrect, his heart hammering. "I told you not to do that! God damn. I feel like my heart is going to come right out of my ribs."

Gabriella laughed a nasty laugh. "Oh, oops."

"You fucking did that on purpose!" He accused, heart still racing.

"Well, no shit, Juan. As Sienna says, I don't want to become boring to you."

"Fuck. You never have to worry about that. I have seen you how often, and just a sniff and I am gone again. You will never become

94

boring. If anything, it'll get more intense, because I will anticipate it all. Please don't do that when I am driving. I seriously could cause an accident."

"Yeah, having to explain that to the insurance company might be fun though: 'How did the accident happen?' 'My girl sexually stimulated me too much and I ran into the tree.' 'How did she do that?' 'She said she was too fucking hot.'"

Juan laughed.

At Gabriella's apartment, he logged into the forum on his laptop. There, under the heading he had written last week, it said simply, "American Café, De Lairessestraat two weeks."

"Well, that narrows this down." Juan muttered. He took out the little notebook he always had with him, usually to write information for work on. He needed to write this down, chancy as that was.

"M- Contact made. American Café, De Lairessestraat, two weeks, both of us. Vis-a-viz. Extract there. –J"

Gabriella read it over his shoulder. She nodded. It was probably vague enough for what they needed it for. He smiled at her.

"Well, beautiful lady, want to go with me to Amsterdam?" He asked brightly.

"Of course. Take me there, sexy man!"

Juan quickly booked two roundtrip tickets. He wanted to send a definite message that he intended to come back. Subtle, he was not. They were for a week and half away. It was cutting it close, but he had to give Mason time to plan, and he needed time to get to a good stopping point at work.

Thank God Mason had given him an account with a card, otherwise this would be all blown already.

"All done." He shut the laptop decisively. "Want to say good night for the next hour or so?"

The next day was Saturday. The Diamond Nest would be open early, because it was always open early. Juan wanted to get going on this while he was fairly sure no one was out tailing him. He knew Porter opened at 8:30. Juan would be there at 8:35 if possible.

Sienna was working on something on a laptop when he opened

the door and it tinkled softly.

"Oh, hello sir." She smiled professionally at him. It was like he was just another customer. "May I help you?"

Juan nodded vaguely, looking at the cases. "I wanted to buy something special for a very special lady."

"We have several designers who contract with us exclusively. Do you have anything in particular in mind?"

"Well, I thought perhaps a bracelet."

"Ah, yes, let me pull a tray for you." Sienna unlocked a case and set a tray of bracelets on the top for him to peruse. Juan palmed his note and slipped it under the case. Sienna carefully winked once to let him know she had seen it. Juan leaned over the case, looking more closely at the bracelets. He recognized Porter's unique touch in some of them, but he didn't want that, not yet. This was a throw-away bracelet. They'd leave it with the identities. Porter's stuff was special.

"Hm, I kinda like this braided look. Do you have anything in gold?"

Sienna picked up the tray carefully to examine the one he had pointed out. She slipped the tiny note expertly from under the box. "Let me check the back for you, sir. Sometimes we have something there, and I can confer with our resident jewelers. If you will excuse me?" She put the bracelets back, locked the case, and disappeared behind the velvet curtain.

She was gone some minutes; when she reappeared, it was with a sparkling braided bracelet. Juan looked at it closely. "May I?" He asked. Sienna handed it to him. It was inset with tiny diamonds and the gold setting was simple. "I like this, quite a bit, but I am unsure of the size. You look to be about the same as my girl. May I try it on you?" Juan asked. If he could hold Sienna's hand she could tell him what was up.

Sienna laughed. "Of course, sir!" She held out her slender wrist. Of course, she was close to Gabriella's size, but it was not exact. As if it mattered; Juan thought it was a genius move on his part; it made him look like a total player. He carefully put it on Sienna and admired it. "Might I see it by the other?"

Sienna got that one, as well, and Juan put it on her other wrist. Now he could hold both hands and pretend to be comparing.

Sienna tapped gently to him, "Smooth."

"I thought it genius."

"Indeed. Porter will be impressed."

"I am glad. Any news?"

"I will meet you Wednesday. Lunch date. I will look different. I am going to go to wherever to extract you both. Mason has not laid it all out."

"Gotcha. Did Porter make these?"

"Both. "

"I will not buy something to throw away that Porter made."

Sienna winked. Aloud, she said, "Is there something else you might like to see, sir?"

"Yes, I think so. These are beautiful, but I do not think they are exactly right."

Sienna nodded, still in her professional mode, said, "Well, let me get some more options for you to consider. As I said before, we contract with several exclusive jewelers, so we should find something that is perfect."

"Anything tribal or animal inspired?" Juan said, going for flamboyant.

"Pacific Islander tribal or African tribal?" Sienna asked.

"African, for an African queen."

"This way, sir." Sienna took off the two he had considered and put them away. James stepped out from the curtain as they looked at some other bracelets. "Miss Sienna, if you would step back here for a moment."

"Can't it wait, sir? I am with a customer."

"I am afraid not."

Sienna sighed. "I do apologize, sir. I must go back again. It must be an emergency. Please excuse me."

Juan nodded absently, looking at the bracelets. Sienna went back with James. She came back within five minutes. "I am sorry, sir. Have you seen something else that appeals to you?"

"Yes, these three. May I bother you to try them again?"

"It is no bother, sir, I assure you."

Juan admired them again, holding her hands gently and turning them slightly.

Sienna tapped, "Mason called. Make that lunch at Smoking Joe's. My code name is going to be Natalya. I am your fling. A prostitute. Behave appropriately. Kiss me. Several times."

"I can do that. I would rather not."

"You have to. Mason said that you'll get out when I get there. When are you leaving?"

"Not next Wednesday. The Wednesday after."

"Time?"

"5 am."

"All right. Be careful. The machines go with you?"

"No, I will leave them. Mason has a key to my apartment. He needs to rob it. Then I can be outraged."

Juan selected the zebra-print bangle and paid for it with cash. "Thank you for all your help. You are the best I have ever had." He smiled at her.

Sienna blushed charmingly and looked aside. Juan could never figure out how she could do that on command. "You are quite welcome, sir." She said, sounding perfectly confused. Juan knew she was acting and he still couldn't tell.

He smiled at her again and left. Wednesday, huh. He'd have to let Gabriella know, just in case. He might have to meet Sienna at least once more before they left. No man stupid enough to have a fling would be smart enough to stay away from her, especially if he was leaving on a trip. Until then, he had a week and a half to get his shit in order.

Chapter 10

By the time it was Wednesday, Juan had most things in order for the upcoming mission. He had the hotel booked for a week, just in case, and he had his clothes ready to go. Mason would have to steal that machine back and there wouldn't be any loose ends for him to pick up. That would give Juan some righteous indignation to level at Phalanx. It would also increase their natural paranoia. It might put them on guard more, but he couldn't help that. If he didn't get them out, Phalanx would probably lift them while he was gone, and he really didn't want those guys to access the command post.

At lunch time, he quietly left the office. He had taken to not covering the red streak. As he had expected, no one noticed. Well, they might have noticed, but no one commented, which meant that they didn't care. Which was good, since he would be losing it soon enough.

Sienna was going to be at a café downtown. She had told him Smoking Joe's at lunch; he had no idea what she would look like other than like a hooker, so this was going to be interesting. She was going to be the hottest prostitute ever though.

Juan went to the bar. It was not crowded. Two or three tables were taken, but there were quite a few open chairs. Juan elected to take a table for two close to the front window. It was one of those ridiculously tall tables, and it afforded an excellent view of the street. It also would allow anyone outside to see them, if people outside wanted to look in.

He had been there about ten minutes when Sienna walked in like she owned the fucking place. Actually, she walked in like she owned the fucking city. Juan never got tired of seeing her disguises, and this was a good one. Her hair was electric blue and spiky. Her makeup was fantastic and bold and she had a slight sneer. She was wearing very little and the things she had on certainly didn't keep anyone from guessing what she looked like without them. Minidress was way too modest a description for what she was wearing.

Juan stared for a few seconds before he caught himself. She sat opposite him.

"Hello, Natalya." Juan said with a slight smile.

"Michael. I hope this is going to have some business proposition attached to it. I don't go out of my way for very many clients, but for you, I make exception." Porter had obviously worked with her on her accent. It was slight, but it was there.

"I can always do a business proposition with you."

"Good. That is later. Let us eat now."

She placed her hand over his. Juan noticed that she wasn't wearing any jewelry with her fingerless gloves. Absently, he wondered if it bothered her to take her ring off.

"You look fucking amazing." He tapped to her.

"I am glad. I hate wearing this makeup. Mason says hi."

"I bet he does."

"Kiss me. No man would leave it."

Juan sighed slightly. He leaned over the table and kissed her. It was never going to be easy, but he didn't have to show how uncomfortable it was. Besides, she was professional, and she could make it less awkward.

Sienna played it up better than Juan thought she would. He knew it was hardly more than just a touch of lips but she acted like it was a lot more. Which actually was damn distracting, especially since he knew what she was wearing. Or, not wearing. Either.

Finally, there was a polite throat clearing. Juan sat back. It was the waiter, who looked way too interested in this whole spectacle.

They ordered, and Juan slid his hand over onto Sienna's leg, which was a bad move on his part, but it was what his character would do. Sienna lay her hand over his. "Mason did say hi. Not like that. He has not got it all in place. You and Gabriella will be extracted explosively."

"What way?" Juan asked. It never hurt to be prepared.

"No. Part of it depends on your surprise."

"Damn. I hate when Mason is sneaky."

"I know. Once out your hair and this Michael person has to go."

"Okay. Bring dye and I will go black. Bring scissors."

Their lunch came and they ate it quickly. There wasn't much more to cover.

Sienna winked at him when he had paid. "Kiss me again. We leave together. You better have your hands on me. If you paid you would not waste it."

Juan sighed softly again. He stood up. Sienna did too, and she put her arms around him pretty damn tightly. Juan followed her lead. She was the expert here.

After an extended wrestling match, or that was what it seemed like to Juan, she let go and he put his arm around her waist and on her hip. They walked out.

"You have your car?" Sienna asked softly.

"Yeah."

Once they were in it, Juan drove away from the bar. "Holy shit, Sienna, I am glad that is done. Fucking awkward."

"I know, Juan," She said calmly, "It is awkward for me too, but it serves a purpose and it will help in the end if you are seen publicly with me. Trust me, and Mason."

"Well, of course, but damn. You look amazing though. You must be the hottest hooker in the world."

She laughed. "Thank you, kind sir! That might be an insult, coming from someone else. From you, though, I don't care. I hate this look, myself, but no one is going to be able to recognize me without it. I really hate how uncomfortable it is to sit down in this."

"Um, yeah, that is something I would really rather not think about."

She laughed. "Drop me off by the FourStar hotel. I am there until I leave. Also, you should be seen coming there, at least once."

"How about next Monday at lunch time?"

"Perfect. I will be there, and then you can leave after about an hour. That is the standard amount of time that one buys."

"Gotcha. I am guessing you won't see Porter?"

"No, not until later. He shouldn't be seen with me. We don't want to give any sort of hints about who else you might connect to. It will be easier to shed the identity and leave it behind if there aren't

101

others."

"Understood. See you next Monday."

She winked at him and got out of the car, the sneer and her dismissive attitude back in place. Juan purposely didn't watch her walk away. He drove off quickly. There were some things he didn't need to see to know how effective they were. This was one of those things. Sienna had the ability to be the center of everyone's attention when she wanted. Juan didn't want to feel more guilty than he did, and besides, he had Gabriella to think of now. He didn't need to be fantasizing about a fake woman, and he certainly didn't want to be confusing his friend with a part she played.

Also, he needed to get back to work. He made certain to wash off the lipstick.

Gabriella was waiting for him Thursday after work. She smiled at him radiantly. Juan felt like the sun had come out extra strongly.

Once they were in the car and driving a roundabout way to his apartment, Juan said, "Sienna is playing a hooker that my guy is involved with on the sly."

"Ooh, I bet she is good at that."

"Yeah, she is. I hope it doesn't make you jealous though. I have no interest in rubbing it in or anything."

Gabriella thought about it for a little while as they sat at a traffic light. "No, I don't think so. I know you are just playing a part, and I know she is beautiful. It must be hard to not look at her."

"It can be. I always feel very guilty about it. I have been to Confession about it multiple times."

"You're Catholic?"

"Yes, but don't worry about it."

"I'm not. I think it makes you much more sexy."

Juan blushed furiously. "I have no idea what you are talking about right now."

"Most men have trouble admitting they are not in control all the time. Saying that you have trouble and admitting it makes you vulnerable, and that makes you sexy."

"Women make no fucking sense. Oh, I bought Sarah a bracelet.

102

Do you want it now, or do you want me to bring it to the bakery?"

"Either. Did Porter make it?"

"No, this will get thrown away. I will buy you all sorts of jewelry, if you like that sort of thing, but I won't buy his stuff for throwing away. It means too much to me."

"Oh. Okay."

"It is just something I have to do."

"I get it, Juan. I think it is sweet."

"Want to go to a drive-in movie?"

"I have work tomorrow!"

"Is that a 'no'?"

"Yes, that's a no. But if you want to have fun, I wouldn't mind staying with you tonight. I have some of my sexy clothes that I bought on break. I want to get your honest reaction before I get your fake one later."

"Uh, okay."

The next few days blew by without a hitch. He dropped by the FourStar on Monday at lunch time. Sienna let him into her shabby room with the television on loudly.

"Sorry that you have to hang out here, Sienna." Juan said very softly.

"It is not that big a deal, Juan." She whispered back. "I snuck out the other day. Porter gets lonely. Besides, my hair is a temporary color, like your gel color. It washes right out. And Porter is stressed about all this. Without alcohol to numb him, he has to deal with it sober. It is very hard for him and I want him to know I am all right. If he thought I was in trouble here, he would knock the fucking doors off."

Juan nodded. "Please tell him about the bracelet. He might want to start designing shitloads for me. I think Gabriella likes presents."

Sienna smiled at him. "I will. He would love to design for you."

"He is the best." Juan shrugged. "I couldn't buy her something that he made for this part. It is almost sacrilegious to throw his jewelry away. Is it hard to leave your ring behind?"

"It can be. Porter worked so hard on it, and it is so beautiful.

However, I know it is safe, and that is more important right now. I will probably only see Porter once before you leave. Is there anything else I need to pass?"

"Is Mason going to get that machine stolen?"

Sienna nodded. "I am not involved with that, but I think you will have a break in during work tomorrow or Wednesday after you leave, or maybe today. It will be gone. It will be safe. You don't need to worry about it."

"Okay. I won't then." He glanced at his watch. "Looks like my hour is almost up."

Sienna laughed softly. She came over. "You need to look the part, Juan. Let me muss your hair a little, and put a tiny smear of lipstick on you. You'll need to wash something off." She ran her fingers through his hair, flipping it around messily. Then she put a touch of lipstick on the back of her hand and rubbed it across his lips gently. "Okay, you look like you had a fling now. Make sure you wash it off at the office or in the car in a public place."

"Will do. How do you ladies wear this stuff? The smell is a huge turn off, right under my nose and all."

"I don't wear it, myself, not unless I am playing a part. I don't like lipstick. But if one is used to it, I think it is easy to wear, just like anything else. Now get going."

"See you in Amsterdam."

Chapter 11

Amsterdam was a nice city, Juan decided. He and Gabriella had checked into Fusion Suites, which was close enough to De Lairessestraat to walk. Juan wasn't always comfortable driving in new cities and he hadn't been to Amsterdam before. Better safe than sorry. Besides, the city itself had interesting architecture.

"Okay, Sarah, let's go take this city apart." Juan said.

Gabriella smiled. "Let me change into something appropriately distracting and we can go."

Juan had to admit, she was very distracting, with that little black skirt and sheer-looking top. "Yeah, that'll totally work. Just stay off to the side of me or I am likely to forget what I am talking about."

She smiled. "Are you sure?" She whispered suggestively and stepped up very close to him. "Don't you want to take a little time before hand? I chose this shirt just for you."

"I bet you did. I notice that it is full of holes."

"It is lace, Michael. Why don't you test it out? I would hate to be caught in defective clothes." She gently started to unbutton his shirt. "Let's not wrinkle your outer shirt though. And the added skin is going to be that much hotter."

"Well," Juan looked at his watch. It was only 10:30. "I guess we have a few minutes." He put his arms around her waist. He could feel her skin through the skimpy fabric. The lace was perfect, he decided.

About an hour later, they left the hotel. "The lace is exactly right." Juan agreed.

"You did seem to enjoy it."

"So did you."

"It is almost like having nothing on. And your hands are extremely gentle and warm."

Juan blushed a bit. "Yeah, well. Uh. Let's get to this place."

They walked to the American Café. It had a dingy door with faded lettering. The windows were either smoked or very dirty. Juan was not very inspired, but what the hell. He was here for the interior, not the outside.

He pushed open the door, holding Gabriella's hand. The place inside had a standard-looking bar. There were couches off to the right side. The lighting inside was just as crappy as the outside had suggested it might be. It was a struggle to even see the back of the small café. Juan noted that there appeared to be people sitting on the couches, around a small coffee table.

The attendant behind the counter looked up quietly. Juan ignored him and stepped over to the couches. He recognized them all from the pictures and the searches he had done in preparation for this assignment.

He sat without asking. Gabriella sat to his left, on the extreme edge of the couch. Juan looked around the group, his eyebrow raised and a sardonic smile on his face.

"So? We're here."

One of the guys, sucking a cigarette, nodded. Fredrico leaned forward. "Did you bring the Commander's machine?"

"No, your guys fucking lifted it out of my apartment."

"What?!" Fredrico stared at Juan. "What's this, you say?!"

"I said your guys already lifted it. Too bad you won't be able to fucking use it. I'm frankly a bit pissed by that, guys. Not a good way to build trust, bitches. First you send your guys to break my fucking door down, then you go and fucking break in while I'm at work and steal the machine? Fucking wrong. It makes me think you don't really want me at all, just wanted access to CommanderRED."

"We didn't lift it!"

"Yeah, whatever. You already fucking tried to get it from the place at least twice. Third time the fucking charm for you?"

The guy with the cigarette inhaled, the orange glow intensifying for a moment. "We didn't lift it." He said softly.

Juan whistled between his teeth. "Well, fuck, then I guess we can both hope that whoever took it tries to open it."

"What, why?"

Juan shrugged. "I left a surprise. It'll blow."

The lone woman hacker, Jayne, leaned forwards herself. "Blow, as in, blow up?"

"Well, yeah. I know how to disarm it, but if someone spins it up without doing that, it will blow and burn the hard drive up. Do you really think I would let it just be protected by software? I don't trust that. We all know how easy it is to get around software."

The guy with the cigarette stuffed it out. Juan saw that he was the Antonio guy he'd researched. He was dangerous, almost as dangerous as the lead hacker, although Juan didn't see Stephen around here. Antonio smiled. "I think that very wise." He said in a peculiarly soft voice. "By the way, may I congratulate you?"

"On what?" Juan asked, a bit wary of this guy. He had real skill outside the hacker community.

"On Sarah. I do not think I have ever seen someone who looked so much better in the flesh than they did digitally. If you ever get bored with this guy, feel free to look no farther, sexy girl." He leered at Gabriella. She gave him a very suggestive smile back. They would mostly see her only as a tool to be used, by anyone. Gabriella knew how to work that. Juan put his hand somewhat possessively on her knee. She smiled a bit broader. It was always fun to be fought over.

"Yes, I have some ability in that area, as well. You already know all that, though."

"Oh yes, we know." Antonio smiled at Juan briefly. "We know a great deal."

Juan thought that meant they knew about Sienna. That would help. "I expected nothing less."

Jayne shook her head impatiently. "Whatever his sex life might be, I am more interested in this break in."

Juan shrugged carelessly. "I think my sex life would be a lot hotter than a fucking break in. If it wasn't your guys, it might be the government, or it might be someone from another group. Does it really fucking matter? It's gone."

It obviously bothered Jayne. She wasn't the type to be sidetracked, which was not a huge surprise, considering she worked with almost no other women. Girl hackers tended to be even more abrasive than their male counterparts. "Who knew you had it?"

Juan laughed sarcastically. "Who knew? Anyone who accessed

the forum fucking knew! You didn't exactly encrypt your instructions! Besides, CommanderRED didn't have any protection on his computer when they grabbed him. Anyone who saw his computer knew about the forum. He had the fucking thing bookmarked! Total noob move! For all that, you guys cracked my computer. Don't act so fucking innocent. I have the logs, I know it happened. I let it fucking happen. If you guys could do it, so could someone else. Or, perhaps, someone did it from inside Phalanx. Did you think of that? How many of your guys have that kind of talent, anyway? Perhaps we should look closer to home before we start looking farther away. It has been my experience that the biggest threat is from somebody being ambitious down the ladder a ways."

Jayne shook her head emphatically. "Impossible." She said shortly. Obviously, she didn't want to address that sort of thing. Maybe she was one of those idealists who thought everyone fought for the flag or some such patriotic shit.

"You are unbelievable. You sell out to the highest bidder and then are surprised when someone else does the same?" Juan snorted.

"We don't sell out!"

Juan sighed. "Whatever. The point is it's gone." He leaned back on the couch. Glancing at Gabriella, he thought he could use a well-placed distraction here. "Sarah, honey, would you see if that guy at the bar is asleep? I need a bottle of water or something."

She caught on right away. "Of course, Michael." She said in a silky, sexy voice, standing up and walking with a slightly exaggerated sway towards the bar. Juan noted with satisfaction that the guys watched her simultaneously. It was quite a show. Jayne glared at them all angrily. She didn't feel very secure in her femininity. She wasn't unattractive, if one could see past the permanent scowl. The fact that she didn't see herself as attractive practically oozed out of her. It heightened her insecurity. Juan figured she used her anger and aggression to intimidate the men, since they had a view of women as objects anyway. She would have set herself apart from other women that way, and now she may even regard them as lesser than herself. That view was undermined by the simple fact that Gabriella could

108

command attention more completely without even saying anything.

Antonio glanced back at Juan and smiled slightly. "You do have good luck with women." He said softly.

"There is no luck with women, man. You either have it, or you don't."

"Well, seeing the two you have so far…"

Juan cut him off. "It isn't luck. Would you like some lessons? First, you have to talk to them like they are people. Women love being the center of your attention. Then, you have to act like you are interested in their minds. After that, you are so fucking in that they will give anything up."

"Perhaps." Antonio said, his eyes back on Gabriella and a fresh cigarette wafting smoke towards the ceiling. Jayne looked disgusted. She wretched her own water bottle open with undue force.

So far Stephen hadn't made an appearance, and Judah hadn't said anything. Juan was going to just wait and let them ask him questions. He was too good to appear too eager.

Gabriella came back with two bottles of water. "Thanks babe." Juan said, taking one.

She smiled at him and gave him a kiss after she had sat back down.

Juan sat, drinking his water occasionally and letting the silence grow. There must be something they wanted or were waiting for. He would make them work for it. Come to me, bitches, he thought. You know you want to.

The silence stretched. It must have been half an hour, or so, before there was a tinny ringing sound. Judah pulled out a cell phone and looked at it. "Gray Wolf." He said in a low voice. Juan didn't recognize the handle. It was either a lower-level hacker or a new handle for Stephen. Either way, Juan didn't care. His position was defensive. He only had to wait two days at most and he would be out. He could hold them off that long.

Judah answered and spoke quietly. Juan didn't try to overhear. Just keep cool, he thought, and don't look at Gabriella right now. She was just a plaything in this place.

109

Judah hung up. "The hit is a go for next week. Everything is in place."

Antonio nodded, snubbing out his cigarette. "Good. I think it is movable then. We will have to wait until Romeo gets back before we give the command."

Juan knew Romeo was Stephen's most common handle. He took a drink to hide his excitement. Finally got around to naming him, had they? And where the fuck was he? Juan wouldn't ask. They would have to give him the information. Jayne gave him a calculating look. She seemed to expect him to say something. Juan didn't much care what she wanted. He could wait. If the worst that happened was that the feds missed Stephen, they at least knew where he had been hanging and would have the computers of these. It would be enough. Unlike these hackers, Juan knew that the white hats employed by the government were just as good at extracting information as they were.

Antonio lit another cigarette. This was going to be a while, Juan figured. He could feel the fatigue of the trip starting to creep over him. Fuck. He was done playing their stupid games for now. If he got too tired, he would be complacent. That would be dangerous. He and Gabriella needed sleep. He stood up abruptly. Gabriella stood up beside him quickly.

"We're done here. Sarah and I need sleep. We flew in this morning. Since you don't have anything else, we'll be back this evening around six. Unless that won't work for your busy schedules. In which case, we will see you tomorrow around noon. It's been real interesting. You have my number. Feel free to let me know if you don't want to see us tonight."

He put an arm around Gabriella and walked out.

"That might have been a bit harsh." She said very softly.

"I don't care, love. I am tired, and they are being annoying. Besides, now they can talk us over and bitch and whine. Then they will be burning to get to know more. They can't leave it like it is. I haven't really told them anything at all and they will not want that. They have to have information. If I don't give them any, they will be panting over what I might or might not have. They can't let me go now."

110

She smiled. "Whatever. I like it. I was bored, just being a figure-head."

Juan yawned. "Fuck them. Let's go get some sleep. Then let's eat. I am hungry."

"Sounds good to me."

Chapter 12

After a nice nap that lasted a few hours, Juan felt much better. Now about that food. He had noticed that they passed a little market on the way. Gabriella was still asleep, so he wrote a quick note and slipped out without waking her.

The market didn't have tons, but it did have some fruit and bread. That was about all Juan wanted anyway. He paid and left, trying to be as inconspicuous as his outrageous clothes and hair would allow. The only thing that made it a bit better was a group of leather and studded young people pushing past him to get in. They all had mohawks and looked straight out of the eighties. Juan smiled to himself. He'd be forgotten quickly with that group in there now.

He stopped outside the room to listen, noting that it was quiet inside. Gabriella had not turned on the television if she was awake. He searched briefly for the key and then opened the door. She wasn't awake. Juan set the bag on the table and went to the bed. He could be romantic, when he wanted to be. He kissed her cheek.

"Mmm." She smiled and opened her eyes. "What a nice way to wake up."

"Would you like something to eat? I went and got some food."

"That would be very nice. Have you heard from Phalanx again?"

"I didn't take my phone with me. I will look now." He went back to his side of the bed for it. "Ooh, two texts!"

"Well, what do they say?"

"Jayne says the group wants to meet us again at six tomorrow night. Antonio says the same thing, a little differently worded. Hm. I wonder."

Gabriella looked at him curiously. Juan put a finger to his lips warningly. She nodded.

Juan switched on the television for background noise. He said very quietly, "It seems a bit odd to me that they would have two different contacts. Something feels weird there. Like there are two groups operating."

Gabriella nodded, taking a bite from an apple.

Juan said a little louder, "Well, it is four now. Want to do some shopping this evening?"

"No, thanks all the same."

Gabriella finished her apple and stood up. She said softly into Juan's ear, "Want to go clubbing?"

Juan shrugged. "If you want to, I guess."

She brightened. "I bet I can make your night very interesting at a club. Yeah, let's go!"

Juan thought he should probably reconsider at that point. He went anyway. The clouds had decided to rain, finally. It was loud, and close, and the music was ghastly, but who cared? There were lots of people, and really, all a club needed was a solid bass line and a good floor. This one had those. Gabriella and Juan clubbed for about an hour, then they left. There was only so much pounding bass that Juan wanted to endure after a trying day. It had been fun though, and Gabriella was so attractive, even in uneven shitty light and fog machines.

"Well, I hope you are feeling better." Juan said as they walked the streets aimlessly. Gabriella had seemed a bit disconsolate to him earlier. The night was nice enough; the rain wasn't cold, yet. Juan really wanted to clear his lungs and head after the club.

"Yes, I do. Thank you. You seemed to have trouble looking somewhere else, and that makes me feel special."

"You are special, plus why would I look anywhere else? I have the best right here."

"Aw, you are sweet." She yawned.

"I think maybe it is time to go to bed. Again. But I need to shower first."

"Dibs." She said immediately.

Juan sighed dramatically. "Fine!"

They slept in the next morning and lounged around the hotel room until it was close to five. Juan had no new texts so he assumed the time was still on. "Ready to go?" He asked Gabriella.

"Should I change from what I wore yesterday?"

"Up to you. I don't even know what all you have."

"I think I will. Turn around and let me throw on a different shirt and a really short skirt."

Juan looked at the opposite wall, blushing slightly. "Ready?"

"Yes." She said. Juan turned back and saw that she also had on a light jacket.

"Oh, is it that cold? It isn't raining anymore."

"When a person is only wearing enough cloth to cover half an ass, yes, it is that cold."

"I hadn't really thought of that. Shall we?"

The inside of the American Café was pretty much the same. The lights were on, but they didn't illuminate it anymore than the sun outside had. There were a couple of other people lounging around the place, and one couple was enthusiastically trying to find out if it were possible to simultaneously give each other mouth-to-mouth resuscitation.

Gabriella looked at them with a raised eyebrow. "Amateurs." She sniffed. "Their technique is terrible."

Juan smiled. "As long as it gets the job done, I suppose."

"It won't. Too sloppy. Too much effort."

"Some people like that sort of thing."

"Wanna bet on if I can make them stop?"

Antonio was sucking at his cigarette. He seemed amused by something.

Juan sat in the same spot he had earlier.

Antonio leaned forward and snuffed out his cigarette. "You seem interested in the other couple, yes?" He said in his peculiarly gentle voice.

"Only as a useful example on how to not make out." Juan snorted. "I don't think I have seen anything that sloppy in a long time."

Antonio laughed softly. "And yet, it works for some."

"Must be a low number of people. Makes me want to get a mop and some plastic covers."

"Yes, you are right there." Antonio lit another cigarette. "I wonder if you might give us all some pointers on that."

Juan shrugged. "If it is what you want, I can probably do that.

But then you better take notes, because I don't stop lectures for questions."

"I thought you didn't do public stuff." Judah volunteered. Juan figured it must have been him on the phone the first night, then.

Juan smiled. "I can make an exception for friends and colleagues." Jayne looked disgusted again, but the men were very interested. Juan decided to try and shake them up a little. "You guys haven't really seen what a real woman can do, have you?" He said in a conspiratorial tone.

Jayne snorted angrily. "Excuse me?"

"Oh, beg pardon. Let me rephrase." Juan said smoothly. "You haven't seen what a woman who embraces and enjoys her femininity can do, have you? I can tell you it is beyond anything you have ever seen online. That's all acting for the camera, boys. Real women, now, they are beyond anything those fake girls pull."

It was pretty obvious that Jayne was angry. She looked around in outrage, but none of the others seemed to care.

"It's all acting?"

Juan shrugged. "Well, think about it. They know the camera is there, and they want to put on a good show. Even if it isn't all acting, a whole lot of it is. None of those girls is being completely natural, and that's why they can't do what a real woman can."

Antonio smiled as he exhaled a cloud of smoke. "And what can a real woman do? Educate me, please."

Juan smiled at him. "A real woman can make you imagine exactly what she wants you to, without taking any clothes off at all."

"Hm. I have a pretty good imagination."

"I bet you do."

"Are you suggesting that women are only sex objects?" Jayne said loudly.

Juan shrugged again. "I'm not suggesting that at all. I am saying, as a fact, that a woman who enjoys being a woman is far more sexy than a woman who thinks she has to be more like a man. And men who force women to act to their own criteria do so at the risk of losing a lot of what makes sex fun to begin with."

115

"Sex is just a power play!" Jayne countered.

"It can be, but it certainly doesn't have to be. Sex can be just as liberating, but not in the sense of people using it to get only what they want from it. Women who know they are women, not toys of men or, worse yet, mirrors of men, are more sexy by far than that."

"You're lying."

"Oh?" Juan leaned back into the cushions languidly. "If that were true, why did all of your comrades there watch Sarah walk over to the bar yesterday morning? I am sure they have all watched girls walk before. They may not have seen a real woman walk though. That is all the difference. And, may I say, you watched, too."

"I did not!"

Juan smiled and let it go.

Fredrico also smiled. He glanced at Jayne and nodded slightly. "We know you are only here for a week."

"Yes." Juan acknowledged. He knew they had accessed his computer and saw how long he had the hotel for and the return tickets.

"Why so short a time?"

"Because. I didn't know how long I would be helpful. I didn't know if you would want me in Phalanx, and I didn't trust your ass."

"Trust is paramount." Judah said softly.

"Can't help that. You haven't given me a reason yet."

Antonio nodded. "He is right, Judah."

"I thought Romeo said no names!"

Antonio snorted. He lit another cigarette. "Fuck that. Like Michael pointed out, it's shit. This isn't secondary school, and I don't have to follow fucking rules that don't make sense."

"Romeo's gonna kick your ass out." Fredrico warned.

"No, he won't. I'm too valuable, and besides, he doesn't have the balls." Antonio certainly was dangerous. He thought for himself, and he flouted the rules. If Stephen didn't watch out, he was going to have an insurrection on his hands, led by this chain-smoker. There had already been cracks in the façade of unity. Juan was just here to exploit those a little, until Sienna did whatever she was going to.

Judah shook his head. "This accomplishes nothing. Our fighting only makes us weaker."

Antonio obviously didn't care. Jayne, who seemed just pissed at the world in general all the time, held up her hand sharply. "It's true, Antonio, and you know it."

He smiled ironically. "If it were true, why are you suddenly using my name? Or is this some play to get me to have sex with you so you can control me?"

"I would never do that!"

"No, you have your little boys for that, don't you now?"

Jayne flushed, although Juan thought it was probably from anger rather than from embarrassment. "You keep talking like that and I will make you sure that you never have the equipment to sleep with anyone, ever. Not even your hand, since you like that so much."

Antonio continued to smile. "It beats the present company."

Fredrico laughed. "It sure does."

Jayne turned on him in a second. "And what does that mean?"

"Oh, fuck off with it. You know you aren't that pretty, and you get all upset when someone else is prettier than you. Well, I am tired of it. Michael brings in a smoking hot babe and you want us to watch you? Fuck that. You could dance naked on this table and it would still be less than her breathing."

"I wouldn't ever do anything for you."

"Good. I'd hate to go blind from it." Fredrico said with extreme distaste.

Antonio laughed. Judah smiled and then looked a bit abashed.

Fredrico turned his face away from Jayne's furious glare. "Well, Michael? Want to prove what you said earlier?"

"Which part?"

Fredrico suddenly looked very intent. "Want to have your girl prove that she is a woman for us? I think we would be very interested in seeing it firsthand."

Juan shrugged. "You know, it is really all up to her. I don't tell her what to do, because then that is just me and what I want." He looked at Gabriella. "Well, Sarah? You heard the boys. They want to see how a real woman can turn boys to men in just a few minutes."

Gabriella smiled easily. She seemed to be up for the challenge. "I would love to prove your argument." She said with a hint of accent. "Who wants to put on some appropriate music for a show, boys?"

"Oh hell yes." Judah whispered hoarsely.

Gabriella stood up smoothly. She still had the light jacket on. As Fredrico went over to the bar to ask for a good stripping song, she calmly kicked Antonio's feet off the coffee table. "I might need the room, you know. You want to see, you have to move this table."

Antonio and Judah quickly pushed it aside. Jayne sat rigidly, looking extremely put out. Then again, she didn't leave, either. Juan figured she didn't want to leave the men of the team alone with him, in case he turned them traitor.

Some techno-sounding music kicked in, with a heavy baseline. Fredrico came back over and sat, his eyes still burning. It might have been a bit fast for a normal strip, but then, Gabriella wasn't stripping. She was dancing. However, she did start it by very slowly unzipping her jacket and letting it slide off her shoulders and onto the floor.

Juan noted that the shirt she had on now was very short, very tight, and zebra-striped. Gabriella smiled a very naughty smile at the men on the other sofas. She knew she was the absolute center of attention, and that was kind of an exciting place to be, Juan reasoned. Women sure seemed to like to be there. She was very sexy, and she was moving like she enjoyed being there.

As a tease, she moved closer to the men on the couch. Juan hoped she knew what she was doing; he had to trust that she did. She put her knees between Antonio's own and forced them open, then she stepped back, mockingly, teasing. He leaned forward, not even appearing to notice he was doing so. The cigarette had gone out. That had to be a first. Gabriella turned her back and came over to where Juan was sitting. Oh, fuck, Juan thought. He hoped she wasn't going to give him a lap dance. He might not be able to keep his composure.

Gabriella gave him a smile. She knew. Dammit. He needed to hide it better. She slid her knee up between his legs and leaned over him. Then the music stopped.

"Oh, too bad. Show's over for now." She laughed at them all and stood up again. Juan noticed that the rest of the bar was watching, too.

"You are disgusting." Jayne accused. "You betray everything women have fought for."

Gabriella shrugged. "You want me to act like I don't like being attractive because you think women shouldn't be. Fuck you. I like being the center of attention, I like having sex, and I like being sexy. Real women aren't ashamed of who they are." She bent over smoothly and picked up her jacket.

Juan smiled as Gabriella sat down beside him again. "I told you all that. Now, then, was that enough lesson for you?"

Antonio was still staring. "God damn. I did not believe it even possible."

Judah inhaled hugely. "She didn't even take anything off, really." He sounded awed.

"I told you." Juan said, gently. It probably wouldn't change these guys at all, but it would show them there was something beyond the internet for things like that. Besides, there really wasn't a substitute for human interaction.

Jayne stood up suddenly. "Get out." She said harshly to Juan. "Get the fuck out and take your hooker with you."

Juan stood up slowly. Time to teach this group what it meant to protect someone. "You can throw me out, bitch, but you don't call her a hooker. Maybe you think I could only get a beautiful woman by paying for it. You can fucking think what you want, but you don't insult my woman that way."

"Whatever. I know you paid for her."

Juan calmly reached out and took Jayne's arm. He bent it with a seemingly idle flick. Michael had taught the move to him, and while he didn't like using it on a woman, it was effective and wouldn't hurt her much. "All right, you can have whatever fucking opinion you want. But you better be fucking ready for me to defend the truth, even against you."

Jayne had been forced around and was arched back. "Fuck off!"

Juan twisted slightly more. "I fucking mean it. Freedom of

119

speech means I get to defend my own, too. Especially against fucking defamation."

Jayne finally nodded. Juan let go immediately.

"Well, gentlemen, lady, it's been real interesting, but if this is really the best you offer me, I find no reason to sell my soul to Phalanx."

Jayne had subsided back into the couch, holding her arm carefully and glaring resentfully.

Antonio, who appeared to be amused with everything tonight, lit another cigarette. "Not so fast, Michael. Please, have a seat."

"I was told to fuck off, I intend to do it."

"Jayne doesn't speak for Phalanx. She doesn't even speak for Stephen, except when he isn't here. Since he's off enjoying himself and whatever girls he can fuck right now, we make decisions. All of us."

Juan looked at Antonio hard. "I don't like being fucked with. Either play straight or I leave for good. Clear?"

"Clear. Sit. We have some things to discuss."

"Fine." Juan sat. "What do we have to talk about now?"

Judah leaned forward, pulling the coffee table back over and retrieving his bottle. "Stephen isn't here. Who the hell knows when he will get back? He is supposed to be back within the week."

Fredrico nodded. "The last time we talked to him that is what he said, at least."

"Who talked to him?" Juan asked carefully.

"I did." Jayne said sulkily.

"Oh?"

Antonio smiled again. "I also talked to him, after you did, Jayne. I don't trust you at all."

"What the fuck?!" She shouted angrily. Juan thought that being that angry all the time had to take tons of energy. "You went behind my back?!"

Antonio sat forward suddenly. His voice was soft, possibly because of all the smoke he inhaled, but he was still intimidating when he got angry. Juan again felt that this was the biggest adversary Phalanx and Stephen had, if they only knew it. He slapped his hand on the coffee table hard. "Fuck you, bitch. Of course I went behind your

120

fucking back. You have tried to manipulate us all from the very beginning. You fawn all over Stephen and then when he is gone you speak for him. Well, listen, and listen good. I don't do being fucked around with. You and Stephen want to sleep and fuck around, fabulous, but you don't try yanking me around with you."

"You don't scare me." Which, Juan thought, was probably true, but he should scare her. He should scare her a lot.

Antonio smiled a very cold smile. "I don't care. I don't want to scare you, bitch. I want you to know what I think, so that when I fuck you over, you will know when it happens. I don't bow to anyone, you, Stephen, nobody."

Jayne smiled back, also coldly. "I know enough about you to keep you in line."

Antonio shook his head at her pityingly. "You think anything you fucking know will blackmail me? Compared to what I know about you, and Stephen too, for that matter?"

Juan perked up. There might be something here to convict Stephen on more than just internet charges.

"You know nothing."

"But I do. I went out and asked her, you know. I know just how old she was." Antonio dismissed the line of thinking with a flick of cigarette ash. "Whatever. Just so you know, there is never an excuse to not follow up on something. In person. Right, Michael?"

"Absolutely." Juan said with a purposely blank face, acting like this meant little to him.

"Now, we have been instructed by Stephen to offer you a position in Phalanx. He wants you and your skills."

"Where and when?" Juan countered.

"Lower than us, but only because he is unsure of himself and of you." Antonio sat back, his amused smile back.

Judah glanced at him quickly, then he leaned forward. Juan irrationally was reminded of a Whack-a-Mole game when they leaned in and out like that. "Stephen wants to meet you on his own. He is, as Antonio said, occupied right now. I am afraid that you will be back in the States by the time he gets back."

"I can arrange to come back, should there be enough reason to. I mean to keep my day job, as it affords cover and gives me the money to keep myself up. But I don't want to do all this shit again. So you guys decide if you want me in. I don't want to keep running over here for this shit."

Fredrico nodded. "Fair enough."

"It is not!" Jayne said sharply. "We can't make that determination."

"We can make a recommendation. When was the last time Stephen didn't take out advice?"

"We don't fucking tell him what to do."

"No, and it doesn't fucking matter now. He wants Michael to get back into the government. We haven't had anyone do it that successfully before."

Juan nodded. "Okay, what do you want in there?"

Antonio leaned forward and snuffed out his cigarette. "We want to know where they are keeping all the Phalanx information, computers, shit like that."

"That is a huge order. You must know that will take months or years. None of that shit is in the same place."

"Yes, we figured it would. And I know you won't want to share your processes. So we want you to start immediately when you get back."

"How much?" Juan asked abruptly.

"The hell?" Judah asked, confused.

"How much is this worth to you, and to Phalanx?"

"Ahh. I understand. Stephen floated the idea of 150k a month."

"I won't do it for less than that, just so we are clear. This is worth a lot of time if I get caught."

Antonio nodded. "We know."

There was a disturbance towards the front of the bar, behind Juan and Gabriella. Juan turned to see what it was. Someone was saying something loudly in a language Juan wasn't familiar with and there was some shoving going on. The view was obscured by a group of

122

people milling around and trying to keep whoever was making the disturbance from getting in the building. One of the men reeled back, apparently shoved off-balance and there stood Sienna in her fake prostitute glory. She looked furious. And totally hot. But she always looked hot. She stormed in, still shouting in whatever language it was and wearing a tiny leather skirt and lace bustier with a fur coat over it all, thrown open. A man stepped forward to try and calm her down, but Sienna threw him off.

Juan knew she didn't weigh too much, but she still had enough fighting experience to use what weight she had to throw people off her. Part of the skill she had was using her attacker's weight to her advantage. Juan knew that Porter, Mason, and Michael had spent quite a while training her in that. Her makeup was streaked, and Juan realized belatedly that it was raining outside. Water dotted her coat. She stormed to the back and stood in front of them all, trembling with apparent rage and screaming in that language. Finally, she gathered herself and shouted, "I find you here! With her!" And then she added some possibly uncomplimentary things in that other language. Juan knew it was the extraction attempt, but he was still a bit surprised. Antonio was staring, Judah and Fredrico were on their feet in alarm, and Jayne was gaping, mouth open.

He held up his hands placating. "Natalya.."

"No! You will not make this okay!" From her coat, she pulled a pistol. Juan recognized it right away, but there wasn't time to warn Gabriella what was going to happen. Still screaming things, Sienna shot Gabriella with it, turned it on Juan and shot him in the chest. Juan was completely shocked. He had kind of expected a bit more lead-up, some actual discussion, something more. He looked down in surprise, noting that he was bleeding. Then the drug in the false bullet started to release into his body. Gabriella had already slumped unconscious beside him. Juan was bigger and had taken some precautionary drugs that inhibited the act of other drugs, so it took longer. He fell off the couch. Feet were moving, running, loud voices shouting.

Sienna was still shouting things in that other language. Then she shot herself and fell. Blood pooled out slowly from under her body.

Before he passed out completely, Juan had to admire this particular extraction. If he was dead, no one would come looking for him. He would have to compliment Mason later. Then everything went black.

Part II

Chapter 13

Mason, Porter, Michael, and Sienna flew into Amsterdam the day before Juan and Gabriella were scheduled to. Mason hated to be there early, but there was no way they could get around it. He had to meet with the soldiers who would be making the sting.

The commander of the group was unimpressed with the way that Mason was going to extract his team members. "Look, why don't we just hit them right now?" He said finally.

"Because," Mason said patiently, "They will exact retribution against my team that way. If your government and mine don't mind having us all dead, then, by all means, hit them now."

The commander sighed. "Whatever you say in this case."

"Thank you. I will be in the café that night as well. We will get the bodies out."

"There will be bodies?"

"Most likely. The two or three who are there are going to be my team. All the rest, you take as you see fit. If there are only two bodies, then the blue-haired hooker is also my team member."

"Blue hair, huh? I hope she plays her part well. They can usually tell when there is someone acting. The government has tried to hit them before."

Mason permitted himself to smile. "She will be very convincing, and she will also not be there very long. She is the extraction, not the plant. We've been working to get my team member positioned with Phalanx for months now."

"All right, sir, we will follow your lead. How will you communicate with us? We'll have to be in a van or truck."

"I can leave one of my team members with you. He is well-versed in how the plan is supposed to work, and he is also very helpful to have in a fight."

The soldier looked over at the rest of the team sitting around the table and eating lunch. "I think either of them would be. But I hope you are going to give us that human mountain."

Mason smiled. "That was the idea."

"Good. We'll look for you in two days, sir."

Then there was nothing to do but wait around. Mason hated waiting, but he was far better off than either Porter or Michael. By the end of the second day, the day Juan and Gabriella actually flew in and made initial contact, those two were almost at the point of fighting with each other. Mason sighed to himself and went out to the market. He was looking for a bottle of vodka specifically, but he would take anything he could lay hands on. They needed the distraction. Besides, that way he could help control them.

"Okay, boys," he announced when he came back into the suite, "The cards are coming out and we are going to not think about tomorrow any more. Deal?"

Sienna caught on right away. "Yes, that is a good idea, right boys?"

Porter shrugged in high bad temper. "Whatever."

"And," Mason continued, "I have brought refreshments. I can't handle you two fucking morons much longer." He pulled out the small bottle he had found. "You'll notice that it is not very big; we should not have to worry about going over anyone limits, plus we won't get blasted. Now, who's in?"

It was a bit later when Mason felt that the room was mellow enough to broach the subject . "All right, are you morons calm enough now that we can talk about this stuff again?"

Porter smiled slightly. "Whatever, Mason. I think you just like being in control."

"When it involves you idiots trying to start fights, yes."

Michael tossed his hand in. "I'm fine. What do we need to talk about?"

"Michael, you are going to be with the unit that is going to affect the arrests. I will station myself inside the bar, to monitor everything in there. Porter, you are going have to be outside with Sienna until she goes in. After she does what she needs to, you can come in and we will take bodies out.

Porter shuffled the cards. "And what is she going to do?"

Mason smiled and went to his suitcase. He took out a long

slender case and brought it to the table. "She is going to use this." Opening the case, he took out the pistol it contained. "Sienna, beautiful, you are going to have to use three bullets. That is the signal. After the third shot, the unit storms the place and pulls the people in there out. Except us, of course. Ideally, you will shoot both Gabriella and Juan, and then yourself. If you are all dead, no one will go looking for you after. Don't insist on it, though. Juan is the important one to get."

Sienna nodded. "I understand, Mason. I'll try to do my best. Also, that bustier you had made has a small pocket inside. I should be able to put a blood pack in there so it looks like I am bleeding more."

Porter looked at the case for a long time. "Mason, there is no way to regulate how much drug any of them are getting. Is that going to be a problem? Gabriella and Sienna are smaller than Juan is."

Mason shrugged. "I really don't know. We'll have to monitor them fairly closely."

"That is hardly reassuring, Mason." Porter accused

"I know that, Porter, but what the fuck do you suggest I do about it?"

Porter sighed. "I guess there isn't much you can do. Sorry."

"Look, Porter, this isn't my ideal plan, okay? If we make them think Juan is dead, they won't come for him for retribution afterwards. I'm a little limited here. If you have something better, then fucking share, because I don't like this option much."

"No, I don't have a fucking better option. I am just worried."

"So am I, and it isn't going to help me to have you bitching about every little damn problem along the way. If you can't be helpful then you can stay here the whole damn time."

"Like hell!"

"I mean it. This job is fucking hard enough without your added help. Either pull your shit together or stay behind."

"Okay, okay. I am sorry. I shouldn't have said it that way. I was just trying to point out a potential problem."

"I appreciate that, I really do, but you sound a lot like you are accusing me all the fucking time. I understand your concern, but I don't need the added stress right now. I know that this could go wrong, especially for the women. You think that makes me happy and warm? It doesn't. Which brings up the next point: Sienna, there is potential for you to die from this. I want you to fully understand that going in."

Sienna nodded seriously. "I do understand it, Mason. I know that you and Porter will try your hardest. I will do what I have to, but I know that, if I die, you tried to keep it from happening." She smiled at Porter. "I will look at you from Purgatory and you better fucking believe that I will forgive you anything you think you did wrong."

Porter shook his head. "This somehow fails to make me feel better, you two."

Sienna put her hand gently over his. "Porter, I can't help that you think everything is your fault. It isn't, you know."

"No, I don't know. That is part of the problem."

Mason rolled his eyes. "Okay, that is probably true, but assuming that you are a victim is just as stupid. The world is not out to fuck you over, specifically. Quit assuming that it is. You're really starting to piss me off."

Porter reshuffled the cards again. "I am sorry, Mason. I apologize. I realize that you are doing the best job you can with what you have. If something goes wrong, I will try to not look at it as aimed specifically at me."

"Good enough for now."

Michael raised his hand slightly. "Question. What am I going to do?"

"You have to cue in the arresting unit. You know our methods, and you will be able to see Porter. Once he gives you the signal, you and your guys need to get in there before the rats start streaming out of the holes."

"Gotcha. I can do that."

"Try to not kill anyone too much."

Michael smiled. "How do you not kill someone too much?"

"I don't know. If you find out, alert me. That could be useful to have, for when Porter is being pig-headed again. I could kill him a little and that might solve the problems."

131

It was Porter's turn to roll his eyes. "You two are just soooo fucking funny."

Michael slapped him on the shoulder. "No shit! That's why you love us soooo much!"

"You better fucking hope so." Porter started to deal a new hand.

Around ten o'clock, they called the game and Michael went to shower while Sienna slipped out to go for a quick walk outside.

Mason gathered the cups and empty bottle.

Porter was still looking at the pistol and bullets in the case.

Mason sighed. "I am sorry, Porter. I don't have a better way to get them out right now."

"I know it, Mason. Anytime I might lose her, it makes me very very afraid."

Mason sat down beside him. "Me, too." He said quietly. "I am afraid that we might lose any of them with this scheme. It is the best way to make sure that Phalanx thinks they are dead, though. I don't have a way to slip them anything more measured."

Porter nodded. They sat there for a few minutes, not saying anything. Mason felt horrible about this. He realized that he probably should have left Porter back home, but he couldn't justify that either. Porter was still working with Sienna to perfect her acting, and he would have worried as much back there. Besides, Mason was worried that Porter might relapse if he were alone too long and worrying. The last thing Mason wanted was Porter to get drunk. Actually, he thought he should probably tell all that to Porter, but it didn't feel like the right time.

Porter gently picked up the pistol and turned it over in his hands. "You know, I have always hated guns." He said softly.

"Why?"

"I am not sure. I haven't had anything really all that adverse happen with one or anything. They just seem so final, somehow."

"I understand, I think. That is one other reason to use it for this. Guns are loud, and they really only have one purpose. Besides, they are easier to fake than knives. As you have demonstrated on occasion."

132

Porter smiled slightly. He set the pistol back down. "Guns scare me, a lot." He said so softly that Mason almost missed it.

"Is that one of the reasons you couldn't shoot yourself the one time?" Mason said gently.

"Maybe." Porter looked out the window without seeing the lights of the city. "Does she really have to do this?"

Mason put his arm around Porter's shoulders. "I think it is the only way. Please don't get so wrapped up in worrying that you lose sight of the fact that Sienna is a highly accomplished and competent woman. She doesn't need you to protect her from everything, you know. She is one of the best marksmen of us all, and she is comfortable with a pistol."

"I know that. It is very hard for me to let her go."

"Well, Porter, I can't help you with that. You can't wrap her in cotton and hide her away any more than you can set her on a pedestal and demand that others look and admire and not touch. She has to be able to grow without you, even though that is hard to accept."

"I know it."

"I know you know. Sometimes it helps to hear it again." Mason sat for a few minutes with Porter. Neither of them said anything further. Mason was thinking about what Porter had said; there was no way to control how much of the drug got out. While he had been assured it would be okay, there was no way to know until they tried it. That made him more nervous than he liked to admit, and he certainly wasn't going out of his way to say so to Porter now.

Finally, he sighed. "Are you going to be all right, Porter?"

"Yeah, man, I think so. Thanks for getting us the vodka, and thanks for talking with me. I know I am not the most fun person to communicate with."

"No, we are going to pull the fun one out tomorrow."

"Ha. Yes. Juan is good for me. He always challenges me and brings me out of my dark moods."

"He challenges all of us. He can see fairly clearly, behind all the joking and optimism. But you know you challenge all of us, too."

Porter shrugged slightly. "Whatever. You know you are too

133

good at this. I could never do what you do."

"So what? I never said you had to, but you see things and point out things that I might miss. Don't you realize how valuable that is? If no one called me on that shit, I would get complacent, and then people would end up getting hurt. I try to see it all now because I don't like being shown up. I am fucking proud, hadn't you noticed?" Porter smiled slightly. "And then you go and humble me, often publically. So, yeah, you make me better. You don't have to do my job to make me better at it, you know. I value your input. It is one of the reasons I asked you to come."

"Oh? Just one reason? What are the others?"

"Porter, do you really want to know?"

"I suppose."

"Well, the biggest reason is that I do not want you getting so emotionally overboard that you go out and drink yourself to numbness. I know you might, and I know you can't do it if you think I can see you."

"Fuck. Well, you are right about the second part." Porter put his hands into his hair and pulled distractedly. "Fuck."

Mason sat silent for a little longer. He knew what he said hurt Porter. The truth sometimes hurt. It was something he needed to realize; his friends cared about him enough to make sure he was safe.

"I'm sorry, man." Mason said softly. "I can't take that chance with you. I love you too much." Porter nodded, his hands still over his face. "Are you okay?"

"No. But I hope to be someday."

"Can I help?"

Porter finally straightened up. His eyes were a little too bright. Mason pretended not to notice. "No, other than what you are doing anyway. Would you be upset if I went for a walk? I promise that I won't go into any place, I just need to get out for a little while."

Mason looked at his watch. "Can you get back in an hour?"

Porter checked his watch too. "One hour. Yes. I will be back in an hour."

He left quietly. Mason shook his head. He stood up and went to the window. Phalanx was so dangerous, and so widespread. He didn't like this mission. Something about it was wrong, but there was nothing to hang his suspicions on. The option he had was the best he could do. It had to be enough, and yet what if it wasn't? Mason had better start planning on when it failed.

If they didn't get everyone, that could be a problem. It might not be insurmountable. If they got more than half the group, they would be able to get half the computers, and then they could trace the others through those computers. Retribution might come against Juan. What did they know about him, for sure? They knew the apartment he was keeping. Michael and Porter had planned to surprise him when he got back and had already moved all his stuff to the house up the hill from Mason's. His car... Ooh, that might be a problem. Mason hadn't been able to get a new car for Juan, mostly because the available options had smart technology and both Mason and Juan shied away from that.

The car might have to go. They had his computer, except it wasn't Juan's. Same with the phone. Gabriella had quit her job at the bakery. She could change her own hair up a bit, to how she used to wear it. The car, though... and Juan didn't have a good option to get home without it. Mason might have to drive him. Oh well, there were worse things. That car was a liability now.

Michael came out of the bathroom. "Porter okay?"

Mason turned. "No, not really. He doesn't like guns."

"Neither do I. I understand that is how it needs to work though."

"I think there might be more to it than that, with Porter. There is always more to it with Porter."

"That's God's own truth!" Michael laughed. "Did he go out?"

"Yes, he will be back in, uh, thirty minutes. We made a deal that he could go out for an hour."

Michael nodded. "It's probably a good idea to give that man limits."

"You are a good one to limit, too, Michael."

"Yeah, I know."

"Do you? You are in the van because I can't necessarily trust you in the bar, you realize that, right?"

Michael winced. "I figured it might be something like that, but it kinda hurts to hear it anyway."

"I am sorry for that." They were both silent for a few minutes. There was a soft knock on the door. Michael moved noiselessly over to the side, ready for action. He glanced at Mason and nodded.

"Yes?" Mason said in normal tones.

"Open the door, please. I don't have a key." A soft voice said. Michael quickly glanced through the peephole. He undid the dead lock and pulled the door open. Sienna slipped through the door.

"You are wet." Mason said, rather unnecessarily. Water was running down her face. She smiled at him ironically.

"Oh, I am? I hadn't noticed."

"Stop that. Is it raining then?"

"No, I managed to fall in the canal." Sienna shook her head hard and sprayed drops of water all over.

"Sienna…"" Mason sighed.

"Well, it's your own damn fault, Mason. You are asking dumb questions. Would you gentlemen excuse me? I would like to shower."

"Please do."

Michael grinned at Mason. "You were asking stupid questions, Mason."

"Yes, I know. I do that when I have been thinking deeply. It is an embarrassing habit. But at least it entertains everyone."

"It sure entertained me."

Porter came back almost exactly at his hour mark. He glanced towards the bathroom. "Sienna showering?"

"Yes," Mason responded. "Did you want to join her?"

Porter blushed a little. "No, you know I am not ready for that."

"Yes, I do know. Is it still raining?"

"Yes. It looks like it might rain all night. Maybe even tomorrow too."

Mason shrugged. "Well, none of us will melt."

"No, but Sienna's makeup might."

"It will just make her look more desperate and deranged. Have you got her all ready to go with what she needs to say?"

Porter smiled. "She is going to call Juan all sorts of things in a Czech dialect. Knowing Sienna, she is going to make up new things to call him while she is in there. It should be fun to see."

"Good. I always enjoy a little theater with my dinner. What did you end up doing?" Porter glanced away guiltily. Mason sighed. "Come on, Porter, you can't hide it from me. What did you do?"

"I went to a church." Porter said very softly, still looking away guiltily.

Mason smiled slightly. "Good."

"Good?"

"Yes, good. You always do better when you can get to a church. But also it is a good thing that you didn't try to lie about it. That means a lot more to me than where you went. You are starting to man up."

Porter smiled slightly. "It was very dark in there. Very peaceful. I liked it."

"Where was it?" Michael asked in a neutral voice. "I might need to go for a walk tonight."

Mason smiled at them both. "You boys!"

"Can't help it, Mason." Michael shrugged. "It helps. Especially when we have all these restrictions on us. It is the one place we can be free."

"I understand, Michael, I'm just making fun of you. Paybacks for earlier."

"Yeah, yeah. Where was it, Porter?"

Michael left quietly. Porter and Mason sat at the table again. Mason was still worried about Porter. This method he had of centering himself was a healthy thing for him though. "Did you just sit in the church?" He asked carefully.

"Yeah, pretty much." Porter said, shuffling the cards absently. "Why?"

"I am trying to gauge your fucking health, idiot."

"Oh. Well, it was very calming. I could hear the rain hitting the stained glass and there were banks of candles, all lit up."

"I like the candles."

"I thought you didn't like Catholicism."

"I never said that; I have looked into it. It makes lots of sense, as a religion."

"Juan said the same thing."

"I know. I went with him when he got baptized and all."

"What? How did I not fucking know about this?"

"You weren't ready for it, Porter. You were still suicidal then. Juan didn't want to burden you with more, although I think he really wanted to ask you to be his sponsor-type person. But not when you were in that condition. You were too focused on your own problems, and rightly so. We can't help others when we are fucked up."

Porter sighed. "Ah, fuck. I have missed so much because of being a fucking moron."

"I am sorry, Porter. Sometimes we have to keep moving, even when it leaves someone behind in life. It has taken you a long time to move past that stage, and I am still not sure you are totally beyond it, even though you are a lot better."

Porter put his hands over his face.

Sienna came out of the bathroom. She looked at the two of them and seemed to recognize that there was something wrong . Quietly, she came over and took Porter's head gently in her arms. Porter suddenly clutched at her and turned his face into her. Mason was a little surprised. He hadn't thought it would matter this much.

Sienna ran her fingers through Porter's hair. "Shh, love. It is all right. Whatever it is, it is all right."

Porter finally sat up, wiping his face. "I've missed so much, so much." He whispered.

Mason closed his eyes sadly. "I'm sorry, Porter."

"No, Mason, I am sorry. I should be present for my friends. Anyone who is willing to put up with me and my shit deserves a little more than I have been giving."

Mason shook his head. "Porter, we love you. We don't demand anything from you. How can you think I would ever ask you for more than you can give? That would be setting you up for failure."

Sienna smiled slightly. "None of us would do that, Porter. We might ask you to do a hell of a lot, but we won't make you fail."

Porter nodded. "I know."

"Besides," Mason said, "There is no way you can be a part of every single thing, all the time, for everybody. I would go through hell for you, but I couldn't be there when you were left behind. And you experienced things that I can never be a part of. Your journey is your own, and I am privileged that you let me share some of it with you."

Porter picked up the deck again and stared through it, focusing on something else entirely. "Well, you are going to have to deal with me a lot more now."

Mason smiled. "I can hardly wait. I bet you are the fucking annoying neighbor who mows his lawn at six o'clock in the morning on a Saturday, just because you fucking can."

"Yeah, well, you probably will let your fucking cat come claw up my door."

"I might. Just for paybacks."

"Want to play cards?"

Mason shrugged. "If you are ready."

"I think so. Sienna?"

She hesitated, then said, "Well, maybe a hand or two. I need to get a lot of sleep tonight, and frankly, I am worried about you, Porter."

"I know you are. I promise to hide it better."

Wrong answer, Mason thought, but he didn't say anything. As he looked at his hand, Mason figured it was probably true; Porter was not going to be able to stop worrying about the team members, but he could hide that from them. He was less adept at hiding it from Mason. As if he knew what Mason was thinking, Porter glanced at him and winked. Mason nodded back. So long as they understood each other.

Michael came in after about an hour. "Still raining, Mason, so you don't have to ask."

"Thanks, I think." Mason said sourly.

"No problem."

Sienna laughed.

"What's this?" Porter asked.

Mason sighed. "You know I sometimes ask really obvious

questions when I have been thinking hard about one thing and have to switch up. I did that, again, tonight. Michael and Sienna will probably never let me live it down."

"Oh."

Sienna laughed again. "It was pretty funny, Mason."

"Whatever."

Chapter 15

The next afternoon, Mason casually walked into the bar American Café. No one questioned his being there. It was not the type of place that encouraged patrons who weren't in on the know, and Mason could be fairly non-descript when he wanted to be.

Sienna had already fixed her hair for the evening. It looked crazy-wild. Mason hadn't necessarily appreciated how much time and effort went into Sienna's disguises before. The blue temporary dye had taken thirty minutes to set, then Sienna had spent a long time and a lot of gel to get it how she wanted it. Porter, Michael, and Mason, none of whom had anything better to do, had watched. Mason suspected that, whatever chemical was used in gel, Sienna had depleted the country's supply by at least half. Oh well, she looked fucking amazing enough to justify the expenditure.

Porter shook his head at Mason at one point. "Ghastly. Making her hair do that is a crime against nature and humanity."

She smiled at them in the mirror. "Wait until you see the makeup, love."

Porter faked a shudder.

Michael laughed. "Spare some for Porter; he looks like he could use a clown face."

"Michael, fuck off. You have no room to talk."

"No, you're right. But just think: we could paint a big ol' smile on your face. Maybe rouge your cheeks up. You'd be so adorable."

"Touch me and die, bitch."

"You don't scare me, big boy. I can take you."

"How much you bet on that, big mouth?"

"A fucking huge amount. Even if you manage to get the upper hand, I'll cheat. Just to beat you at your own game."

Mason sighed. "Fucking drop it, both of you. I'm not up to being a fucking babysitter for two overgrown juveniles."

Sienna laughed merrily and that cut off any other conversation on the subject.

Now Mason was sitting at the bar in the dim, smoky interior of an inferior cafe. He acted as uninterested in his surroundings as the other patrons but he kept his ears open, sifting through any conversation around him. If he heard something useful it could be worth more than the people they had come for. Juan and Gabriella weren't there in the room. There was the possibility that there was some sort of backroom but that idea struck Mason as far-fetched for some reason. This type of place seemed to rely on the fact that it was so overlooked that people naturally stayed away, except true idlers or members of Phalanx, of course.

Mason had already finished one beer extremely slowly and was on his second by the time there was a minor disturbance at the entrance. Juan and Gabriella breezed on in. As they passed behind him, Mason heard them discussing the merits of the couple making out heavily near the front of the room. He smiled into his beer glass. He looked at his phone again; he'd been pretending to do things on it all afternoon, so it made no difference if he actually did something. He texted Porter: "He's in." Porter didn't respond but Mason wasn't upset by that. Porter was a professional and he wouldn't needlessly send a message that might be intercepted. It was time to sit back and await the results, in the enviable form of Sienna.

About thirty minutes after Juan had arrived, one of the group he was with at the back came over to the bar and said something softly to the barkeep about music.

Mason happened to glance curiously over as the music started. Big mistake. Mason hadn't seen Gabriella dance before, and he found he couldn't look away now on his first time. His face flushed a bit and his breathing seemed to stop. The only good thing was that the song wasn't very long. When it stopped, she laughed and stood back up. Mason took a deep breath. It seemed like he had forgotten to do it for the entire time the music was playing. The rest of the clientele seemed to be just as intent on her as Mason had been. He took a huge gulp of beer. All of a sudden, he understood what Juan had meant about getting shit-faced just from watching Sienna. Completely believable.

"Damn, that was hot." The barman said to no one in particular. "I hope they don't chase him off so she will come back."

"Yeah." Mason agreed. "They fucking scare off too many."

"Shit, yes. They fight too much. But I hope they fucking get it together to keep those two." The barman moved off down the bar again to serve someone. Mason filed that information away. It was always good to know about weaknesses.

Then the distraction appeared: Sienna shoved her way in shouting and cursing loudly. Mason stood up hurriedly and positioned himself close to her. When she threw off a restraining hand, he conveniently moved in to grab her. She threw him and he reeled back convincingly, taking several others out with him and opening an avenue for her to the back. It worked beautifully even if it put him on the floor at the front and out of position to help when the actual shooting happened. Michael and the unit were through the door almost before the third shot finished. Porter must have signaled him in. The general stampede never got moving.

They swiftly surrounded and cuffed everyone and began moving them out to transports. Michael roughly put Mason's hands behind him and cuffed them. "All right, buddy, let's get you going. I need to check the carnage before we get you out of here." He shoved Mason towards the back of the building and indicated a stool. "Sit there and don't fucking move your ass."

The rest of the unit moved out with the other people who had been in the bar. Nobody paid attention to Michael or Mason. Porter slipped in during the general confusion and slouched his way back. No one seemed to see him either.

"You know, Mason," he said softly, "I am so fucking tempted to leave those cuffs on you right now."

"And yet, you won't." Mason smiled at him.

Porter made a face. "No, I won't. I need Sienna too much." He unlocked the cuffs. Mason stood up and went swiftly to Sienna. He rolled her gently to her back, ignoring the blood, and checked her pulse and breathing. The drug that the false bullets held depressed both to the point that it was almost impossible to detect them. However, it was short-lived. Sienna seemed to be coming around again already; her pulse and breathing were observable. "She's fine, Porter." Mason said,

143

moving to Gabriella. She also seemed okay. Juan was, too, but his pulse was slower and his breathing lighter. It could be due to the drug taking longer to work. Mason didn't want to take any chances; he carefully measured and injected a low amount of stimulant into Juan's arm.

"Is he alright?" Michael asked quietly.

"Probably, but let's not take any chances we don't have to." Mason said back just as quietly, his fingers still monitoring Juan's pulse. "He's doing better. We need to get out before someone official comes in. Michael, do you have the van in the alley?"

"Yep."

"Then you better get Juan. I'll bring Gabriella, and Porter will kill us both if he doesn't get to carry Sienna. Let's go, boys." Mason gathered up Gabriella and moved to the side exit, dimly visible behind the bar.

Michael had driven a nondescript van around to the alley, beside the reeking trash receptacles. Mason and Porter waited just inside the bar while Michael opened the side. "Get in here, quick. We'll blow this joint and be gone."

Mason swiftly handed Gabriella to Michael and went back inside to make sure everything was cleared out as Porter went out with Sienna. The inside of the bar was still empty. Mason took a bottle of vodka off the shelf and smashed it over the blood pool on the floor, mixing it with the bleach cleanser he saw under the bar. It might help mix the scent up a little for any forensics team. Not that any of them had DNA records anywhere, but why take a chance, even if it was small?

He also picked up the pistol. Anything left was collateral.

Michael had the engine running. Mason got in and had hardly shut the side door before they were moving.

"Where to?" Michael asked.

"The airport. Let's get the out hell of here." Mason checked everyone again. They were all coming around, Sienna even opening her eyes and smiling at him.

"And let's get there quickly so we can get Sienna cleaned up."

"Thank you!" Porter said.

"I didn't mean just the makeup, Porter."

"I know. And I appreciate that. Actually, seeing the blood was quite a jolt. I didn't think it would hit me as hard as it did.

"It's almost all fake." Sienna whispered.

"I know that too, Sienna, but it still gave me a jolt."

She smiled at him. "That's sweet!"

Porter sighed theatrically. "Now she is going to use it against me forever, I just know it."

Mason shrugged. "It helps keep you out of trouble."

Juan struggled to sit up. Mason helped him. "Man, whatever the fuck is in that, it gives one hell of a headache." Juan complained.

Gabriella woke up very confused and a little frightened. Juan gently took her hand. "It's okay, Gabriella. We are out. There was a drug in the bullet. I didn't have time to explain it to you. I am sorry."

"Oh, is that what happened? I can't really think right now."

"Yeah. It seems to work pretty well, although it fucking hurts. Mason, look into that."

"Whatever." Mason said absently as he checked Gabriella. "You would just bitch about something else."

"Bitch? Me?"

"All the fucking time!" Michael said from the front seat.

"Hey, quiet from the peanut gallery!" Juan said back.

"Yeah, fucking make me, Johnny."

Gabriella tried to sit up. Mason caught her has she slipped sideways. "Thanks, Mason. I seem to be dizzy."

"Lean against Juan. He needs someone to keep him grounded anyway."

Porter laughed softly. "So true."

Juan shrugged good-naturedly. "Well, Porter, I gotta say, you might actually be right for once."

"It's more than once, Johnny."

"Hm that I doubt."

Mason closed his eyes resignedly. Porter saw him do it. "Oh, we have to stop. Our fearless leader is getting tired of us. He might start being sarcastic if we don't."

Michael snorted from the front, "Yeah, we might not survive a full barrage of Mason-sarcasm."

Mason's phone rang. "No, you won't. Now shut the fuck up. I have to take this and I might not be able to concentrate if you guys are being idiots." They all became quiet. Mason pretended to be outraged often but he fully appreciated how his team was able to take him seriously when he needed it.

"Hello." He answered the call.

"Dr. Briggs. We have the team leaders apprehended except Stephen, alias Romeo. He is at large still."

"Fuck. Did you get the computers?"

"Yes, sir. Cell phone, too. Hopefully, something in one of them will give us a break or a hit somewhere." Mason was thinking. Something seemed off. What was it? "Dr. Briggs?"

"Just a moment." Mason stared out the windshield. "How long ago where the last calls on each phone placed?"

"The most recent was today around noon, off the woman Jayne's phone. Then there was one off Antonio's. Also Fredrico's. None of them are to the same number or the same location."

Mason shook his head. "Something about this is fucked up. I need to think on it. I will call you later. We are going to be airborne for a few hours. I'll let you know if we need anything else."

"Right. Talk to you when you land."

"What do you think is wrong?" Porter asked.

"I don't know, Porter. We missed the big leader though."

"He may not even be the key anymore," Juan volunteered. "I think Antonio and Jayne are the real players in this drama."

Mason thought about that. The barman had said that there was lots of fighting happening. It could be that the fighting was a power struggle between Jayne and Antonio. "Juan, did you get the impression that there might be some infighting happening?"

Juan shrugged. "I felt like there was the beginning of it, but I don't know how strong it was."

Mason was not satisfied. "Did any of them try to deliberately sabotage you or anything?"

"Jayne tried to kick me out, but that was after Gabriella danced and she might have been jealous."

"Oh, did you dance for them?" Sienna asked. "Good girl."

"Yeah, she did." Mason said, still distracted.

Porter grinned suddenly. "Was she any good?" He asked Mason with a twinkle in his eyes.

"Pretty good, yeah." Mason wasn't giving this conversation much attention. There was something bugging him.

"Only pretty good?"

"Look, Porter, have her dance for you. You decide for yourself. I have the feeling something is wrong about this, and I am trying to nail it down. Leave me the fuck alone."

Porter held up a hand. "Okay, Mason. I will back off. I was merely joking."

"I'm sorry, Porter." Mason sighed. "Something is fucked here. I don't know what, and that makes me nervous. Something about the timing and an off comment I heard at the bar."

"Well, why don't you tell us, then maybe we can help."

Mason glanced at Juan and Gabriella. "Later, perhaps." He didn't want to worry Gabriella right now. She still looked a bit upset. Porter caught on quickly. He nodded. "Maybe after we look like ourselves again?"

Mason shrugged. "We'll be at the airport shortly, and we can get everyone fixed up there, before we leave."

Michael negotiated all the traffic with his usual finesse and they drove into the service entrance of the private airport.

Mason opened the side door. "Everybody out. I have all the shit you need in that bag, by Porter. Juan, you get your hair dyed black again, then we'll cut it. Ladies, you know what you need to do. There is dye stripper in there, and other stuff. Get to it. We'll wait in the food area."

Sienna pulled her bloody coat around her. "You better have some real fucking clothes in there, Mason. I am not sitting on an airplane in nothing."

"Well, Porter might enjoy that, but yes, there are clothes for you ladies in there, as well as a new shirt for Juan. Get going."

147

Mason and Porter sat in the food area, which was a kitchen thing with vending machines. Mason needed coffee. Fortunately, there was s pot standing there. It looked like used motor oil but it was close enough.

Porter sat at the table. "What is bugging you?"

Mason put his hands over his face in frustration. "I don't know. That's what is fucking annoying. I heard something from the barman about Phalanx scaring away or chasing away other potential members. Then there is the fact that Stephen isn't present. It makes me think he is a rather ineffective leader and that a lot of the decisions are made with the lieutenants, so to speak, and that worries me. If they are fighting among themselves, it might mean something different than what we expected."

Porter thought about that, tapping his fingers nervously on the table. "This could be a lot more messy than we thought if Phalanx has dispersed beyond the leadership."

"I know. I didn't like this mission to start with because it put so much on Juan. I have the feeling that it is unraveling worse than before and that makes me tense. It's like when Sienna got double-crossed that one time: this whole game is changing in the middle, and I am not sure I know the rules this go around."

Porter nodded. "It is a problem."

"What is?" Michael asked, coming in and pouring himself some of the motor oil. "And what the hell is this?"

"I think it is pretending to be coffee. There might be a problem with this whole Phalanx wrap-up. I don't have anything specific though. It is pissing me off."

"Well, share. Pissing is better shared."

Porter snickered. "Do tell?"

"Fuck off, you know what I meant."

Mason smiled slightly. "This wrap-up feels too easy, somehow."

"Oh, is that all? Well, fuck, let's make it more messy then."

Mason leaned forward in interest. "Yes, let's! That is exactly what I need."

"I was joking, Mason."

"Well, I'm fucking not; we pulled this group, it is supposed to be a cohesive ruling group, yet Juan tells us that they are fighting, sometimes hard. I heard from the barkeep that they chase off or scare off potential hackers. That should make them a fairly ineffective ruling group, right?"

Michael nodded. "One would think so."

"Yet they aren't. They command respect and attention from high-level and moneyed terrorist groups and totalitarian regimes. Why? What is it that we are missing?"

Porter shook his head. "I don't know, but you are right. It does feel wrong. Where are we going to find answers?"

"I think once we get back, I will start with Phalanx itself. I might need you to come along, to observe. You both catch things I miss. I am not so proud that I can't ask for help."

"You will be able to interrogate?"

"I can manage that sort of clearance, yes."

"Damn. Okay, seriously, Mason, how much clearance do you have?"

"Pretty high, but I asked that it only be specific to our missions. I don't want to be involved in the political shit that goes on at the high levels of FBI, CIA, NSA. Those places are hellholes that I have no interest being involved in."

"So who hires us?"

Mason smiled. "I have no fucking idea, Porter. The less I know, the less I can reveal."

Porter laughed. "True, that."

Michael finished his coffee. "Well, Juan and the ladies should be done. I kind of got the impression you didn't want this general knowledge."

"There isn't any knowledge to be general yet, Mikey. I only shared it with you two because you can spot things that I don't."

Porter nodded. "I think you are right. What do you think is the next move then?"

"I think I will get in to interrogate. I only worry that Phalanx or whomever is really behind them will act before we can."

149

"Yeah, thanks for the fucking happy thought there, Mason."

"Sorry, but you knew the fucking rules when you started. Let's go shear Juan." Mason drained his coffee and stood up.

"He won't let you touch him with scissors." Porter warned, also standing.

"I know which is why you are going to do it."

"Ah, fuck, that is not in my job description."

"It is now."

Chapter 16

Juan had just washed the dye out of his hair. It was all black again.

"Looks good." Mason approved. "Now Porter is going to cut it."

"What the hell?" Juan protested.

"Well, I could do it for you instead."

"Oh fuck that. I'll take Porter any day."

"I rather thought that would be the case."

Porter didn't actually have to do much, just even some of the more exaggerated pieces out. Juan looked a lot less like a comic-book character and more like a normal person.

"Okay, okay, that's enough, Porter! Don't fucking shave me bald!"

"You know, Juan, you just bitch worse and worse."

"Practice makes fucking perfect. Now get away from me with those things."

Michael laughed. "Yeah, it's his kryptonite! Cut it off and he reverts to a normal geek!"

"Hey, it's 'nerd', Mikey, and shut the fuck up."

"Enough, nerds and geeks and muscle freaks." Mason said loudly. "We have to get out of here. Let's go check on the ladies."

"You have such a way with words, Mason!"

Mason ignored that. He knocked softly on the door to the women's restroom. "May we come in?" He asked, pushing the door slightly open.

"Of course." Sienna's voice said.

Mason jerked his head to the others. "In. Let's go."

Sienna and Gabriella had both washed the stripping compound out of their hair and changed clothes. Sienna had also removed the strong makeup. They looked very different, and very beautiful. Gabriella's hair wasn't usually all black. It had dark brown highlights through it. Mason saw that Juan was quite taken with her all over again. Good. She could keep him under control.

151

"You look very nice, both of you. Are you about ready?"

Sienna smiled. "Of course. I was just throwing away everything left of Natalya."

"Very good."

Gabriella looked a little wistfully at the bracelet she had on still. "Ah, well, goodbye, Sarah." She pulled it off and threw it in the garbage.

Porter smiled. "Do you like that sort of thing, Gabriella?" He asked carefully.

"No, not usually, but Juan gave it to me."

"Well, I probably shouldn't say anything..."

"Which means you are not going to shut the fuck up." Juan interjected disgustedly.

"Naturally. But, Gabriella, Juan has given me a rather lengthy list of ideas and I am currently in talks with James to produce some pieces for you."

Gabriella looked at Porter sharply. "Are you joking right now?" She asked suspiciously.

"No, my dear," Porter said gently. "I don't purposely joke with other people's feelings. Not over something important. I am quite serious; we are both very interested in turning out the best that we can."

Gabriella's eyes suddenly filled with tears. "You would do that for me?" She whispered.

"Of course we would."

She didn't say anything else, but she did give Porter and Juan very hard hugs.

Mason smiled and winked at Porter. He winked back. Juan shook his head at Porter. "I told you to keep it a fucking secret."

Porter shrugged. "She was upset about throwing the bracelet. I am trying to ease her past it."

"Whatever. I think you just like pissing me off."

"Sometimes."

"You know," Mason cut in, "Much though I would love to stand here and listen to you two insult each other, we need to get on that plane. So let's get going and continue this on the way home."

As they boarded the small jet, Mason called the agent back. "I don't have anything concrete yet. I want to interrogate them, though, altogether, and perhaps separately. I want some of my team to witness. They might be able to help."

"Whatever you need, Dr. Briggs."

Juan had heard the conversation. He looked at Mason penetratingly. "Something is bugging you, Mason. I can tell." He said softly. "What is it? You obviously don't want to bother the ladies, or you would have said something in front of them."

"You're right, Juan. The thing is, I have a feeling that there is something more, and something we are missing. It is just a feeling, though."

"Gotcha. I will try to help you out with it, if you want."

Mason shook his head. "Not right away, Juan. You have done enough, and I don't want you walking around with a target on your back. You are dead, so let's leave you dead for a while."

Juan grinned. "No complaints here! But if you need something, let me know."

"I will." Mason turned off his phone and they climbed in.

Porter looked at Mason searchingly as he came in. Mason shook his head slightly. Porter looked out the window. Mason knew he hated waiting for things to happen. Mason didn't much like it himself. It gave rise to the very real possibility that they would be outmaneuvered, and quickly. He didn't like playing defensively in these situations. It was better to be the surprise strike, not the considered and patient reaction. That was the way they had to play, and Mason didn't like it.

Sienna looked at Mason. "Everyone they wanted weren't there in the bar, I assume?"

"No, we missed the head honcho."

"Damn. Hopefully they will pick him up quickly."

Juan looked up suddenly. "Hey, Mason, I just remembered something. Antonio, the smoking guy, he mentioned something during one of the sparring matches between himself and Jayne. She said something about having some sort of information on him, and he said something similar to the effect of, 'I have enough on both you and Stephen. I went and found her and I know just how old she really was.' I don't think Jayne understands how dangerous he is as a player in this whole thing. He also said something about Jayne fucking around with Stephen, and how she used sex to subdue people."

"Hm. Good job, Juan. Is there anything else?"

"I don't know, Mason. What do you think, Gabriella?"

She shrugged. "I got the feeling that Jayne thinks and acts like she is in charge, but the guys are pretty much arrayed against her, although I think Judah is the least strong of them all, from the limited view we got of them all."

"Or he could be hiding it." Mason added a bit sourly. "We didn't have enough to work on going into this and we don't have enough coming out. I am not taking another one this vague. It's too dangerous for you all."

"And for you." Sienna said.

"I don't much care about that, Sienna."

"Maybe not, but we do."

"I appreciate that." The talk went into other channels and Mason sat still thinking through this whole debacle. It should have been a straight-forward snatch, and instead it was turning into a nightmare. He wouldn't be taking another job for quite a while. The people hiring needed to get their shit together. This was the second mission that had been botched by a lack of information and he refused to take the chance again. He intended to take a hard line on it when they got back. This stress wasn't worth it for him. He would not be risking the lives of his friends needlessly anymore. This was fucking bullshit.

He stared out the window at the ocean flowing beneath in uncounted miles without seeing anything. What did he have, really? He had a chance comment and a general feeling of unease. Juan had heard that there might be some illicit behavior from someone. There was definite fighting happening, or a power struggle. There was almost no information on the principle players, other than Juan's and Gabriella's direct observations. Mason would bet on them more strongly than any other information, but they hadn't been in long. Their chances to observe were circumvented by short time.

"Damn it all." He muttered under his breath. There was so much he needed and no time to get it. Phalanx could strike anytime, or no time. It might not even be Phalanx they were looking for. It could be someone in the background, someone manipulating. It was possible that Phalanx didn't know they were being used. Too damn vague! When they were back and he had something more concrete, he was going to the secretary of Homeland Security. He might take Porter and Juan with him. This was going to be dealt with high up.

Sienna put her fingers gently on his arm, recalling him to where he was. "Beg pardon?"

Sienna, who was certainly no fool, looked at him quite seriously. "Mason, I asked you what we would be doing when we land. Are you not listening?"

"No, I was not. I do not like how these missions have devolved into messes. We are having too many slips. You should know that, better perhaps than I do."

"Oh. You are right, there, I suppose. I assume you will be taking steps?"

"I intend to take it as high as I can."

Her eyes widened in surprise. "You do?"

"Yes. Now, you are all free to go as you wish when we land. I have something to take care of. Juan, I would like you to ditch your car though. I don't know it is safe anymore."

Juan made a face. "Damn. I liked that car. Well, okay, I will. Can I at least get my CDs out of it?"

"Sure. I'll drive you around until you get another."

"Okay. Then you will at least have good music in that tin can you drive."

"Whatever. The shit you listen to sounds like auto-tuned dying mammals in a woodshed."

"Yes, but they are popular mammals. Makes all the difference."

Once the plane touched down, Mason turned his phone back on. He immediately redialed the number that he had been talking to before.

"This is Dr. Briggs. What news?"

Juan and Gabriella had pushed past him and were going out of the plane, followed by Porter and Sienna. Michael was behind him.

"Well, Dr. Briggs, there has been one slight hitch."

Mason felt his stomach tighten. "What fucking hitch?"

"The woman let something slip. She said to one of the initial intakes that Antonio wasn't going to win."

"Win? Win what?"

Mason stood at the open door of the small jet, absently watching Porter and Sienna getting ready to leave and Juan and Gabriella walking towards Juan's car, laughing about something.

"We don't know, Dr. Briggs. She stopped talking right after that, but she seemed to be alluding to something beyond the present situation."

"What the fuck?" Mason suddenly had a premonition. Maybe there were multiple ways of chasing people away from Phalanx. He dropped his phone. "Juan! Get away from that car!" He shouted, sure he was right. Something was wrong and he couldn't tell what.

Juan looked back, obviously puzzled. He and Gabriella were already by the trunk and he had raised the keychain and pushed the keyless unlock. He must have heard something, because he suddenly jerked himself into Gabriella , both of them falling sideways. The car exploded. It was obviously a bomb, and the engine blew spectacularly. Juan and Gabriella were thrown back by the blast.

"Fucking hell!" Michael shouted.

Mason was already running. Porter, who was faster even if he had been further away, right behind him.

Mason got to Juan first. He quickly checked him. Juan was bloody and unconscious, but he was alive.

Porter was shielding Gabriella form the heat of the burning car. "She's alive but this is serious, Mason! We have to get her out of here!" He shouted to Mason.

"I know!" Michael pounded up. "Michael, get Juan out of range, now! Porter, is anything broken?"

"Her legs look bad, Mason, real bad."

"Is her spine good? Ribs?"

"They seem to be."

"Then get her out of range, now, Porter! If she loses a leg, that is better than having her die! Go!"

Sienna had her phone out already. Mason grabbed it and dialed.

"Hello, Samaritan Hospice." A gentle voice answered.

"This is Dr. Briggs. I need a transport at the Fairway airport, now. There's been an accident and there will be two to get. I am tending them until you get here."

"Right away, sir!"

Mason ended the call and handed it to Sienna. He checked Gabriella again. She was stable. Thank God.

Porter, covered in blood and whatever shit the fire was putting out, gestured for Sienna to stay back. "No, love, I don't know what that car is burning. I don't want you to breathe it if you can avoid it. I am fine. I promise. Can you follow the ambulance to the Hospice?"

Sienna, very pale but completely self-possessed, nodded. "Of course, Porter. "

"Do you have keys?"

"I do."

"Why don't you go and get ready to go then? I am not excluding you, you understand; I am worried that some of those fumes might be dangerous for you after the drugs you've had today and with your history."

"Porter, I understand you. I trust you, beloved." She ran to the car.

Mason looked at Porter and Michael. "Here are the keys to my car. The hospice doesn't have a big ambulance and you two together stretch even normal-sized things."

Porter grabbed the keys. "On it. Let's go, Michael. I know where it is. We need to be there as soon as we can." They ran to Mason's sedan and left, Sienna following closely.

The ambulance screamed its way in. Two orderlies who Mason

recognized jumped out. "These two, and step on it." Mason said, getting out of the way. If he hadn't known the two men, he would have refused to let Juan and Gabriella go, it was that serious. Until he had answers, no one was getting to his team without his knowing it. This was fucked up and he was pissed. Mason got coldly angry when he got pissed. Unlike Porter or Michael, who tended to get physical and beat things or people up, Mason grew more focused and furious. It might not have been the best response, but he couldn't help it much and in this situation it would probably help.

Juan and Gabriella remained stable through the ride. Gabriella worried Mason more than Juan. Her legs were very troubling. She was going to require surgery at the very least, and her abdomen looked to have taken some trauma. Juan was heavier, and he had been moving a bit more. He seemed to be in better condition, for whatever reason, at least on the outside. Mason was more worried about Juan's emotional stability when he woke up and Gabriella wasn't there.

When they got to the hospice, Mason jumped out and let Dr. Harris take over. Mason was no surgeon and he wasn't going to go shoving into a field he didn't have expertise. Porter, Michael, and Sienna were waiting for him at the front desk area.

"Okay, Dr. Harris is taking them. We'll know more soon. In the meantime, none of you are going any fucking place without me, got it?" They all nodded. "All right. Here is what we are going to do. Porter and Michael, I want you two to take showers. There are some here. I will get you clothes. Sienna, you stay with me, physically, until these two are done. Let's go."

Porter was angry, Michael was furious, and Sienna was composed but seething.

Mason led the way to the showers. "Here you gentlemen go. We will be back, and I will be probably chewing various people's asses for a while. If you need something, I want you to tell me, got it?"

Michael raised his hand slightly. "Karen?"

Mason nodded. "We'll go get her. I don't think I can avoid startling her, though."

"She is stronger now, Mason, she can handle more."

"Good. She is going to be with us until this gets sorted. Fucking pisses me off."

Porter looked at Mason warily. "Are you going to hit somebody?"

"No, you should know I get pissed differently than you do."

"Yes, and that frankly scares me."

"Too fucking bad. Get in there."

Chapter 17

Karen was worried, but once Mason had assured her that Michael was all right and that he needed her with him, she calmed a bit. Mason was glad that she didn't get too worked up.

"The thing is, Karen, there's been a glitch, and Juan and Gabriella have been hurt. I don't want anything to happen to anyone else if it can be avoided."

"I trust you, Mason." Karen said, handing him some of Michael's clothes and getting in the car.

Sienna quickly got some clothes for Porter and they rushed back to the hospice. Porter and Michael were finished showering and were patiently waiting for clothes. Mason quickly handed them in and stayed out with Sienna and Karen. It took only about five minutes for Porter and Michael to get ready.

"Okay, let's go. I think we should camp out in the chapel until I have something more to go on."

Porter shrugged. "You know I won't complain about that."

"Good. Go." Mason was already dialing his cell phone. "This is Dr. Briggs. We had a situation. It will be contained, do you understand? No one is to know the details, other than that there was an explosion and some people were hurt."

"Understood, Dr. Briggs."

"None of this is to get to the prisoners. None. If it does, it will be fucking hell for someone."

"Understood."

"I will be in when I can, but no one is to interrogate without me, and I will not leave until I can be assured that my team is safe. This is the second huge slip and I will not stand anymore."

"Yes, sir."

"Also, I will be meeting the Secretary. This will not stand."

"Sir! Are you sure you want to do that?"

"I said I will be meeting the Secretary. Until I can have assurance that this sort of fucking shit does not happen again, we will not be accepting any jobs from the department. Now you will make that meeting and give me the details."

"Yes, sir."

Mason ended the call. Porter raised his eyebrows in admiration. "Hot damn."

"You and Michael are coming with me to that meeting, you hear me? I was going to take Juan, but that would be a mistake now."

"Sir, yes, sir!"

"Shut the fuck up." Mason was still furious. This should never have happened and while some of it was probably his fault, it certainly wasn't all his. "Sit your ass down and listen. There is something big here. I am going to find out what it is. Until I know, none of you are going anywhere that I can't secure first. Any of you. Period. We'll know about Gabriella and Juan shortly, then we can plan more. For now, sit and shut up."

They all sat in the quiet, dark chapel. The lights weren't on, so the only light came through the narrow windows. It was peaceful, at least. Mason closed his eyes and took deep breaths for a few minutes. It was calming. He could sure use some fucking calming. It was perhaps half an hour later and there was a soft knock on the door.

"Dr. Briggs?" Mason recognized the voice of Dr. Harris. "Would you step out please?"

Mason stood. He hesitated. "Doctor, would you mind just saying whatever you need to in here? These are all good friends. They deserve to know."

Dr. Harris nodded. "Very good. Juan is going to be all right. We had to put some stitches in one of his cuts, and he will undoubtedly be sore for days. We gave him some light pain relief. He'll be waking up within the hour. The young lady is more concerning. She'll probably be all right, but we had to amputate some of her toes. We couldn't save them all. Her legs are pretty well torn up, you know. We had to do some reconstructive surgery on her muscles. There isn't any way to predict how that will heal. I am sorry. We tried the best we could."

"Dr. Harris, I know that you are one of the best. I have no doubts at all that you have done all that was possible. We knew when we saw the injuries that it was possible for complications. We are, I

161

think, all relieved that you have saved her life." The rest of the team nodded. "Thank you for your hard work." Mason shook hands with Dr. Harris. "When can we see them?"

"Juan should be awake soon. You may visit him any time. Gabriella will be later, I think. She is going to be in a great deal of pain for a while, so we are going to hold off on visits for a while yet."

Mason nodded. "Michael, why don't you and I go see if Juan is awake? Porter, please stay with the ladies here. If any of you need to leave, you let me know."

"Of course, Mason."

Dr. Harris led them to a hospital room. "Here is Juan's room. His vitals are good. I have no doubts that his physical recovery will be fine. You will have a better idea of his mental state than I would, Dr. Briggs."

Mason inclined his head. "Thank you for everything, doctor. I am very grateful that you and your hospice were able to take my friends."

"It is never a problem. I will go and check on Gabriella. If you will excuse me."

Michael and Mason sat, one on each side of Juan, waiting for him to regain consciousness. Michael shook his head in frustration. "Fuck, Mason. What the fucking hell happened?"

"I don't know and I will find out. I have a suspicion, though."

"Good, because this is fucked up."

"Yeah, pretty much."

They sat in silence until Juan stirred. His eyes fluttered and he groaned. "Fuck. What the fuck happened?"

"Your car blew up."

"Goddamn. Where am I?"

"Samaritan Hospice. We brought you here."

"Fuck, my head hurts." Juan struggled to sit up. He managed it after a few moments. "God damn fucking hell. I liked that fucking car, too."

Michael and Mason didn't say anything. Juan closed his eyes again and rested a little. Finally, a nurse came in. "Dr. Briggs? Dr.

Harris says that your friend can join you out of the room, if he would like. It is best if he gets up and moves around."

"Very well, thank you, nurse."

Juan smiled slightly. "Yeah, that'd be great. Especially since you brought the human mountain with you. I can always lean on him."

"That's right." Michael said softly.

They helped Juan slowly down to the chapel. His movement was very slow.

"In here, Juan." Mason opened the door.

Juan smiled again. "Trust Porter to find a fucking church."

"I heard that." Porter said from inside.

"I don't care." Juan said back. They went in. Porter stood up and helped Juan sit down.

Dr. Harris came back in. "Dr. Briggs, I think I need to talk to you privately." Mason stepped out and shut the door. "The young woman is almost awake, but I think you need to come and talk to her as soon as we get her stabilized. She could a bit disoriented, and I think there might be help you can give her. We had to do a hysterectomy. There was extensive internal damage to her right ovary and uterus from the blast. The trauma was too much. You may need to provide support for her." Dr. Harris handed Mason a file.

"I'll be along in just a few minutes." Mason said. "I haven't told Juan about her yet, and he is going to need support with him before I leave him."

"Thank you, Doctor."

"You're welcome, Doctor." Mason went back into the chapel. "Porter, do you have that priest you like on speed dial?"

"Uh, yeah, why?"

"Trust me, you want to see if you can get him here."

"All right." Porter pulled out his phone and stepped to the back of the chapel to call.

Mason sat down beside Juan. "Johnny, here's the reason I want that priest to come here: Gabriella has had some pretty serious injuries. She has been in surgery while you were out. I am going to see her now, and you might need to see her soon, too. But you are going to need

163

support, any support we can give you, right now. Do you get what I am saying?"

Juan had clenched his fists tightly. He stared straight ahead at the simple altar. He nodded once.

Mason put his arm around Juan's shoulders. "I'm sorry, Juan. I am terribly sorry." He said softly.

"It's not your fucking fault."

"That somehow doesn't lessen my guilt."

Porter had come up so quietly that Mason hadn't heard him. "Mason, he's coming. He was out at a house call anyway. He should be here within the next ten minutes. Will that be soon enough?"

"It will have to be."

Juan had covered his face with his hands. Mason strongly suspected that he was crying. He just sat with his arm around Juan's shoulders until the priest came in.

Porter touched his arm softly and motioned towards the door. Mason nodded. "Juan, I have to go see how Gabriella is doing. Father Greg is here, if you need someone to talk to."

Juan nodded from behind his hands. Porter sat beside him on the other side. "Go, Mason. We got this."

Mason shook hands with the priest at the back of the chapel. "Thank you for coming, Father. I appreciate it." Father Greg smiled slightly and nodded. Mason slipped out the door.

Outside, he slammed his hand on the wall as hard as he could. "Fucking hell! Somebody is gonna pay for this!" He went to the nurses' station. "Dr. Harris asked me to check on Gabriella?"

"Yes, Doctor, right this way." The young nurse led him down the hall to another room. There were many more machines in this room, though not all of them were being used. Gabriella was breathing lightly, her eyes still closed. Her legs were wrapped in gauze and she had several monitors hooked to her.

Dr. Harris was checking something on a chart. He turned. "Ah, there you are, Doctor. She is almost awake, I think."

"Very good. You have done a marvelous job."

"Mason?" Gabriella whispered very softly. Her eyes fluttered and opened.

"Yes, I am here." Mason came quickly to the side of the bed.

"Where am I?" She asked, very confused.

"In a hospital. Do you remember what happened?"

"Well, let's see. I remember getting off the plane. Juan was making fun of your music. Then you said something, and, um, I don't remember."

"That's just fine, Gabriella. The truth is that there was bomb in the car and it went off. You and Juan were close to the car when it detonated, and you were hurt."

"I was? Is Juan okay?"

"Of course; nothing can hurt him too badly. Well, that's not true. One thing hurts him." Mason said as he checked her medicine drip.

"What's that?"

Mason looked at her compassionately. "He is afraid that you are going to be afraid of him, of course. He blames himself and he thinks you will blame him."

"That's ridiculous."

Mason shrugged. "People in love are often ridiculous. Anyway. You have, in fact, sustained some serious injuries. Doctor Harris assures me that you will fine, but you have had some reconstructive surgery on your legs, and you have had to have a partial hysterectomy. Unfortunately, even the genius that he is could not save your toes. You have had four amputated, from both feet."

"Four? How many do I have left?"

"Six, of course. You'll have scars, but you have legs still. You might have bled out but for Juan and Porter. Juan knocked you out of the main blast and Porter put some bandages on you to stop the bleeding as much as he could."

"Oh. Well that is good. May I sit up?"

Doctor Harris nodded. "That should be fine. Let us help you." He and Mason carefully supported her up.

"Ah, that feels better. May I see my feet, doctor?"

"They are wrapped in bandages right now, but we could

probably give you a peek later. I'll need to look at the sutures."

"Okay. I don't think there is anything wrong with what you have had to do. I just want to get acquainted with my new feet."

Dr. Harris smiled. "That should be fine."

Mason looked at Gabriella hard. "Are you all right, then?"

"I know what you are asking, Mason. Yes, I think so. It is hard to say for certain, of course, but I think so."

"All right. I think Juan might need me more right now."

"You had better go and see him then. Doctor, will I be able to go and see him? Maybe in a wheel chair?"

Doctor Harris considered. "I think that might be acceptable, if it is a quick trip and you don't try to stand or anything that might pull your leg muscles yet."

Mason left. At least one of them was okay, sort of. She had handled the news about her feet better than he thought. He was slightly concerned that she hadn't addressed the hysterectomy though. Now he had to get Juan stabilized and get down to interrogating these asses who played fast and loose with people's lives.

The chapel was lit up now that it was dark outside. The priest was already gone, but Juan looked better. Sort of. He was kneeling, which had to hurt, and had his face on his arms. Porter still sat beside him. Michael, Karen, and Sienna sat a respectful distance away. Mason slipped in beside Juan. Porter went over by Sienna.

Juan glanced over at Mason. "I hope she is okay. I should have been faster."

"Fuck that, Juan. You were fast enough. If you had been slower she would be dead."

Juan shook his head. "I heard you and I still pushed the fucking button. Total idiot that I am."

"Fucking stop. You had no reason to think what I said was that important. You reacted much faster than I could have, and you are both alive because of it. I won't let you do that."

Juan sighed and put his face back into his arms. "Whatever, Mason. You know it's my fault."

Mason resisted a sudden urge to shake him. "Look, Juan, you

166

are starting to piss me off more, which is not a good thing for either of us right now. How about you shut the fuck up for a while? I have asked someone to come in and have a look at you. Then you can make a better informed decision."

Juan shrugged. "It won't change."

Mason didn't say anything. He did take several deep, centering breaths. He understood what Juan was feeling and it was perfectly valid. He would have to work through the misplaced guilt. However, Mason didn't want to deal with it right now; not on top of everything else. At least Porter had a grip on himself for the time being. And Michael. Juan was smart; he would get through this.

The door opened after ten minutes or so. The nurse backed in, carefully pulling a wheelchair. Gabriella looked fairly alert, considering. Her legs were still covered by a blanket and she dragged the IV along with her.

Juan didn't even look up. He was still roiling in his own thoughts. Mason nudged him, not very gently, in the ribs.

"Ow! Damn it, Mason, that hurts!" Juan glared at him.

"I know, and the person I wanted you to see is here. Try to be a good listener." Mason pointed to the other side of Juan.

Juan turned with the air of someone doing a chore and not expecting to enjoy it. Mason watched with a slight satisfaction as Juan stiffened sharply when he saw Gabriella.

"Hey, baby." She smiled at him slightly. "I know I don't look that great, but you look as good as ever." Juan didn't say anything. He couldn't. He threw himself on the floor beside her and put his head in her lap. "Oh, Juan, it is okay." Gabriella said gently. "I am fine, really."

Juan shook his head, not looking up. "No it isn't."

"Juan, it is. Look at me, please." He couldn't resist that sort of command. "Look, I am hurt, but I will get better. I always get better. I might have some fun scars to show off though. I am afraid my legs aren't going to be quite so attractive to the general populace anymore."

"Who fucking cares? You are beautiful and scars don't matter at all."

"You're so sweet. I might have to use a cane to walk. Doctor

Harris warned me about that possibility. I have lost toes and that sometimes throws off balance."

"I don't care."

"Oh good. I had hoped so. The other thing is, I can't have children. There was too much damage inside; they had to take steps."

"I don't care about that either. If that matters to you, we can work around it someday. I love you, and you are here. All of you. I don't love who you were. You are here, you are who I love."

Mason looked at Porter and winked. Porter smiled. It was pretty damn similar to something he'd said once.

Gabriella sighed. "I was worried about that."

"You shouldn't ever worry about that." Juan said gently.

Mason nodded. "True. He's been in here beating the hell out of himself with guilt since he woke up, you know."

Juan sighed. "Do you have to say that, Mason?"

"Yes. You are pretty damn smart, Juan; you should have figured it out on your own. You didn't, and Gabriella deserves to know it."

"You make me sound so fucking stupid."

"You were fucking stupid. Now you aren't." His phone buzzed in his pocket; a text had come in.

Juan shrugged. "Oh well." He kissed Gabriella gently. It was obvious that he wanted to do more but he was worried about hurting her needlessly. She felt the same way, Mason was fairly sure.

Mason glanced at his phone. "Meeting today, 8:30 pm, office. Text to confirm."

It was 6:30 now. It would be tight. "Okay, team, here's the deal. I have a meeting with the Secretary at 8:30 tonight. Porter and Michael, I want you to come. That means the rest of you are going to be without us until later tonight. Sienna and Karen, you can go to my house if you would rather be there. We have to leave now to get to this meeting. Is that all right with everyone?"

Sienna nodded. Karen looked hesitant but she also nodded.

Porter stood up and looked at Michael. "Shall we? I would like to knock some official heads around, myself. Kick some ass, you know, the usual."

168

"Fuck yes." Michael stood up as well.

"Be careful." Karen said to him.

"I will." Michael kissed and hugged her. He went over to the door. "Let's do this, Mason."

Mason looked back at Juan. "You'll be all right, both of you?"

Juan smiled wryly. "Yes, I expect so, now. You do know how to bring in the experts to make me better, don't you?"

"Whatever fucking works."

Gabriella smiled and made a flipping motion with her fingers. "Go, go. Have fun."

"I intend to." Mason stepped over to the door. "Gentlemen. Let us go have a little discussion with a head of state."

Chapter 18

The small jet they had arrived on hadn't left. Mason had expressly told the pilot to wait, even though Mason strongly suspected he was an Air Force pilot of no little rank.

As they boarded again, Mason stopped and said to him, "Thank you for your time, sir. I know you are probably an officer. If I were you, I might make myself as scarce as I can when we get there."

The pilot smiled. "I had planned to do maintenance, for as long as I might need to."

Mason nodded. "Wise decision. We'll need to fly back tonight, too; I can't leave my team for long now."

"I understand, sir."

"Thank you, sir."

Mason was still furious and he was getting more so as this dragged on. Porter leaned over and touched his knee. "Mason, breathe, man. You are fucking pissed and you are starting to make me wary."

"Good. Maybe I will impress them as such, too."

"You might also come across as slightly homicidal, since you haven't changed and you have blood and stuff all over you."

"Again, good; maybe that will also impress them as such."

Porter smiled then. He looked at Michael. "This is going to be so much fun!"

Michael sighed. "You have a fucked-up sense of humor."

"Of course, but Mason is going to go batshit crazy there. Come on, haven't you ever wanted to see that?"

"Not since the last time he chewed us up one side and down the other."

"This is different; he's chewing someone else."

Michael shook his head. Porter laughed. Mason didn't respond at all. He was gathering his thoughts on this matter. He intended to go in and lay his groundwork all at once. If there was to be argument, that was fine, but they would be well aware of what he thought before anything else was said. To that end, he began to draw a mental list up.

He didn't appreciate being hung out to dry; these missions already came with the risk of death or capture. To not give him all the information at the beginning only made it more likely that they would fail. Then there was the problem of when they succeeded and the ball got dropped somewhere else. It wasn't happening again. He was going to refuse all attempts to sooth his feathers or to double-speak him out of the office. Mason grew sterner as the jet flew closer.

By the time they had landed, Mason was ready, come Hell or high water, or both.

They disembarked and there was a discreet black sedan waiting, with some service man standing there, in black. Mason nodded curtly and got in. Porter and Michael squeezed in, too.

"Damn it, Michael," Porter said in irritation, "Could you not sit on my damn hands?"

"Fuck off, Porter, I have no room here."

"You fuck off; I can't even buckle a seat belt, even if I wanted to."

"Good thing you don't want to, then, huh?"

The sedan purred to a parking garage. They were out of the car almost as soon as it had stopped.

Porter stretched. He looked pointedly at the security man. "Next time, could you please ask for something bigger than what they use to transport kindergartners?" The security man didn't even smile. Porter shrugged. "Just a thought, since I do like to be ready for things, and I can't when I can't even fucking breathe."

"This way." The security man said, leading the way to a door and a staircase.

"Hmm," Michael said, looking around a little nervously, "Nothing we can do if we are stuck in here."

"Thanks for that fucking pleasant thought, Mikey." Porter retorted. "Things like that only make this that much more pleasant."

"You could have stayed in the fucking car."

"Fuck that; you don't get to have all the fun."

Normally, Mason would have joined the banter. He didn't mind it and it was fun, but not right now. It didn't bother him, especially since he sensed that the security guard was getting exasperated by it, and because it was still fun to listen to.

They came out of the concrete stairwell to a carpeted hallway. "This way, sirs." The security man said in his neutral voice.

Porter elbowed Michael. "Hey, we've been upgraded to 'sirs'."

Michael shoved Porter back. "They must not know you are coming."

"True, that. Mason likes to keep secrets. Sometimes I think he even keeps secrets from himself."

"How the fuck do you keep secrets from yourself?"

"Well," Porter said in a voice Mason immediately knew was his straight man set-up for a joke, "When he gets dressed, he doesn't turn the lights on. That way, he doesn't have a clue what underwear he has on. See? A secret."

Michael started laughing. "So that's how that works! It explains so much!"

"It does, indeed." Porter said, still straight-faced.

Mason looked over his shoulder. "Better than you, Porter. At least I have the underwear on."

Michael laughed again. Porter shrugged calmly. Whatever he was going to say was cut short when the security man stopped by a door. "In here, sirs."

Mason stood back. "Feel free to open the door, sir." He said coolly. He wasn't walking into something now. The security man stared at him for a second, then set his teeth and opened the door. Mason glanced in and nodded to Michael and Porter.

They walked in and the security man shut the door again.

The room was empty, of course. Important people could afford to keep minions waiting. Porter sprawled his long form into a comfortable chair. Michael, who was obviously keyed up, walked aimlessly around the room, looking at things. He gestured to a statue at one point. Mason came over. There was a small pinhole in the decorative base. Might be a bug, or it might not.

Mason was suddenly gripped with a ridiculous notion. He pulled out a stick of gum, chewed it for a few seconds, and stuck it over

172

the hole. It probably wouldn't do anything to the statue. Probably.

Michael grinned. "I like it! Why the hell do you have gum?"

"Sometimes my patients don't smell so good." Mason shrugged.

Porter laughed. "That is the best solution I have seen in a long time. Obvious, and yet, juvenile. It certainly sends a message."

"It would have worked better with something totally nasty like bubblegum, but I can't stand the flavor."

"Yeah, that would have been better. Oh well, cinnamon is good enough."

Michael resumed his nervous prowling. "When is this guy gonna show, anyway?"

"When he feels like it. He will condescend to it."

Five minutes later, the side door opened and a young professional lady stepped in. "Hello, Doctor Briggs. I am the assistant to the Secretary. He asked me to extend his regrets, but he will be unable to attend."

Mason stared at her for a good two minutes, ignoring her outstretched hand. He turned abruptly. "Let's go, gentlemen." He said shortly.

"Sir! Wait!" The assistant sounded alarmed.

Mason turned back and faced her down. "You can tell the Secretary that I came to talk to him. If he doesn't have the decency to clear his damn schedule for those he employs to clean up his shit, then he can go fuck himself. I don't pander to anyone. Either he gets his ass in here in the next fifteen minutes or we are gone and he can go to Heaven, Hell, or Purgatory to find us again."

"Sir, I can't just dictate to the Secretary!"

Mason let the silence stretch again. Then he said very quietly, "I can, and I will. Go tell him." He turned back towards the door. He could tell by her nervous footsteps that the young woman was vacillating on what to do. Then he heard her go to the side door, open it, and pass through to wherever the hell she came from.

Michael smiled when the door was closed again. "That'll do it, I bet you on it."

173

Porter put his hands behind his back. "No bet. Besides, I told you this was going to be fun."

"You were right. I shouldn't have doubted."

"Better than a fucking play. I only wish we'd brought popcorn or pretzels."

"Or pizza. I am fucking starving."

Mason suddenly realized that none of them had eaten for hours, since before lunch time. "Oh, fuck, I am sorry. I forgot about food."

Porter shrugged. "We'll survive. This is more important right now."

"Thanks, Porter."

Porter smiled. "We are here to support you, Mason. We can do that for you; you have done it often enough for all of us."

"Thanks. Really." Mason looked at his watch. "Mr. Secretary has only seven minutes before we walk out. He might be cutting this rather fine."

"His choice." Michael said dismissively. "If he doesn't show, we get to eat sooner."

"There is that." Porter mused.

They waited. The minutes dragged by. When there were two minutes left, the door opened again. The assistant came back in. "Sirs, please, he will be here in five minutes, I promise. He has been held up in the Capitol."

Mason looked at Porter. He shrugged slightly. Mason looked back. "Five minutes. Otherwise we leave. I don't mean to put you in such a position, Miss. I would not want this to fall on you. Five minutes."

"Thank you, sir." She sounded very relieved.

Mason looked at his watch. Three minutes ticked away. The door opened and the Secretary swept in, looking flustered. "Now, then, what is this? You can't make demands on me like this! Do you have any idea how much I had to drop for you?"

Mason jerked his head at the assistant and she scurried out. Mason fixed his eyes on the politician. "Oh, I know exactly how much

174

you had to fucking drop. Now let me tell you how this is going to work from now on. You hire me. Well, your department has been dropping the fucking ball far too often. First you miss a key player on one of our missions, now you fucking forget to tell us who is really behind Phalanx. Here's the deal, Mister Secretary: we're done with you. Either up your fucking game or you can start cleaning up your own shit, publically, and with political consequences. I don't do games. You guys have held out on us one time too many. I almost lost members on American soil in a retaliatory attack that you could have helped us prevent."

"But we don't know who is behind Phalanx!"

"No, but you fucking know someone is! This is the shit I am talking about!"

"Okay, we did hold that back, but we don't have any information about it."

"I don't fucking care!" Mason slammed his fist into the desk. He leaned forward menacingly. "You know someone might be behind them. That should have been given to me. You fucking think I am some pawn in your little political game. Wrong, bitch! I don't answer to anybody, and I don't fucking play politics. You can't afford me, not anymore. I won't take anything from you until you get your priorities fucking sorted."

The Secretary recoiled slightly. "You did know you have blood on you, right?"

"Nice try to change the subject; yes, I do know it. It is my team's blood. They are only alive because the bomb didn't detonate right away. I am perfectly willing to put it all over you, though. You can go try and explain that to your reporters. Remember, we don't exist, so far as anyone knows. I hold the trump cards, Mister Secretary. I can bring your whole damn regime down, from the inside, no less, and you can't really stop me." The secretary's face blanched slightly. Mason straightened up. "Your decision, of course."

"I need time to get it worked out."

"Of course. And I won't be taking any jobs from you again until you do. I want tangible changes. And until then, I will be involved with tying up Phalanx. If you can't give me better than 'we don't know', then

175

I will find out."

The Secretary was getting angry. Good; Mason wanted him angry. He might make more mistakes that way. "You can't just barge in here with your hired goons and expect me to cower for you."

"Hired goons?" Michael said from behind him. Bad move, Mason thought. Oh well, he was gonna pay consequences now, that was damn sure. Michael put his fist through the wall, literally. "Nobody calls me a hired goon, Mason. This goes down now. I'm done talking with little fuck-offs who don't have a fucking idea what they are talking about."

Porter stood instantly and grabbed Michael. "Now, now, Michael, I am sure the Secretary was just subject to one of those unfortunate slips of the tongue that plague people. Right, sir?" Porter looked coolly at the frightened Secretary. "I am sure you didn't mean to fucking imply that we only do things for money."

"You can't threaten me! This is my office!"

Porter drew himself to his full, considerable height. He glared down, looking for the entire world like an avenging angel or something worse. "I can do whatever I fucking want. You seem to think we should be intimidated by you. We aren't. We just watched two friends thrown to the ground by a bomb. I just had to carry a young woman from a blast zone. Before that, I had to watch the woman I love more than my life itself shoot herself for your fucking political gain. So fuck you. This might be your office, but I will turn it into a garbage heap. Michael here can do whatever the fuck he wants to you. I will take your status symbols instead."

There were running footsteps outside in the hallway. Mason looked at the Secretary calmly. "You can call off your men, Mister Secretary. If you don't, this is going to look very ugly on you."

The Secretary hesitated. He pulled himself together and when the security men opened the door, he gestured slightly. "It is all right. These gentlemen are finished with their meeting and will be returning to their transportation now."

Mason inclined his head very slightly. "Think about what I said, Sir. I have some things to attend to, and then you can decide what you

176

are going to do."

He smiled at Michael and Porter. "I think we have taken enough time here. We really should get back."

Michael was still glaring at the Secretary. He snorted and turned without acknowledging him further. Porter smiled a caustic smile. "Thank you for your hospitality, Sir. We truly couldn't have found you more accommodating if we had wanted to."

Mason left after Porter had stalked out. He turned in the doorway. "Goodbye, Mister Secretary. Do try to stay in touch, under the conditions we laid out."

They shut the door firmly. Mason looked at the security man who was their detail. "We are hungry. Stop by a drive thru so we can get some food."

The security man shrugged. "All right, sir."

"Thank you."

They stopped at an In-n-Out burger on the way back. Mason ordered what seemed like ridiculously large amounts, but then, he had Michael and Porter with him. The security detail had to hold it all since the back seat was crammed so tight with Michael and Porter together.

Back at the airstrip, they got out and took the bags of food from the security man.

"Let's get out of here. I am tired of the smell of bullshit, and this place positively reeks of it." Porter said, climbing up into the jet. Michael was right behind him and Mason lost no time himself. He offered some food to the pilot, who politely declined.

"All right, you two. Let's eat. We have enough time to get that done before we get back."

"Amen!" Porter said, buckling his seat belt and reaching for the bags. Michael had already opened one and shoved something in his mouth. He nodded. Mason realized he was famished.

"Don't let me forget to eat for that long again."

Porter shook his head. Nobody said any more for at least fifteen minutes as they demolished the huge stack of food.

"Ah. I feel better now. I might regret it later though." Mason sighed.

Porter shrugged. "Who cares? I always overeat when I have forgotten. I think it is a human thing to do."

"Maybe so but I will still regret it."

Michael shoved his empty wrappers away. "What's the plan when we land, Mason?"

"It will depend on if Sienna and Karen are still at the hospice or if they went to my house. Either way, I will stay with Juan and Gabriella. They are the most vulnerable. You and Porter will be able to handle anything directed at you if you stay together."

Michael nodded. "Sounds good."

"And tomorrow, I want you two to come with me to the interview I am going to conduct on Phalanx. You can be behind the one-way mirror. I want someone there I trust who can help me."

Porter and Michael both nodded. "We'll be there." Porter said.

"Thank you. You guys have been amazing through this whole shitty mess."

Porter smiled slightly. "Mason, you have pulled my ass out of shit far worse than watching you chew a politician down to size. You don't need to thank me. I will never be able to pay you back for standing by me all this time."

Mason smiled back. "Porter, I have told you before, I don't keep tabs. You shouldn't, either."

"I know, but I still do. Maybe it is the gambler in me; I have to know how much I have compared to everyone else."

Michael laughed. "That's it. If it makes you feel better, Porter, I do the same."

"It does make me feel better, Mikey."

Mason sighed. "Let's land this fucking jet and get back to our friends and loved ones. Tomorrow, we get answers."

"Well said, Mason."

Chapter 19

Mason knew that the interview was going to be difficult. He'd already blown off the steam he'd been collecting and he was calmer now. Porter and Michael were going to have to come and watch his interviewing though. He needed that other set of eyes on these hackers.

As he got ready, he deliberately mussed his hair a little, not enough to be obvious, but enough to look inexperienced. He also took his dress shirt and squeezed it to give it some wrinkles. Nothing objectionable, but there. And his tie was just this side of shabby.

Porter raised an eyebrow at his appearance as he came out for coffee. "Where on earth did you find a tie like that?"

"Thrift store, of course. I have to give them the psychological edge that they think they have. They won't be as on guard if they think they are superior."

"I get it, Mason. I'm not an idiot. I meant that the tie is fucking perfect."

Michael shook his head. "Whatever. You guys are too damn sneaky sometimes."

"Sometimes." Mason agreed as he poured a cup of coffee. "Now, I am going into this pretending to be a low-level interviewer. I have to depend on you two to watch them for me."

"You're doing them all together?" Michael sounded surprised.

"For the first part, yes. If I can get something that way, they will all know about it and I can use that. If I don't, oh well."

Porter nodded. "Let's get this bitching day started. I want to do something. I hate waiting."

Mason sighed. "No shit, Porter. Chill. I want to get some caffeine in me before this."

"Because you are a fucking addict."

"Because I have to fucking work with you!"

Michael snickered. "He's got you, Porter."

"Fuck off."

Mason drank the rest of his coffee. "All right, let's go." He said, purposefully checking his reflection.

They were quickly whisked through security and Mason was given a low-level entry badge. It helped him look incompetent, or at least inexperienced. They followed the uniformed guard through the halls to a room that was obviously on the viewing side of a one-way mirror.

"This is the interrogation room we'll be starting in." Mason gestured. He had procured Styrofoam cup of the ready-made coffee that the bureau had for its normal employees. Porter, always keyed up, nodded tersely. Michael grunted and sat down. Mason looked at Porter pointedly. "Keep it under control, gentlemen."

"Yeah, whatever, go do your job."

"Of course. Just a reminder." Mason squared himself and went in.

He arranged his files and cup while the hacker elites were brought it. Once they were all sitting across the steel table from Mason, he looked up. He was careful to slouch his shoulders and squint slightly. All of that would lull them towards where he wanted them. "Gentlemen, lady." He nodded to them. Antonio, the one Juan thought was the real powerhouse, nodded, smoking a cigarette. None of the others returned his greeting, although Jayne looked about ready to kill somebody.

"I see here that you all have been brought in on charges related to internet crimes."

Antonio, still smoking, looked quite amused by something. He sent a cloud of smoke wafting towards the ceiling. Judah glowered at his hands, his lips pressed into a white line. Fredrico looked downcast, and Jayne still glowered.

"Well, let's start at the beginning then. Do any of you know why you've been brought here?"

Antonio took his cigarette out of his mouth. "Because we trusted somebody. But he must have been an agent. Good thing he's dead." He said, his voice very soft.

Jayne turned on him immediately. "Shut up! Anything we say is going to be used against us!"

"I don't care."

"What?!" Jayne screamed at him, going from normal voice to full volume with no buildup. Mason winced.

"I said I don't fucking care, bitch, and quit screaming at me. Maybe you think we need to preserve your precious unity shit, but I don't. I never bought that fucking line. All it's done is landed us here while Stephen is out playing Romeo, just like his fucking handle."

"Shut up!" She screamed again, half standing.

Antonio blew smoke right into her face. While she coughed and sat back, he leaned over the table towards Mason. "I'll deal. I want out of this shit. I'm done with this group. They're spineless anyway."

Mason looked at his file quickly. "Okay, so who is this Stephen guy?"

Antonio looked amused again. He took a fresh cigarette out. "He's the leader of Phalanx, of course. Except he's not. Not really."

"Oh?" This was the sort of thing Mason wanted to pursue. "Then who is?"

"Don't know. That's the thing. Normally, this bitch thinks she runs it, but she doesn't, either. She and Stephen have all sorts of fun together, but neither of them is really in charge of us."

Judah nodded very slightly. Mason glanced at him. "You agree with that?"

Judah looked at his hands and mumbled, "They have sex a lot, and they both go out for encounters elsewhere, and we run it together without them."

"So you three lead Phalanx?"

Fredrico shook his head. "No, not really. We still get orders from Stephen, and he sends Jayne to make sure we do it, but I think he gets orders from someone else. A lot of his shit now is high-level and involves lots of money."

"It involves paying you lots of money?"

"I fucking wish. I mean it brings in money, but I don't know where it goes. Do you guys?"

Antonio shook his head. "I tried to trace it, but I hit a fucking dead end twice. Pisses me off. I want to nail him just for that."

Mason suddenly understood why Juan considered Antonio more dangerous than the vocal Jayne. He could hold a grudge. "A dead end? Do you think he laundered it and put in Swiss accounts?"

"He might have. I couldn't trace where he got it, either. I only got that it was from somewhere in France. Ironically, he goes there a lot now, doesn't he, Jayne?"

She refused to look at any of them.

Antonio smiled maliciously. "Of course you remember, Jayne. You meet him there, don't you?"

"Why does he go to France?" Mason interjected quickly.

Antonio laughed softly. "For the girls, of course! He never was particular about his girls. Neither were you, were you, Jayne?" His eyes glittered at her. She didn't look at him still. Antonio continued as if she had agreed. "He likes them all. They both do. Once they get started, they don't get enough. But that is beside the point slightly. I think the fucking backer he has must be there."

"Where, in Paris?"

"It might be. The last place I traced him to was in Paris somewhere, but he covered himself pretty well. He always was one of the best."

Jayne suddenly lunged to her feet and slapped Antonio as hard as she could across the face. Antonio was on his feet like a cat, and he threw her to the floor with little effort. "Try it again, bitch. I can end it right here, right now, if you want."

Jayne seemed about ready to take him up on the taunt, but several guards burst in and took her out at Mason's gesture.

Once they had settled back, Mason looked at Antonio. "Will you need something for your face?"

"No, that bitch always had a worse bark than her bite. She hated me anyway."

"Really?"

Antonio laughed. "She tried to keep me out of Phalanx." He casually lit another cigarette.

"How do you know?"

"Because Stephen told me, of course. I think he didn't trust her.

However, Stephen is not the most courageous person I know."

Fredrico nodded vigorously. "No way. He wouldn't stand up to anyone face-to-face."

"Hm." Mason was thinking quickly now. Obviously these three were perfectly willing to talk, especially if it meant screwing Jayne in the long run. "Would you excuse me for a minute? I have something I wanted to ask my superiors."

They didn't seem to hear him, so Mason stood up and left. Once he was back in the room with Porter and Michael, he nodded towards the room. "What do you think?"

Porter was staring into the glass. "They seem pretty genuine. Do you think this Stephen is in Paris?"

"It seems a good place to start. We probably won't be able to find him exactly, as Antonio is pretty good and he couldn't do it. But then again, he didn't have all the computers we do. If we can figure out a more precise area, we should be able to find Stephen."

Michael smiled. "You probably won't get the location out of Jayne, though. I wouldn't even try."

"I wasn't going to, Mikey. I don't give a flying fuck about her. Antonio interests me, though. Why is he doing this, and why now?"

"Go find out."

"What a stupendous idea! I will!"

Michael sighed and poked Porter. "This is your influence, right there."

Porter poked him back. "It's yours, not mine."

"Whatever."

Mason smiled to himself as he went back to the room.

The three were discussing something when he reentered the room quietly.

"I only wish that crazy bitch hadn't shot them both. She was smoking hot." Fredrico said wistfully.

Antonio nodded and blew out a cloud of smoke.

Mason sat down again. "Who is that?"

Judah smiled slightly. "That girl Michael brought with him. Whatever her name was."

"Oh. Well, speaking of that Michael Douglas guy, did you hear that his car exploded the other day?" Mason said, looking distractedly for something through the files and other stuff.

"What? No, I didn't hear anything like that." Fredrico said. "What happened?"

Mason was still looking and sounded plausibly distracted when he answered. "Um, it seems like the airport went to impound his car and it blew up. Killed the guys hooking it up." He sat up triumphantly, having found a little scrap of paper that had found its way into one of the file folders.

Antonio looked very interested. "Really. Hm. I wonder."

"You wonder what? It seems like someone put a bomb on his car to take him out."

Antonio nodded slowly, smoking. "I wonder who would have done that."

Mason shrugged. "Maybe it was a message. Or the wrong car. It was parked close to a diplomat's car."

Judah shook his head. "No, it was for him. I bet you anything on it. Remember how Jayne said something about how he would never get a chance to regret it if he left Phalanx?"

"Oh, yeah." Fredrico agreed. "That was the night before the crazy bitch hit and took him and his girl out."

Mason frowned. "You guys think Jayne ordered a hit on this Michael? That makes no sense. He was going to do something for you, wasn't he?"

Antonio smiled. "Well, we were going to pay him. Those aren't necessarily the same, now are they?"

"No, but a hit is different."

"True." Antonio looked absently at the mirror, thinking. "A hit, huh. That doesn't seem like Jayne's style. If the hooker hadn't shot herself, I would have put that on Jayne, but she wasn't in that. Jayne's done shit like that before."

"She could still have done that." Judah suggested. "The hooker could've ended up falling for that Michael guy. He was fucking good with the ladies."

184

Antonio nodded. "True, that's true."

Mason wanted to get them past Sienna. He already knew about her side. "Well, that makes sense. But then that means Stephen put out the hit."

Antonio shook his head very slowly. "Maybe, but I don't think so, somehow. I mean, he might have ordered a hit, but I don't think it originated with him. He's pretty spineless."

"That's the kind of person who would hire a hit, you know." Mason pointed out.

"I know, but I still doubt it. Stephen is not that interested in the people who work for Phalanx anymore."

Judah nodded. "Yeah, he gives us jobs but he doesn't care about who does them, not anymore."

Antonio blew some more smoke towards the ceiling. "He's been giving jobs that target the US government a lot more, too. That's what Michael was supposed to be doing for us. And then last year he wanted us to target Israel."

"Did you?" Mason asked.

Antonio smiled at him. "Well, I won't get anyone else in trouble. I will just leave it at saying he wanted us to target Israel. Although, now that I think on it, Jayne set that one up. Which was a mistake, because then she started to get really annoying."

Fredrico sighed. "Yeah, the power went to her head big time."

Antonio looked over at Judah and Fredrico. "Did either of you ever fuck her?"

"No way, man, she scared me." Judah shook his head.

"Yeah, me, neither. She sure liked the boys though."

Mason thought he should pursue this a bit, since it might make them reveal more about Phalanx. "The boys, huh?"

"Absolutely. I tailed her once. She went to one of the boy clubs in Amsterdam and picked up a fourteen-year-old. Disgusting."

"That's illegal here; she might get a long time for that."

Antonio smiled again. "I know. That's why I am telling you now."

"Do you have details?"

"Of course. They're all on my computer, which I know you guys already have."

"You seem to be quite good at this." Mason noted.

"I want to take her down if I have to go down. And Stephen. He goes and holes up in France with his little girls and fucks around there while we take his hits. I don't do that. He is going down, too. I am sure you will find some juicy stuff on him in my files, too."

"Good to know."

Judah smiled at Antonio. "Bet that hooker of Jayne's could've pulled him out of France. Or Michael's girl. We should have sent him pictures to try and get him to come back."

Antonio shrugged. "I think Stephen is finished. He hasn't really been in control since the hacktivist attack on PETA that one time. Somebody is pulling his strings. I bet they give him enough to keep him happy and satisfied in France so he issues commands and gets his blowjobs at the same time."

Fredrico nodded. "You're right, Antonio." He glanced at Mason. "I'll only speak for myself, but I will talk to you guys in return for some leniency."

Antonio also nodded and Judah seemed interested.

Mason pretended to think about it. "Well, guys, I can't make the deal myself, you know, but I think that, if you are able to provide useful information and are some way accountable to keep from these hacker activities again, we might be able to deal. I will be sure to pass it on to my superiors."

Antonio smiled. "Let's all hope they listen to you."

Mason shrugged. "They always have in the past. I don't think you should say anymore right now, though. I will get someone in here to talk to you in a little bit." He stood up and took his files off the table. "Just whatever you do, don't sign anything without a lawyer here."

They all nodded and Mason left.

"You cut them a lot of slack, Mason." Porter said.

Mason shrugged. "I don't care. They are going to bring down Phalanx from the top down. They deserve some. Besides, Juan is right; we absolutely need to neutralize Antonio somehow. This might be the

186

way to do it."

Michael stood up. "Well, I think we're done here."

"Yes, I think so. Let's get going. I want to submit my report and recommendations. Then I think we are going to have to get ourselves to France. Porter and Michael, if you don't want to come, I understand. I don't want you to be worried about the people here if you go."

Michael nodded. "I think I will stay. I can keep everyone safe if I am here."

Porter put his hand on Michael's shoulder. "Thanks, Mikey. I would really like you to watch out for Sienna and Juan for me. They might be worried and you will help with that."

"Of course, Porter. I will keep them safe. You go nail this bastard and whoever put him up to this."

"You know you can bet on that." Porter looked at Mason. "When are we leaving?"

"It'll be a few days at least. I have to get identities and shit like that."

Porter nodded. "Good. I think we might need Callie, too. We might need a female presence somewhere, and Sienna is too vulnerable right now."

Mason thought about that. "Yes, I think that might be a good idea, Porter. Let's ask her."

"I have to get some things ready at the store, but Sienna can handle most of the usual stuff. Just give me the dates and we will be ready."

"Thank you, Porter. And thanks, Michael."

Michael grinned. "Bring back some good wine!"

Mason laughed. "You can bet on that, too!

Chapter 20

Mason had set up covers for himself and Porter. He was going to be running a bookstore for another embedded agent, ostentatiously because the owner was going on vacation. Callie would be his daughter. Porter would be delivering meat for a grocer, and Callie's boyfriend. They would share the flat that Mason already had in Paris. He went there at least once a year anyway.

There was one small detail that Mason needed some help with, though. He sighed and called Sienna. "Hey, it's Mason. Can you help me out with something?"

"Of course, Mason! Just tell me what you need."

"I need grey hair."

"You know, you may be the only person who would ever seek that out."

"Yeah, yeah, I know; can you do it? I don't want this outside of the group, not even Emma."

Sienna paused for a moment. "Yes, I think I can, Mason. Should we do something for Porter at the same time?"

"Yeah, that'd be a good time. Don't tell him though. I think it will be more fun if it is a surprise."

Sienna laughed. "You are evil sometimes!"

"I know. When can you do it?"

"Tonight good? Maybe around six?"

"Absolutely. Thank you in advance."

"You might want to hold off on that until you see the job."

"Nah, I doubt that."

True to her word, Sienna was outside Mason's door at six sharp. "Porter will be over a little later; he's trying to get everything wrapped up before he leaves." She wrinkled her nose. "He always worries that he is giving me too much to do, when he fucking pays me to do the exact work he won't let me do."

Mason smiled. "He doesn't want to burden you."

"I'm his employee, Mason. He can't let it go though. Anyway. That is really between me and him. Let's get to your hair."

It might have taken longer than Emma would have been, and Sienna wasn't as sure with the scissors, but Mason wasn't worried about either time or exactitude. The security that no one would know what he looked like was worth it to him.

Sienna sighed. "I'm sorry this is taking so long, Mason. I know I'm not as fast."

"Who fucking cares? I get to have the most beautiful woman I have ever known running her hands through my hair. Take all the time you want!"

"You are outrageous!" Sienna laughed. "I'm almost done. Then we'll have to let it set for a long time, at least thirty minutes. Your hair just doesn't take dye as well as some."

Mason shrugged. "Whatever. I am willing to wait. Although the foil does make me look a bit demented."

"That, my dear, is not the foil."

"Oh, that was just mean."

"Possibly, but it was funny."

There was a soft knock at the door. Sienna quickly went and looked through the peephole. "It's Porter." She said and opened the door.

Porter came in and smiled when he saw Mason. "Oh, I didn't realize we were having a makeover night."

Mason smiled back. "And it's your turn now!"

"Damn. I was afraid of that."

Sienna pointed imperiously to a chair by the bar. "Shut up and sit down."

"Yes, Ma'am!" Porter sat across from Mason. "Am I allowed to ask what the hell you are going to do to me?"

"Anyone else could. You may most certainly not."

Porter sighed dramatically. "I don't deserve this!"

Mason grinned. "You do, you know it, and you like it."

"That was unkind, Mason, even if it was all true."

"Boo fucking hoo. Want a beer?"

"Damn straight. Got anything good?"

"I have some Dead Guy Ale." Mason offered.

"That'll work." Sienna was putting some few foils into Porter's hair. Mason noted that she was doing a lot less than she had in his own. Oh well, Porter was supposed to be young enough to be packing shit around Paris. If he looked too old it wouldn't be believable.

After a long time, Sienna looked at Mason's hair in one of the foils. "A little longer, Mason. It's not quite there."

Mason sighed. Porter laughed.

When Sienna washed all the dye out, Mason was amazed at how different he looked. "Damn. That is quite a difference. You did a great job, Sienna!"

"She always does." Porter noted. "You look way different, Mason. Lighter hair makes your skin darker. Do you have some glasses or something?"

Mason smirked and pulled a pair of wire-rimmed glasses out of his pocket. He slipped them on and stooped his shoulders forward.

"Perfect." Porter nodded. "They won't know you."

"That's the idea. I don't want anyone to recognize me from a picture or description."

"They won't."

"Good. Now, I told you where you're working. I'm in the little bookstore just up the road from the flat. It'll be a good place to be stationed, especially since the latest information the government has given me from the computers they have is that Stephen likes to frequent some of the boutiques that are in that area. Of course, he seems to frequent boutiques all over the fucking city, but there too."

Sienna nodded. "Callie is coming by in just a few minutes. I will get her hair darker, much darker. She can help in your bookstore if you think that would work, Mason."

"That will work, but I want her there only rarely. She's really going to be bait for Stephen, but not as a prostitute. He doesn't seem to really care for age or profession. He thinks of himself as a ladies' man and he likes to conquer as many as he can, paid for or otherwise."

Callie came in about ten minutes later as Sienna was washing Porter's hair out. She had given him some bleached-out streaks. Porter could change how he appeared more expertly than anyone else, so it made sense to do little to him anyway. Callie looked at the two of them appreciably.

"Very nice, Sienna. You did a great job."

"I'm not finished yet, Callie. You're next."

"I was afraid of that."

After about half an hour more, they were all finished being altered. Callie had very dark red hair. It was obviously dyed, but it didn't seem to matter as much on women.

"All right. We leave tomorrow morning. Once we're there, I start immediately. Porter, you aren't supposed to be in until the next day, so you can feel out the city. Callie, I am afraid this is going to be a bit boring for you initially, but that is the way this is going to go this time."

She smiled. "Whatever you say, Mason."

"My name is Alfred now. Porter is Giles. He has that rakish, Cockney feel to him, doesn't he?"

"Rakish, certainly."

Porter struck a heroic pose. Mason rolled his eyes.

"And you, my dear, are going to be Mercedes. And you are my daughter and Porter's girlfriend, so there is the connection. That may mean you have to kiss or hug him at some point. Also, you're really there to be bait for Stephen; basically, we need you to be subtly sexy and beyond his reach. Nothing drives men crazy more than the unapproachable. We feel like we need to conquer."

She nodded. "I understand, Mason. Let's go and get this guy."

Mason smiled. "We leave tomorrow. Don't go out tonight, please. I don't want people seeing you before you are in character. This should be a good way to ease you and James into this type of stuff, too. If you find that it is not in your comfort zone, then we can always pull back next time."

Callie smiled. "Okay." She glanced up at Porter. "You are going to be the hardest part to adjust to, sir."

He shook his head. "Not 'sir', Mercedes; Giles." He'd already slipped into a slight accent.

She laughed. "That will make it easier, Giles!"

"Good."

Sienna was looking seriously at Callie. "You know, if you are uncomfortable you may have trouble acting like you are in relationship with him. Would you like some lessons on kissing?"

Callie blushed slightly. "Um, I don't know."

"Well, to start with, it can help to make your mindset be that this is the person you are being, not the character you are assuming. You might need to think only like who you want to portray. So if Giles here walked by and you are in public, how would a somewhat reserved lady react to her lover?"

"I think I understand, Sienna. I am a little worried about kissing him, though. He is James' boss."

"Partner." Porter corrected absently.

"You know he doesn't believe that."

Porter shrugged. "I can't help his hang ups. I have my own; I am not borrowing his. But the point isn't that, the point is that you are going to have to suspend everything you know about me and react only to Giles. I can act like him all the time, if that will help."

Callie laughed. "I think it will be fine, once we are there and no longer sitting in Mason's kitchen with Sienna here."

"That is acceptable." Porter looked over at Mason. "Is there anything else we need to go over?"

Mason thought about it. "I don't think so. Here is the guy we want." He passed a picture to Porter and Callie. "My bookstore job is right beside one of the elite bordellos, ironically. He is sure to get around to it soon. All the high-class ladies are there, and he is willing to go for anything wearing a skirt, it sounds like."

"Really?" Porter raised his eyebrow. "Maybe I should get one."

"God, no!"

"It was just a thought, Mason."

Mason faked a horrified shudder. "If you're looking for something like that, it sounds like that Jayne will go for anything, period. Although her stuff seems a lot younger than we are. Which is just disgusting."

"Amen, brother." Porter drank the last of his ale and set the bottle down. "Want to play some cards? Since we're stuck here anyway."

"Sure. Sienna, you in?"

"Of course. This is the last night for a while that I get to beat Porter at poker."

"My dear," Porter said, shuffling quickly, "You are not going to beat me."

"I will if you don't cheat."

Porter merely smiled. He started dealing. Mason wasn't totally sure if that meant he wasn't going to cheat or if he was. That was probably the whole reason for the smile to begin with. Oh well, it would be fun trying to catch him. Mason almost never could, but the challenge was worth it.

Later, after Sienna had swept them all clean, the ladies retired to Porter's house next door to do woman things. Mason handed Porter another beer and dealt a hand of Gin Rummy. "Just curious but did you cheat tonight?"

"At dealing, you mean?" Porter asked, looking at his cards and shifting them in his hand. "No, I usually don't. It's not fun to cheat friends."

Mason nodded. "I wondered. I can't usually catch you."

Porter smiled slightly. "It is even harder when I am not doing it."

"There is that. We should probably not play too late; we'll have to blast out of here tomorrow early."

"Yeah, well, you are about to get fucking steamrolled, so there won't be lots of incentive to stay up and prolong the torture."

"Whatever." Mason rearranged his hand. "By the way, how's Juan's house working?"

Porter shrugged. "We put Gabriella in the one side bedroom. Karen and Sienna painted it all yellow and cream and put lots of girly fringes around it. It will be a nice place for her to get stronger. The physical therapist is scheduled to come out three times a week, and Juan is still on leave, so he can be there. Also, Michael and Karen are going to be in one of our houses here, so they will be close. Michael can

193

be relied on to protect everyone and their fucking cat." Ninja had wandered in and jumped into Porter's lap. It was obvious that he was not moving anytime soon.

"You say stuff like that but then you don't exactly get rid of him. I think you are faking your cat feelings."

"Shh. They can sense things like that."

Mason looked pointedly at Ninja, who was now curled up and had two paws to the ceiling. "Really? You think?"

Porter smiled and gently scratched Ninja under the chin.

They decided to get to bed after another hour. Porter called Sienna to see if she wanted him home or if he should stay. He hung up with a slight smile. "She told me to stay the fuck over here."

"That's my girl. You know where everything is. See you in the morning." Mason got up and went to his room. He caught a glimpse of himself in the mirror of the bathroom and got a jolt. He had forgotten how different he looked. Perfect.

Chapter 21

The flight had been unspectacular. Porter had spent an hour with Sienna before they left, and Mason wisely didn't ask what happened between the two of them; he knew that it was hard to leave her when there had been such a violent retribution on Juan.

Porter still seemed preoccupied as they got to the flat. Mason looked at him and said, "Out with it."

Porter shook his head. "It's nothing, Albert."

Mason lowered his voice. "Fuck that, Porter. Out with it, now."

"I just feel a sense that something is wrong with this." Mason waited; Porter would elaborate when he was ready. It wasn't long. "After that car bomb, I am worried that they will find her." There was no difficulty guessing who he was talking about.

"There's always that chance."

"I know. This time just feels more immanent."

"So let's get rid of the head of the snake; it's hard for snakes to bite that way."

"Good point."

Callie gently laid her hand on Porter's arm. "You know that no one will let her get hurt. James is in on this. He has arranged some things, too."

Porter smiled down at her. "I am glad. Thank you." He said slmply, kissing her on the cheek. "Now, Albert, aren't you due at this book store? Should we walk you there so you don't go doddering off somewhere else?"

"If that is what you want." Mason shrugged.

The bookstore wasn't far. It would be easy to walk to it from the flat. It had a nice little sidewalk patio space with umbrellas and tables for patrons to sit and read if they wanted. Inside, it was laid out like most bookstores, and dust created sunbeams from the windows. The man behind the desk was an older man who looked up when they entered.

"May I help you?" He asked.

"That depends." Mason said in a soft, weak voice. "I am Albert.

I have come to take the shop over."

"Oh yes, that's right. If you would come to the back, I will give you what you need."

Mason followed slowly. The back office was not large. The other man handed him a sheet with very small writing on it, a finger on his lips in warning. Mason nodded and took the sheet. Most of it dealt with the usual agents who used the shop, and who had bugged it recently.

Out loud, Mason said, "Yes, this seems most complete. Do you have any specific instructions regarding new shipments or anything like that?"

"No, there should be nothing out of the ordinary. I shall enjoy this holiday; I have not had one for a few years now. Thank you for taking over."

"It is no problem. Enjoy!"

The agent handed Mason a key ring, put his hat on, and left the shop. Mason went to the desk. Porter and Callie came over. Mason passed the sheet to Porter, who read it swiftly. He nodded and handed it to Callie. When she had finished, Mason took it back and lit it with a lighter. He set the burning paper on a plate and they watched until it had been reduced to ashes. Porter stirred them with his finger and threw them out the front door.

He was smiling faintly when he came back. Mason looked at him curiously. Porter put the plate down on the desk, leaning over and breathing into Mason's ear, "The bordello is two doors south. I may have even spotted our mark already. Down the street. He left it and is walking away. He'll be back."

Mason nodded. "Good." He whispered as softly back.

Porter took Callie's arm and they left. Mason settled into his job and opened an old book. The rest of the day passed pleasantly if uneventfully. Mason made certain to go out at least once an hour to clear the tables or fuss with umbrellas or make up something to do. He did not see anyone that seemed either to be watching the shop or their mark. He did notice that the bordello seemed to be doing business and that business picked up later in the afternoon. He closed the shop at around five. While he was lowering the umbrellas, very slowly, he noted that there was man across the street that seemed to be watching. Mason continued to lower and put the umbrellas away and when he tottered back out, locking the door, the man was still watching from the café across the street. Mason shuffled back to the flat, pausing once to look at a display in one window. He didn't see the man in the reflection, but he was certain that it was someone with an unhealthy interest in the shop at least.

Porter was making food when he made it to the flat, chatting with Callie. Mason sighed, straightening back up. "That is going to destroy my back." He complained.

Porter didn't even look around. "You enjoy it anyway."

"Of course, but it is still going to hurt." Mason took a bottle of water off the counter and drank it. "There was someone scoping the shop out."

"Official or otherwise?"

"Can't tell yet. It might be nothing anyway, but we never know."

"True. I think it is a good sign; we can capitalize on any interest."

Mason nodded. "I'm hungry; that had better be done soon."

"It will be. Now get the hell out of here until it is."

Chapter 22

Porter went out early for his job the next morning. He had
made some coffee and left it for Mason and Callie. They ate some quick
sandwiches for breakfast and drank the coffee. Then they left for the
bookstore. Callie was wearing a lovely swing skirt. Skirts were always
attractive in a society where women mostly wore jeans or pants
anyway. Something about skirts was so much hotter than pants were.

Mason shuffled his way along, his shoulders bent. Once they
got there, Mason went it and Callie took care of getting the tables
ready. She would be going to see Porter later, at his lunch break.

The morning was uneventful. Only two people came in to
browse. Mason had some interesting books to leaf through, but he
made certain that he didn't get too absorbed to be alert to people
outside. Callie left around 10:00 in the morning. Mason figured she
would get back when she was ready. If she didn't make it again today,
that was fine.

The most interesting thing happened sometime after lunch
time. A young lady came bursting into the shop, looking wildly around.

"Excuse me? May I help you?" Mason asked mildly, looking up
from his book and blinking through his glasses at her.

"You've got to hide me! The police, they are after me! Please,
sir!"

Mason shrugged. "All right, all right, calm yourself. You may be
in the back room until the danger is past." He led her to the door to the
store room. She went in and he shut it again. As he went back to his
desk, he was thinking this over; she seemed genuine, but then, why
would she go into the very store where she would be noticed? It would
make far more sense to go into the bordello a few doors down. People
were always going in and out of there. There was almost no one in
here, ever.

Mason smiled slightly. Something was definitely rotten in
Denmark. It might not be a big deal, but then again, it might. He would
get to the bottom of this soon enough.

No one followed the woman into the shop. No one even looked

interested outside, with the one exception of the same loiterer across the street. How convenient. This stunk, for sure.

After an hour, Mason opened the store room. "No one has followed you, child; you are free to go." He said, stepping back and holding the door open.

The young woman came out, blinking in the light. She was attractive enough, Mason supposed. He wasn't terribly interested in things like that, though. She smiled up at him. "Oh, thank you so much, sir!" She said, moving closer than necessary to him. Mason thought she was trying to distract him from something. "I would never have dodged them without your help. May I repay you somehow?" She didn't give any doubts to what she meant because she ran her fingers gently up his sleeve.

Mason stepped back, saying coldly, "You misunderstand, mademoiselle. I am a widower with a daughter your age. What you suggest is beyond inappropriate. Please leave. Now."

She stared at him, her cheeks reddening slightly and then she flounced out. Mason chuckled softly. Now he would see what she was really up to. He sat back behind the counter with an affected sigh. As he pretended to read his book again, he saw the young woman cross the street, looking around carefully. She seemed to note that he had not followed her, but she had no way of knowing that his eyesight was quite good and he could see her easily. She paused for a moment beside the man across the street. Then she moved off. Mason was certain she'd passed some information of some kind to him.   There wasn't much she could say, really, so Mason was not worried. Maybe the loiterer would go find something else to do now.

At closing time, he began to totter around and getting ready to go. Porter appeared, without Callie, and helped him shut the place up. Then they moved slowly back towards the apartment.

"I have someone watching the shop." Mason said softly as they walked.

"Hm. I wonder who." Porter mused.

"No clue, but I did have a plant run on in and try to seduce me."

"That has got to be the most thankless job ever."

"Shut up. I knew what she was doing. Maybe they'll find something more entertaining to do somewhere else."

"I just meant that you are as easy to get a rise out of as the average stone."

"Fuck off. You know Sienna can do it in two seconds flat. So can most women. I try to hide it is all."

"Yeah, well, she gets that out of everyone."

"Does it make you jealous?" Mason asked.

"Not really, because I know she doesn't mean it for anyone else. Before, though, when I wasn't sure she was interested in me, I used to get ragingly jealous. Then I would go on a bad bender for at least a day. Get shit-faced drunk, pick fights, that sort of thing."

"Well, I am glad you are beyond that."

Porter smiled slightly. "So am I. I was a real jerk. God knows why she even wanted to see beyond that, but I am so glad she did."

"There is a lot in you that you don't see. We see it, and that's why we even bothered putting up with you. Plus, you are the best scam artist ever."

"Well, that is nice of you to say. How do you know I am not scamming you now, by acting straight?"

Mason shrugged. "I don't know it, but I believe it. Besides, I see you changing."

"Oh, good. We're almost home. Who wants to make dinner?"

"You do."

Porter laughed. "All right! Now that we decided that, let's go eat!"

The next day started the same way with almost no one stopping into the shop and Mason watched the street outside. However, around lunch time this time, he saw Stephen walk by, headed, evidently, to the bordello. Quickly, Mason texted Callie: "Get here. Now."

She was there within ten minutes. "What is it, Papa?"

Mason gestured her over and whispered softly, "Get a book and go out. Stephen went by. I want you out and visible when he comes back. You know what to do from there. Try to get him to set up a meeting or something here tomorrow. We should be able to get some authorities to jump him then."

"All right." She adjusted her glasses and picked up a book. She stationed herself outside, fully visible to both sides of the street and opened her book. Mason brought her a cup of iced coffee and she set it beside her.

Results were not long coming. Stephen, fresh from whatever the hell he did in there, came out and looked up and down the sidewalk casually. Mason was out adjusting one of the umbrellas, so he saw Stephen catch sight of Callie and make a beeline for her. He smiled to himself and went back inside to give Stephen an open field.

From inside, Mason watched Stephen stand in front of Callie and smile, saying something. She looked up from her book and responded. Stephen stood there, talking for a few minutes, and finally he took Callie's hand. Then he walked off. She picked her book back up and continued reading for a little longer. Once she was finished, she shut the book and came back in with her empty cup.

She rolled her eyes at Mason.

He smiled slightly. "Later. Tell me at home."

"Yes, Papa. I think I will stay here for the afternoon and we can go home together."

"As you wish, Mercedes."

There were, somewhat surprisingly, several clients during the afternoon. Mason was attending to a pair of older women when Porter stopped by.

"Mercedes." He kissed her on the cheek in greeting. "I did not know you would be here."

"I thought I would help Papa this afternoon. Besides, you were busy at the store, Giles."

"And you were bored."

She shrugged and continued to shelve books. The two clients left and Mason began to get the store ready to close. It took much less time when there were three of them doing it. Then they all began to walk home.

"We've picked up a tail." Porter said casually.

Mason nodded. He'd seen the loafer follow them this time.

"Yep. Same guy as before. They should've used someone else."

"Maybe they don't have that many to spare. No, Callie, don't look back. Pretend to look at your face in your compact and you will get just a glimpse of him as we go."

"Oh, him." Callie said as she put her compact away. "He watched the whole time that Stephen tried to pick up on me. Kind of creepy."

"It is indeed. However, I am more interested in if he is official or not. Maybe I will go out later tonight and see if he is still out."

"Another bar?" Mason smiled.

"Why not? It usually works. Besides, I can pretend to drink better than some people really drink. And I have lots of experience acting drunk."

Mason smiled again but said nothing. He wasn't going to insult Porter that easily, even though he knew Porter probably wouldn't mind. It was time for Porter to move beyond the sins he'd given up, and that included Mason reminding him of them.

Once they were inside the apartment, Mason straightened. "Goddamn it, this is hurting. Okay, Callie, give us a run-down on the contact and then we'll decide what to do."

"Is that a good idea, Mason? Won't the guy outside hear us?" Callie asked nervously.

"I doubt it. I had cork put in the walls and door. And if they have planted any bugs, I have Juan's special jamming devices all over this place."

"Ah, very good. All right. When Stephen got past the ogling and all the lame pick-up lines, he suggested that he would come by again tomorrow at around noon."

Porter nodded. "That'll have to work, Mason. We can't keep him on the streets much longer."

"Yeah, let me pass it to Agent Kyle and he will make the arrest. Then, once we are back and look like ourselves again, I will question him. You gonna go and see who that one guy works for? I know you enjoy that sort of thing far too much."

Porter grinned. "If that is all right with you."

"Of course it is. Have a good time. I'll tell Sienna not to worry about you."

"I would appreciate that. See you in a few hours." Porter left quietly.

"Well, Callie, what should we eat?" Mason asked as he opened the cupboards.

"Will Porter really be all right?"

"Of course. He is the best. But you knew that."

"I know. I just don't want him to get hurt. He means a lot to James and to me."

Mason nodded. "I understand, but you will just have to trust him. He knows what he is doing and he is always careful. Even when he used to get drunk fairly regularly, he never let his character slip. Besides, it might be important that he find out who this guy works for, and I can't do it."

"Why not?"

"Because I am already established as an older man who has a daughter and doesn't drink or smoke or anything fun. Porter is a young enough character to do all those things." Mason began to cut some vegetables to prepare a stir fry.

"This is very confusing."

"Yes, but it is fun all the same. It is all just a big con, and the best cons involve making the mark believe what you want them to. Porter has always had the soul of a charlatan, and he is the best. I am not exaggerating in the slightest; I have seen him convince a group of police and thieves simultaneously that he was an army captain and therefore had the authority to lead everyone. Then he got each group alone long enough to tie them all up. And it was only as a distraction, because I only needed them out of the area for ten minutes."

Callie laughed. "I bet he loved that."

"He did. He enjoys playing the part. Will you excuse me for a moment? I need to text Sienna. I did promise I would, and she will tell everyone else."

Chapter 23

Mason was sitting at the table and Callie had gone to bed when Porter slipped in. "We have a problem, Mason." He whispered.

"What?"

"That guy is official. Like, real official, EU level official. They were going to pick up Stephen on their own, but he has got wind of it and gone to ground. I found someone who can help us. We have to go meet him now. Without Callie."

Mason snorted. "Of course he got fucking wind of it! Nothing else has gone fucking right, why should this? Fuck!" Porter nodded. Mason sighed and stood up. "Let's go tell Callie and get this shit over with."

In Callie's room, Porter gently put his hand over her mouth and shook her awake. "Mason and I have to go out. You stay here, and do not, under any circumstance, open that door for anyone. I don't care if it is us or not. It must stay locked."

She nodded. Mason had to give her some credit: the girl was hard to phase.

"We'll try to be back soon. As far as you are concerned, this apartment is empty. No lights, no sound. Got it?"

She nodded again.

Porter and Mason slipped out the front and Mason locked the door and the deadbolt. He heard Callie slide the interior lock into place. If he lost the key to the back door, they were stuck outside.

As they walked quickly up the sidewalk, Mason asked, "How did you find out he was EU?"

"I lifted his credentials. Had to make sure."

"Gotcha. Where are we going and who are we meeting?"

Porter smiled. "We're going to a cabaret and we're meeting a priest."

"That has to be the most ridiculous line ever uttered."

"It is all true, though. Brother Ambrose has heard something from one of Stephen's regular girls."

"Yeah, okay, but how do you know him?"

"He saw me lift the creds off the agent. He waited until the agent was passed out and he admonished me for it. I told him enough to convince him."

Mason shook his head. "You have the most fucking luck of anybody I have ever known."

Porter smiled widely. "Well, no shit, Mason. Can't lie to a priest, you know. Anyway, he said he would help us. Here is the joint."

It was a very shabby, low-end cabaret with dark interior and bored girls. Mason could care less, though. Porter and he slipped into a booth at the back, their backs to a wall and a full view of the rest of the room. A figure in a black robe came in a few minutes later and joined them.

"Father." Mason nodded respectfully. "If my associate had told me you were a Jesuit, I would have been less incredulous about this."

The priest smiled broadly at that. "Yes, we are in charge of everything, aren't we?"

"That's the word on the street, I guess."

Porter smiled. "Well, Brother, I told my boss here what you said. He is the one who needs the information."

"Ah, yes, the information on Romeo?"

"Well, we call him Stephen."

"Oh, is that his name? The young lady didn't know it."

"No, she probably wouldn't." Mason agreed. "We need to get him and get him off the streets. Can you help us?"

"I believe so. You see, Stephen believes that he is being hounded by agents, according to the young woman. She came in to speak with me yesterday, after she thought her room had been searched. I can't give you any information on her. Confidentiality, you understand."

Mason nodded. "I am no official government agent. I don't need witnesses or anything like that."

"Very good. She was quite frightened. She said that Stephen often hides out in the Blue Lotus, he has private rooms there."

Mason nodded. "Thank you, Father. We will do our best to get him out of your fair city and into some sort of detention."

The Jesuit looked shrewdly at Mason. "You are no official government agent, yet you wish to detain him?"

Mason smiled. "There are many forms of detainment, Father, and most of them are not, strictly speaking, legal."

"Ah. I will ask no more, then. God be with you, my sons."

"Somebody needs to be." Porter muttered.

Mason elbowed him. "Shut the fuck up."

Brother Ambrose smiled again and slipped back out.

Mason played absently with his cup. "That's the bordello by the book store, you know." He said softly to Porter. Porter nodded. Mason thought about it some more. "We could try and pick him up there, but that might be noisy. He made an appointment with Callie though. If she was inside the bookshop, he would come in to talk to her. We can pick him up then. Brush off your agent part. You are gonna be the one to arrest him. You have what you need?"

Porter took a sip of the beer in front of him. He wrinkled his nose in disgust. "Goddamn awful. Don't drink it. Yeah, I can pick up what I need pretty fast."

"Papers?"

"I can fake it tonight."

"That's the new plan, then. Once we have him, we need to get him to the flat, and we can 'interrogate' him there."

"This is going to take time to set up. Like all night."

"I know, so let's get started." Mason stood up and left with Porter beside him. He was still thinking his way through what they would have to get done. "Damn this whole mess. I am still fucking pissed."

"Good." Porter said, ducking under a low-hanging branch.

"Good?"

"Yes. You need to be pissed. You are way too rational most of the time. The fact that you can experience emotions makes you more human."

"Fuck off. You know I get emotional."

"I do, but not everyone does. Besides, I would rather have you be pissed than flat."

"Yeah, whatever. Let's get this done. What do you need?"

"Papers. Official stamp on them. Something that looks like some sort of warrant or order. A gun."

"A gun? Like fucking hell."

"Mason, you have to trust me. No real agent is going to be apprehending someone who is a flight risk without a pistol."

"I have one that should work. You better be fucking careful though."

"Guns still scare me, Mason."

"Good. Stay fucking scared. And give it back when you are done with it."

"Yes, sir." Porter paused. "I think I will need to take these highlights out, too. I am going back to the normal black. But I will cut it. Sienna is gonna be pissed, so you have to explain it to her."

"Why is she going to be pissed?"

"Because she likes my hair like this."

"Oh. Well, I guess you don't have to cut it, if you don't want."

"Agents aren't allowed to have hair this long, in general. It goes tonight. I have a suit and tie that should work. The paperwork is the sticking point now."

Mason nodded. They started up the alley that ran behind his flat. Mason quickly unlocked the door and they slipped in. All the lights were off and there was no discernible noise. Mason switched on the kitchen light and found himself staring into a pistol. Callie, very pale but determined, had it trained on them both. "Oh, thank goodness it is you two." She lowered the pistol.

"God damn. You scared me pretty much shitless. I didn't hear anything." Mason said.

"I tried to be quiet."

"You succeeded very well. Holy shit. Okay, let me recover a second." He took a deep breath or two. "New plan. Again. You are going to have to be in the store all tomorrow. Theoretically, Stephen will come in to see you, and Porter will be acting as an agent to apprehend him. We'll bring him here to set up a false interrogation of him, and we'll see what we can get out of him. You'll have to be quiet when you are here until you go back."

"And when is that?"

"Tomorrow evening. If he doesn't come in to see you, we will go after him. You don't need to be part of any of that." Callie nodded. "Now, you go to bed. We might be up a while longer. See you in the morning."

After she had disappeared, Mason nodded to Porter. "Let's get this going."

Porter pulled off his jacket. "Got scissors?"

"Porter, now really, what do you think I am? Of course I do." Mason went to his own room and returned with his smaller suitcase. He put it on the table. "Here's the damn scissors. And some dye, but not a lot." While Porter took them, Mason pushed aside some of the toiletries. Underneath there was a small seal press and some heavy card stock with an aged appearance. There were also several official-looking papers and forms. "Warrant, warrant, I had something in here that would work. Warrant. Oh, here is close enough." He pulled out a form and put it on the table. "Now a license for an agent. What's your name going to be?"

Porter was cutting his hair shorter at the sink. "Dunno. You're going to have to get the back, Mason. I can't see it enough to make it even."

"Fine; stand still."

"Just don't take all fucking night like last time."

"Bitch and moan too much and I might accidently slip and cut off a big chunk." Mason warned as he carefully began to trim Porter's curls.

"You wouldn't fucking dare."

"Keep it up and find out."

It didn't take very long, even with all the complaining, and then Porter carefully covered the bleached streaks over.

Mason went back to the table. "Now, what name are you going by?"

"Hm. How about Arthur Dent?"

"Fucking no!"

"Damn. Okay, then how about Charles Douglas?"

"Better. All right, Charles, you are going to be FBI now because that is the identification I brought. You better start signing stuff so you get a good signature. And stand over by that wall there. Let's get a picture. The lighting is better for it over there. Then you can sign the thing and I can laminate it with the official-looking paper stuff they have now." Mason grinned suddenly. "It has a holographic effect in it; you're going to be covered in rainbows!"

Porter looked disgusted.

It took the better part of two hours to get the credentials all done and drying. Porter was still perfecting his character mentally. He washed the dye out and had returned to dark, nondescript curls.

"Now if we could just make you shrink and uglier, you'd be fucking impossible to identify." Mason grinned.

"Fucking shut up." Porter said absently. "Let's get that room I'm in set up for the interrogation place."

"All right. I have the one hole in the wall already, to the pantry."

"I know. Let's put a one-way mirror over it. You have one of those, I presume?"

"Of course I do. I come prepared."

Porter laughed. "Only very unique people would come prepared to interrogate a person in Paris!"

Mason shrugged. "Whatever. Let's get the bed out of there, too. Just the table and the one chair."

"You have some serum, too? Let's get him a little disoriented before we do anything else. Not enough to be troublesome, but enough to alarm him."

"I like it. Yes, I have the serum. Once we grab him, I'll use it. The big problem is going to be getting him here."

Porter nodded. He stood looking blankly out the window for a few minutes. "Well, how about in a big box? I've been hauling them all over the city anyway. If I have a hat on, no one will know I have changed my hair, and then I can be more inconspicuous going into the book store anyway."

"All right. He is likely to be heavy."

"Mason, I am not a fucking weakling."

"No shit. I meant that the box has to hold up."

"Oh. Yeah, I have been hauling some in wooden crates. I think they were huge cheeses. Anyway, I can slip in and snag a crate. Will that work?"

"Better than a box."

"You're right. Let me go get that right now. It'll take me about an hour. No more. If it takes longer, come looking. I might have been apprehended and I will need to get out."

Mason looked at his watch. "All right. One hour. You have a key?"

Porter pulled out a small metal tool. "Yep."

Mason nodded. "Get going. I don't think it will be hard to pick a lock on a small grocer."

Porter winked. "It really shouldn't. One hour." He slipped out the back door silently.

Mason went and began to redecorate the room in the back. The bed was too awkward for him to move on his own without too much noise, but he did cover the vantage hole with the small one-way mirror and put a heavy blanket over the small window. Porter hadn't exactly left his stuff around, so Mason knew it wouldn't be difficult to get it out. He threw it all on top of the bed. There was a little painting that he took off the wall and that was all he could do on his own. The painting he tucked under his arm and went back to the kitchen.

The falsified documents were done. He put the FBI badge into a leather case for Porter. Mason chose the cover that wasn't new; that would be a mistake. The badge should look used. No new agent would be on assignment like this.

Porter knocked softly and came back in. He had a large slatted crate that he stood in the corner.

"Porter, that thing has holes."

"I know, Mason, but we can't just shove him in a box anyway. He's going to have to be knocked out."

"All right. You do it, though."

"Naturally. Documents?"

"Yeah, they're done. Here." Mason handed Porter his badge.
Porter flipped it experimentally.

"Good, Mason. No one will be able to tell. Especially not here.
I also got the rest of what I needed for the suit. These stores really
don't have good locks."

"Thanks." Mason yawned. "Help me move that fucking bed
and then I need to sleep."

"Yes, we wouldn't want you to miss your beauty rest. Really
don't want you to miss that."

"Fuck off."

Chapter 24

Mason and Callie walked slowly to the bookstore the next morning. Porter would come in later with his worker's smock over his suit. Mason reasoned that no one would notice him and he could whip it off in the back room. The box would come with Porter. Now they just needed the mark to show up.

The morning was slow, which was fine with Mason; the fewer spectators and potential witnesses, the better. By noon, Mason was getting a little nervous. It was possible that he and Porter would have to storm the bordello and that sort of thing was harder to get right.

The agent who had been watching the store wasn't in his usual place. Porter had gotten him very drunk; perhaps he was still sleeping it off. Good. The less the EU knew at first, the better.

Porter came in with his large box, giving the impression that it was full and heavy. He disappeared into the back room after a nod from Mason. Everything was in place now. They just needed Stephen to show up.

Rather surprisingly, he did. It was just after 1:00 when he looked in the door of the bookstore. Mason pretended to be reading and gave no hint that he saw Stephen sneak in. Callie smiled distantly and continued to shelve the book she had in a basket beside her. Stephen stopped beside her and struck up a quiet conversation.

Mason shuffled to the back room and knocked softly on the door once. Porter opened it immediately and came out in his suit, looking every inch the federal agent. Mason nodded and shuffled back to his desk. He sighed for effect as he sat down and picked up his book again. Porter would know exactly how to handle this.

Stephen had taken Callie's hand and helped her to stand. She smiled graciously, still slightly distant. Stephen and she continued to talk.

Porter slipped in from behind Stephen. He put his gun barrel against Stephen's back. "Don't move. You are under arrest by the FBI on internet charges." He whispered. Callie backed away in alarm. Porter expertly frisked Stephen, pulling a small automatic from under his shirt and flicking it to Mason. Callie quickly left the store, acting confused. Porter made sure that she was out, then he hit Stephen a sharp blow to the side of the head. Stephen crumpled. "Quick, Mason, help me get him out of here before anyone notices."

Mason grabbed the unconscious man's feet and Porter took his shoulders. They rather unceremoniously slung him into the back room and shoved him into the slated box.

Mason looked at Porter. "You going to take him now?"

Porter nodded. "I had better. You should come, too. We can't have just one of us. Too dangerous."

"You're right. Just let me call the agent who runs this shop from the flat."

Porter nodded, zipping up his coveralls and hoisting the box to his shoulder. "God damn! What the fuck does he eat?"

"You really don't want to know, Porter."

"You're probably right about that. See you in a few." Porter walked out of the store and turned towards the flat. Although he was strong, Mason knew that the weight had to be extreme, especially to carry in a box. Oh well. Porter could handle it.

Mason tottered around shutting the shop up and left. As he walked, he made sure that he wasn't tailed. Having that EU agent turn up would be terrible. He saw no one he suspected and he slipped into the flat with no problem. Porter was waiting for him.

"He's still out. Call that one agent, then we need to get Callie out of here."

Callie came to the front room. "Are you sure?"

Mason smiled at her. "Yes, I think so. I do not want you hurt. We don't really know what might happen here, so let's get you back to James. You did a splendid job, Callie."

She smiled at him. "I bet James doesn't even recognize me when I get there."

Porter laughed. "Good! Shake his ass up a little!"

Mason called the agent first. "We had to leave. The shop is secure."

"Very good, sir. I hope it worked out for the best?"

213

"Good enough. You had an agent watching. EU."

"Hm. I wonder why he was there. Oh well."

"He got a little drunk last night. Perhaps he will be reprimanded for it and removed."

The agent laughed. "I wondered! Well, good luck to you, whoever you are."

"The same to you." Mason hung up. "All right. Callie, get your stuff together. James is going to be meeting you in a few hours." He was already calling.

Once Callie was off, Porter came back from the room. "He's still out. I think he will wake up soon, though."

Mason nodded. "I think you should do the initial interrogation. Did you take him out of the box yet?"

"Yes. I threw it in the alley."

"Excellent. Now we just need to wait for him. Who wants first watch?"

"If you take it, I will make some food."

"Deal."

It was perhaps fifteen minutes later that Stephen began to stir. Porter brought Mason a sandwich in the pantry space. "How's it going?" He asked softly.

Mason jerked his head towards the mirror. "It's about to get interesting. How you want to do this?"

"I'll start, and if you hear anything, you can fill me in or back me up."

"Will do. I'll watch from here and we can tag-team him later. Although, to be fair, I think he is going to crack quickly. Antonio mentioned to Juan that he had no balls. Antonio might be wrong, but whatever. Start simple."

"I know what I am fucking doing, Mason."

"I know. Chill a little, man. No need to bite my fucking head off."

"You're being fucking obvious again. You deserve it." Porter left and Mason stayed where he was, still eating.

Stephen had sat up, rubbing his head and looking around.

Mason knew he was a smart guy, and he would quickly come to the totally erroneous conclusion that Mason wanted him to come to. Slowly, Stephen stood up and examined the room. It took almost fifteen seconds. He tried the door, which was locked. He moved over to look in the mirror. Porter opened the door and stepped in.

"Ah, Stephen, please, have a seat." Porter took the hacker by the shoulder and forcefully directed him into the chair facing the mirror. He occupied the other. Mason snorted to himself. Porter was too damn tall and was blocking his view. He went and tapped softly on the door.

"Excuse me." Porter said from inside and cracked the door. "What?" He breathed.

"You're blocking the fucking view."

Porter sighed and rolled his eyes. Mason shut the door and went back to the observation post. Porter had moved his chair over by the table. Mason smiled to himself. Way to take it to the illogical extreme, Porter.

Porter sat and let the silence grow in the room. Stephen began to fidget. Porter sat calmly. Finally, it became too much for Stephen. He blurted, "What the hell is this? Who are you? Where am I?"

Porter calmly pulled a cigarette box from his shirt pocket and lit one. He used his left hand. Mason assumed that it was characterization, but there was the chance that Porter had added another bad habit. The left hand made Mason think it was part of the character he was.

Porter blew a cloud of smoke towards the ceiling. "Why, I think you know some of those answers." He said calmly.

Stephen looked wary of that answer. "What do you mean?"

Porter took another drag on his cigarette before he answered. "Really, Stephen, let's cut the innocent act. You've been hitting sites for how long now? Did you really think you were untouchable?"

Stephen looked worried. Extremely worried, in fact. He didn't say anything. Porter shrugged. "Well, we have some time to wait for you to start being helpful." He stood up and glanced at his watch. Mason noticed absently that it was on his right wrist. "I'll be back in a while." He left and shut the door behind him.

Porter rejoined Mason in the pantry. "What do you think?" He asked quietly.

"I think he is getting the idea. Give him a few minutes to get really alarmed and then continue. You know what you are doing; I'll just watch for now. If I get anything you might use, I'll let you know. We need to know who's bankrolling him. He must have some idea of who it is, even if he doesn't really know beyond the lowest level person he talks to."

Porter nodded. "On it, Mason."

"By the way, when did you take up smoking?"

"Oh, let's see." Porter glanced at his watch. "About ten minutes ago."

"I rather thought that might be the case. Don't get too attached to it."

"Mason! How dare you! I am appalled by the very suggestion!" Porter protested in an overly-dramatic voice. Then he grinned and left.

Mason smiled to himself. Porter was just too much sometimes.

Back in the room, Stephen was looking around again. His face had a guarded, hunted expression. He was getting the point.

Porter reopened the door and quietly resumed his chair. He had a coffee cup in his left hand. "Well, Stephen? Where were we?" He asked genially.

He sat again, taking a sip from his coffee cup. Mason wondered what he was drinking. Evidently so did Stephen, who was staring longingly at the cup as Porter set it down. "Want to get me some of that?" He asked a bit petulantly.

Porter shrugged. "Depends."

"Depends on what?"

"Depends on if you are going to be helpful or not, of course. Now then, you must know we have quite a bit of information on you by now, Stephen. I don't mind sharing with you, privately, that the charges of internet-related terrorism are probably not going to be the most damaging for you. I think the sexual offense charges are going to sink your ass."

216

"What are you talking about?" Stephen asked in an outraged voice, not sounding very convincing.

Porter shook his head. "Really, Stephen, don't act like an idiot. You did know we picked up all of Phalanx's command group, didn't you?"

"What?!" Stephen sat up very straight. Apparently he didn't know.

Porter paused for effect. "Well, we did. Several of the seized computers have some very incriminating files on them, you must know. Both you and Jayne are going to be facing some serious trafficking and assault charges." Porter must have been making it up, since no one had said what was really on the computers, but it sounded perfectly plausible.

Stephen clearly believed him. He began to bite at a fingernail distractedly. "Wait, wait a moment." Porter sat back and took another drink of coffee. Then he lit a cigarette. Stephen sat up again. "What can I give you to cut a deal?"

"Beg pardon?"

"What can I give you to cut a deal? I don't want to go down on sex assault charges."

"I can't guarantee anything on that front. However, if you start outlining the way Phalanx has been funded and operated, it might be possible to get you into some sort of program or witness system."

Stephen nodded again. He was caught between a bad place to be and a worse one.

"Although," Porter added, "You'll probably be monitored, and that means you better fucking be clean from here on out."

Stephen nodded again. "All right." He squared his shoulders. "What do you want to know?"

Porter pretended to think about it for a second, smoking reflectively. "Let's start with the shift in Phalanx. When did it happen exactly? You were being standard hacktivists at first. What changed?"

"We got a proposition to hit a big target."

"Bigger than PETA, right?"

"Yeah, bigger than that. Hacktivists don't make any money,

man. I got a suggestion that I meet a guy; he was interested in hiring Phalanx for a job. If we did it well, he might be interested in coming back, with more money. What do you think I did?"

Porter snuffed out his cigarette. "I assume you took the job."

Stephen snorted. "Of course I took the job! He was offering big money, big risks, big challenge. Hackers live for the challenge, sometimes even more than for the benefits. We like to flout the rules that we think shouldn't apply." He smiled wryly. "I think that most of Phalanx probably thinks that rules and laws are for other people, not for the elite who are smart enough and strong enough to take what they want."

Porter lit another cigarette. "The way to anarchy is paved with misconceptions like that."

Stephen shrugged. "Probably. I know better, myself. I just like the challenge. But I gotta say, this guy kinda scared me, somehow. He seemed all smooth and friendly, but he never let me question the jobs. It was either all in or all out, no in between. And I started to feel hunted. Guys kept showing up, and I knew they were the same guys. Scary." Stephen suddenly looked a bit relieved. "I am sorta glad you guys picked me up. I feel a little safer, knowing that a government is interested in keeping me safe, at least for a little while. I haven't even been visiting my girls anymore; too freaked out."

Porter was quiet, smoking and apparently thinking about how to proceed. Stephen waited for another question. Finally, Porter snuffed out the cigarette. "Okay, well, we need to know who this guy is."

Stephen sighed. "I don't actually know. That's the most aggravating part. Trust me, I have tried to trace him. I really have. I have had no success."

Porter made an irritable jerk with his head. "Dammit."

"I know. I have been able to get his real name, that is all. And I only just got that a day ago."

"Well, give me that and we will see what we can do."

"His name is Jean-Paul Croidon."

Porter nodded and stood up. "Let me get you something to eat and drink. Excuse me."

"Thank you."

The name may not have meant anything to Stephen, but Mason knew it. This shit just got real.

Chapter 25

Porter came back into the pantry. "You heard it all?"

"Yes. He may not know who that is, but I do."

"You do?" Porter sounded surprised.

Mason nodded. "Yes, but once I explain it, you won't be so surprised. Let's get Stephen handed off to real agents. I'll prep him for it after I call our contact here."

"Gotcha. I did say I would get him some food, so I will do that while you make your calls."

Mason nodded again, already putting the number into his phone. "Agent Kyle? This is Briggs."

"Ah, yes, I take it there was a change of plans?"

"Yes, there was an EU agent watching the place. We have picked up Stephen alias Romeo. We'll hand him over to you in person, at the Rue Cassette in an hour. We'll be in front of the Café Café. My partner is very tall. You will not miss us."

"Understood. We'll be there with the appropriate paperwork. I will have a uniformed officer and an undercover agent along with me. I will have on an obnoxiously flamboyant tie."

Mason grinned. "We'll look for you then."

He went into the room where Stephen was still sitting. "Stephen, I am the presiding agent in this area. We are going to have to transfer you to another group. Don't worry; we will feed you. My agent did promise that, and I try to not contradict him. Also, I warn you, strenuously, do not sign anything without a lawyer present, and do not share any information without a lawyer present. As far as what my agent and I know, you should know that information will go no farther than us, officially. Do you understand what I am saying?"

Stephen looked very surprised. "You are saying, as far as I can tell, that you won't be putting anything I just said into a file anywhere."

"Correct. I don't trust computers anyway. You know how easy they can be to crack."

Stephen smiled slightly. "I might have some idea that way."

"I rather expected you to. What you have said is something that we will be following up on ourselves. Make sure that anything else you say to anyone else is only in the presence of your lawyers. That is your right."

Stephen nodded. "I understand. Thank you, agent."

"You're welcome." Mason looked at his watch. "We have to hand you off in forty minutes. Eat fast."

"I will!"

Porter came in with some food and Mason left. Once they handed this guy over, they were going to have a fun conversation with the backers of Jean-Paul Croidon.

The hand-off went smoothly, as Mason had expected. Porter could be fucking conspicuous when he needed to be. Mason did not prolong the process. If Stephen was even half as smart as Mason suspected, he wouldn't be talking on his own.

Porter smiled as he took a drink of his café latte and watched Stephen walk off with the agents. He glanced at Mason. "What next, O Exalted Leader?"

"Fuck off. We're going to go have a little chat with Jean-Paul and his superiors."

"Who is that, anyway? You said you knew who it was."

"Of course I know him. He is a state psychologist. He is employed by the French Government to advise public policy and diagnose high-level patients."

"Holy shit. This is going to be fun."

"Fun, my ass. The French are in this up to their fucking eyeballs and I want to jerk them around a bit."

"That's what I mean by fun, Mason. I love watching you fuck people over."

Mason grinned at him then. "Let's go do it, then. I've had it with this fucking mess. The sooner we get their attention, the sooner we can get back to America and make sure those people we love are okay."

"Agreed. I appreciate your concern, Mason."

"Fuck that, Porter. I am way past 'concerned'. I love you all way to fucking much to be merely concerned for you all."

221

"I know. That is what I appreciate. How is Sienna doing?" Porter asked as they stood up.

Mason shrugged. "It is hard to read emotion through texts, but she seems all right. Worried about us, and especially about you, of course. She has been helping Juan and Gabriella out."

Porter shook his head in disgust. "Juan is too fucking lucky. He gets a hot roommate and the hottest nurse God has conceived of."

Mason smiled. "I think he once said that it isn't luck, Porter. You either have it, or you don't."

Porter snorted. "Whatever."

Mason laughed. "Let's go to the official residence first. It is just possible that he is there in clinic today. They can call him in if he isn't."

Porter shrugged. "I am following your lead on this."

"Okay. Just be careful. He is very smart and he can mentally manipulate people easily. Don't let your guard down, not for a second. And try to not give anything away."

"I have a good poker face, Mason."

"I know. This is the highest stakes we've ever played for."

"I understand. I guess I better drop this identity, too."

"Yes. I don't want you picked up for having falsified documents."

Porter nodded and pulled his false credentials out of his inner pocket. He causally lit the entire thing with his lighter and left it to burn out on a café table. He tossed the cigarette pack into a garbage can at another café.

"Where did you hit on the idea of smoking, anyway?" Mason asked curiously.

Porter smiled. "From Antonio. I rather thought that Stephen must know of the threat he poses, so reminding him of it by adopting one of his obvious habits was easy."

"You're undoubtedly right. You smoke like you've done it for years."

Porter shrugged. "It's not too hard if a person doesn't inhale it all the way. Just suck it into the mouth. That way much doesn't get into the lungs. Still tastes awful and makes a person reek though. How far is this office?"

"Not much farther. I might have to try that smoking thing sometime. It would be very helpful in some disguises."

"I know. I developed it back in high school, when smoking was the way to rebel. I didn't like really smoking, and this looks like it."

"Yeah, and you like making people think you are doing something they want you to without really subscribing to it."

"Well, there is that too."

Mason shook his head. "You never have been who you really are before, have you?"

Porter sighed. "No, not really. I was always afraid that no one would want that loser. So I tried to make myself the winner."

"It makes sense, Porter, even if it is fucked up."

Porter nodded.

"Besides," Mason continued absently, "Sienna saw through enough of your shit. Thank God for her."

"Amen." Porter said fervently.

They were in front of an imposing marble building. There were the standard massive columns and doors that were fifteen feet tall. Porter looked at the façade and grimaced. "Why the fuck does everyone have to be overcompensating with the buildings?" He complained.

Mason grinned. "Because it is the easiest, and people are fucking lazy."

"True, that. Shall we?" Porter offered his arm.

Mason bowed. "We shall, dear sir." He linked his arm with Porter's airily and they breezed into the building.

The receptionist gaped at them as they came in, arm in arm. Mason found he didn't give a flying fuck what anyone in this place thought of him. "We're here to see Dr. Croidon." He said to her.

She continued to gape at him.

Mason disengaged his arm from Porter's and leaned over the counter. "Did you not hear me, young lady? I told you that we are here to see Dr. Croidon. I am not accustomed to being ignored."

"Oh, uh, sorry, sir." She looked down in some confusion. "Uh,

Dr. Croidon is not in right now."

Mason shrugged. "Then we will wait until he is in."

"Sir, he, uh, he is not available today."

"Then we will wait until he is."

"No, sir, I mean, uh, he is not available without appointment."

Mason was pretty much done with fucking around with this. "Look, young lady, you trot yourself into his office and give him this card and tell him that I am here on account of his fucking up with Phalanx." Mason took one of his calling cards out of his card carrier and threw it across to her. Then he turned dismissively, leaning on the counter and looking at the wall opposite. He heard her hesitant footsteps walk off somewhere.

Porter grinned at him. "You can be truly offensive when you have a mind to." He complimented Mason.

Mason shrugged. "I'm not playing games. Besides, I have fucking learned from the best in the field."

"I'm glad you paid attention during the fucking lessons."

Mason shrugged again. "Yeah, well, the professor was fucking full of himself. Unless there was vodka involved."

"I do miss the vodka."

"You'll get better, and then you can have it more often."

Porter nodded without replying. Mason noted that the paintings were all abstract and the colors were all carefully designed to be pleasing without being obvious. Boring-ass building. Mason wrinkled his nose.

"What?" Porter asked quietly, catching the look on Mason's face.

"This has to be the most boring building I have been in."

Porter looked around. "Yeah. Well, I stand by my original statement: he's obviously over-compensating."

"With boring shit?"

"Of course. Boring people can't help being boring, so the fact that it is boring just reinforces it."

"Okay, that was about three 'borings' too many in one sentence." Even as they made light conversation, Mason stayed alert

224

for anything. Porter probably did, too, but he was hiding it well. Also, he was the back up on this one. That always made a huge difference.

There were some hesitant footsteps coming back. Mason adjusted his mental state a little. He was not the one who had to explain himself; Croidon did. He would just assume the role of aggressor. Of course, that came with its own pitfalls. He had to be careful not to bull too hard. That was a good way to fall into a trap.

"Uh, sir?" The administrative assistant said quietly.

Mason turned back lazily.

"Dr. Croidon will see you. Will you be able to wait ten minutes?"

Mason pretended to think about it. "No. You tell him that I will not wait for his pleasure."

"But, uh, he is on the phone with the Secretary of State!"

"I don't give a flying fuck one way or another. You just trot on back and tell him I am coming in."

The young woman vacillated, clearly unsure of how to handle this situation. Then she meekly went back. Mason jerked his head to Porter and they followed her quietly.

Chapter 26

They paused outside the plain door the secretary had gone through. It was slightly ajar, and the sound of voices was clearly audible from the hallway.

"Sir, I apologize again, but they won't leave."

A man's voice growled something at her in French. She responded.

Mason looked at Porter and nodded. He opened the door loudly. The secretary jumped guiltily and turned. The man behind the splendid desk looked up sharply in alarm. He had a phone held to one ear. The standard white coat and dark tie that many scientists wear looked fastidiously pressed. His dark hair was smoothed into perfect alignment. Mason smiled slightly. He wanted to ruffle this immaculate person up.

"You may go." He said dismissively to the young woman. She hesitated, looking fearfully between Mason and Dr. Croidon. "I said, 'you may go'." Mason said slightly louder. She scurried out quickly, shutting the door behind her.

Mason casually reached across the desk and took the phone. He hung it up. "You are now free, Doctor. We have only a few things to discuss, and then you may continue your call."

Croidon was a little thrown but he was still clearly in control of himself. Mason did not underestimate him; to keep control, he would have to make sure Croidon didn't get the upper hand at any point.

"Well, Doctor, you know who I am. I had my card sent in, which I assume you conveniently ignored. However, I have no interest in being ignored. You see, I know who you are. I have actually interacted with you before, and I have been to one or two of your little talks at various conferences. I realize that you think I am just some low-level practitioner who is out to puff myself up at your expense." Croidon's face betrayed a slight agreement. Mason smiled. "I can assure you that is not the case. Not at all. You see, Doctor, I am in every respect your superior." No doctor with a self-image like Croidon would like that. He shifted in his chair irritably and opened his mouth. Mason merely raised his voice and continued right on. "Oh, I know it seems childish to say that. You are, undoubtedly, a very smart man. Since I respect that intelligence, allow me to give you some advice."

Mason put his hands on the desk and leaned in menacingly. "Get your fucking self out of politics. You aren't very good at it and you are starting to piss off the people in real power. You think that your little office here will protect you? You and whoever gave you the mandate to use Phalanx have targeted the US government. I know it, and I am perfectly willing to bring it to light publically. You will be fucking dispensable at that point. I don't give a fuck about your precious little power play here. I don't like people who fuck with my friends. You have tried to fuck with us, and you are in my sights now. I hear anything from you again, anything at all like this shit, and your ass will be buried. Do I make myself clear?"

"You can't bluff me!" Croidon said loudly, half-starting from his seat.

Porter laughed softly. "Oh, believe me, Doctor! He isn't bluffing. I have played cards with him enough to know that he isn't using a poker face. Not this time. Everything he said, I fully back, except that I don't have the same influence, so I will just have to come and beat your ass to within an inch of death."

"You two can't just come in here and threaten me! I have rights!"

Mason sighed. "You're right, you did. You jettisoned them once you entered an illegal monetary arrangement with a known hacktivist group to target government installations. We have all the leaders of Phalanx. They are talking. You are fucked. I suggest you and your government start scrambling to cover your asses for when this fucking shit comes out. We'll be going now. Thanks for seeing us." He turned and gestured to Porter. "Shall we?"

Porter bowed gracefully and took his arm. "We shall. Your lead, or mine?"

"You may." Mason said graciously. They were both being highly ridiculous, and it was fucking awesome. Porter waltzed him right out of the room and shut the door. "Now we better get the fuck out of here. Fast. We are going to be targets very, very soon."

Porter nodded. "How soon can we get on a plane and out of here?"

Mason considered. "I think we can probably swing it within an hour."

Porter considered as they hurried out of the building. "Might be tight."

"Yeah, it will be. But they can't take us off the plane without there being a scene. It is the airport I am worried about. We are vulnerable there and on the street."

"How about if we drive across the border to Switzerland?"

Mason considered. "All right, but we have to get going within the half hour. There could be a lock on our passports and shit."

"I know, but it's probably still safer than Charles de Gaulle now."

"True. All right, let's do it."

Chapter 27

The border patrol was bored; Mason could see that right away. The soldier slouched over and gave no more than a precursory glance to their passports. Mason was privately glad that the soldier hadn't been more alert. They would have been in a world of hurt if he had been.

There had been a watch posted for their names before they had made it far from Paris. Porter had been scanning the official channels with a handy little device pioneered by Juan. When he heard the call go out, he glanced meaningfully over at Mason. "We got out of there right in time, I think."

Mason nodded. "Your idea to go through Switzerland is brilliant. I think we might have had trouble in France."

"We're still in France, and we still have the border crossing."

"So start praying to all the saints you can think of that we will get through."

Once they had made it, Porter winked at Mason. "Well, at least one of those saints petitioned God correctly. Now let's get out of Europe. We are a liability until we can be back in the air or on US ground."

Mason nodded. "I have us on a plane already. I arranged it while you were swearing at the traffic in Paris."

"Me, swearing?"

"Like a fucking pirate."

Porter laughed gaily. "Well, let's get going! Pirates who fight and run away live to plunder France another day!"

Mason laughed.

Once the plane had taken off, Porter relaxed visibly. "God damn. I half expected some soldiers to barge in and take us off the plane, treaty or no."

Mason smiled. "I did, too. They can't touch us now. Besides, we are non-existent, so far as any government besides the French one is concerned."

"You think they are gonna have political repercussions?"

"They had fucking better! I hope Stephen spills all their fucking secrets! Antonio, too. They are the two with the cred."

"Yeah. And they don't like each other, so that boosts their cred."

"Always. Maybe I will set something in motion with a journalist or two, give them some hints to go digging after. France deserves a little squirming over this debacle, especially after their 'holier than thou' attitude concerning spying and undercover activities."

Porter snorted. "Fucking hypocrites."

"We're all hypocrites, Porter, they just got caught at it."

"Think they'll liquidate Croidon?"

"I doubt it. He is the pawn, but he has power. It is the powerless that they would have liquidated, like Phalanx. That is one reason Stephen was so worried. He isn't stupid and he must have realized that they were the real fall-guys."

"Probably. I wonder if the EU was onto it, too."

Mason shrugged. "We may never know, but I might give them a nudge, too. Once we are back, that is. Now let's talk about something else. I am done with this shit."

"Thank God!" Porter pulled out the ubiquitous deck of cards from his shirt pocket.

"Absolutely; thank God. Once we land, you better change and shower. You smell like smoke still. You can do it at my house, if you want."

Porter nodded, dealing a hand of gin. "Enough of that. Wanna see if your luck is still holding up?"

The rest of the flight went by smoothly in cards and a little alcohol. By the time they landed, Mason and Porter had left Paris behind them. Mason's car was still parked in the small side lot. He eyed it hesitantly. Porter glanced between him and the car. "Oh, yeah, maybe we should do a quick look over it."

Mason nodded, suddenly profoundly grateful to Porter for his understanding. He would never be able to put it into words, but the fact that Porter took his feelings seriously was a huge comfort.

The car looked fine. They drove out to Mason's house without any incident.

"The shower is there. I will run over and grab you some clothes."

"Thanks, man. Sienna will appreciate it, even if she never knows."

"Will she be there? Am I going to startle her?"

"I doubt it, Mason. It is only 2:45. She should still be at the store."

"Oh, yeah, I hadn't looked at the time. Too intent on driving."

"Uh-huh. Whatever." Porter went into the bathroom and shut the door.

Mason smiled to himself. He went to Porter's house and came back with the clothes quickly. The water was running when he got back. He knocked on the bathroom door and shouted, "They're out here, Princess!"

"Fucking thank you, I think!" Porter shouted back from inside.

Mason laughed and went to find Ninja. Cats tend to handle themselves well, but Mason wanted to make sure.

Ninja was lying across his desk in the sunbeam and ignoring him. Mason smiled. It might have been more believable if he hadn't had his ears back to make sure of where Mason was, and if his tail wasn't flicking.

"Yeah, I missed you, too." Mason said, petting the cat, who growled at him.

He stood for a moment, looking out the window and absently scratching Ninja under his chin. It would be nice to not have to worry any more, at least not for a while.

Porter finished in the bathroom and came out. "You want the towel?"

"Nah, just leave it there. I will get it later." Mason said dismissively.

"Your choice." Porter said. "Did you need anything else?"

"Nope. Get your ass over to your store and surprise your lady."

"Thank you, I will!"

"It had better involve some serious public kissing."

"Are you speaking professionally?"

Mason smiled at him. "Yes, and as your friend, idiot. Get going."

"Sir, yes, sir! Will you need an extensive debriefing on the operation later?"

Mason laughed. "Whatever the fuck makes you happy!"

Porter grinned and left.

Mason stretched. Yes, it was definitely good to be home.

Epilogue

Mason finally got an invitation to go to a house-warming party for Porter and Sienna. It had taken long enough. He smiled as he wrapped a nice glass vase for them. Porter would complain about it and Sienna would love it. Mason wasn't stupid; he knew who he needed to impress.

When he knocked on the door at 7:00, there were already sounds of conversation from inside. Porter opened the door and Mason saw that everyone else was there.

"About fucking time." Porter griped.

"Shut the fuck up. I had to finish at the office." Mason said calmly.

"Whatever. You like being fashionably late."

"Was there some time limit?"

"No."

"Then shut the fuck up." Mason walked in and handed the box to Sienna with a smile.

"Mason, you shouldn't have." She smiled back.

Mason shrugged. "And yet, I still don't care."

She laughed and opened it. "Oh, this is lovely! Thank you!"

Porter sighed. "I bet it gets broken in two days."

"Whatever, man." Mason elbowed him in the side. "She likes it."

"Yeah, yeah. Excuse me, I have to get dinner finished."

Mason hadn't been in the house before, so while Porter messed around in the kitchen, Sienna showed him around. The front room had a beautiful hardwood floor.

"I love this flooring, Sienna."

"Yes, Porter had it put in specifically. I think he must have a reason he hasn't shared yet."

Mason smiled slightly. "And it is driving you crazy."

"Of course it is." She smiled resignedly.

Mason laughed.

The dinner was spectacular. Porter had done a fantastic job.

Juan and Gabriella were sitting opposite Mason and Sienna, with Michael and Karen next across from James and Callie. Porter got to be at the head of the table.

Towards the end and after the dessert had been served, Porter winked outrageously at Sienna. "Ready for the entertainment, my dear?"

"Of course. Let me put on the mood music." She stood up and went somewhere. Porter also stood and when the strains of music came wafting through tastefully hidden speakers, He bowed and extended his hand to Gabriella.

She looked very flustered. "Here? Now?"

Porter smiled gently. "Of course. When else?"

Gabriella carefully stood up, put aside the cane she used, and Porter gently lead her in a waltz.

When it was finished, he helped her back to the table. Then he looked at Juan. "That is your surprise. We have been working on it for a while now, helping to rehabilitate and all that. Gabriella wanted you to be able to dance again, you know. Don't fucking waste it." Juan couldn't respond, he was so choked up. Porter nodded. "Good."

Sienna returned. "Looks like it worked." She observed with a smile.

"Perfectly." Porter agreed gravely. "Now, there is a slight surprise for the rest of you all."

"I hope it isn't that emotional." Michael piped up.

"Kind of depends, I think." Porter shrugged. "Sienna and I wanted to extend an invitation to you all: we'll be getting married in six months, and we want you all to be there."

Mason felt a bit emotional himself. While Porter and Sienna answered the usual question from the others, he allowed himself to just sit back and bask in the happy feeling he got from being with his friends. It had been one of the worst months he'd ever had, but it was turning around, finally.

Maybe, as a present, he should get them a cat.

www.ingramcontent.com/pod-product-compliance
Lightning Source LLC
Chambersburg PA
CBHW021234130626
46554CB00004B/1494